D0391435

Also by Daniel Reveles

Enchiladas, Rice, and Beans

Salsa and Chips

DANIEL REVELES

ONE WORLD
Ballantine Books • New York

A One World Book
Published by Ballantine Books

Copyright © 1997 by Daniel Reveles

All rights reserved under International
and Pan-American Copyright Conventions. Published
in the United States by Ballantine Books, a division of Random
House, Inc., New York, and simultaneously in Canada
by Random House of Canada Limited, Toronto.

http://www.randomhouse.com

Library of Congress Catalog Card Number: 97-91885

ISBN: 0-345-40509-9

Text design by Holly Johnson

Cover design by Kristine V. Mills-Noble

Cover illustration by Linda Messier

Manufactured in the United States of America

First Edition: September 1997
10 9 8 7 6 5 4 3 2 1

This is for my three Muses of Joy
Brenda, Valerie, Andrea

CONTENTS

ACKNOWLEDGMENTS

The author gratefully acknowledges the contributions of many people on both sides of the border. I am indebted to Valerie Ross, that wonderful Hatchet Lady whose keen editorial eye is priceless. I must thank the long line of musicians, poets, hagiologists, lawyers, doctors, and working women who stop by my corner table at La Fonda and so willingly share their experiences with me over a margarita: Bertha and Roberto Perretta, genial hosts at El Passetto Restaurant; Lic. Gloria Lopez, Tecate's first woman judge; Dr. Rafael Elizondo; and Lic. Luis Fernando Angúlo, a walking *antologia de refranes mexicanos*. My thanks to Denise Paccione because she is always there with the xxooxx when needed. Special thanks to Jim and Sharon Coffman for their warm midwestern hospitality while I was on tour in Kansas. And, of course, a warm *abrazo* to my friend and publisher at Ballantine, Cheryl Woodruff, who once shared my corner table while mariachis filled La Fonda with *alegria*.

—D.R.

Tecate, B.C., Mexico

Salsa and Chips

APERITIVO

Listen!

The mariachis are playing that gay melancholy music that touches all the human emotions. Violins summon tears, a trumpet lays a garland of silver notes around your heart. Welcome to my little pueblo of Tecate. I am nothing less than delighted you could join me here at my corner table at Restaurant La Fonda. You're just in time to savor a frosty margarita to smooth out all the little wrinkles of your day and bring summer to your soul.

And as long as you're here you might as well stay a little longer. I have some wonderful tales to share with you. I want to take you to places you've never been. I want to introduce you to people you might not otherwise have the opportunity to meet so you'll know how Mexicans live, how they think, what they feel. You'll meet working women, single mothers, macho rancheros, the gentle sisters of the Order of Santa Brigida, genuine witches, along with an assortment of colorful scamps and scoundrels.

Tecate, B.C. (no zip), Mexico is, even by Mexican standards, a small pueblo. One square block anywhere in the USA has a higher Barbie doll population than Tecate has people. The dusty little town lies in a shallow placer under the cosmic fallout of Mount Cuchumá, the enchanted mountain of the Pai Pai. A lot of the magic still clings; to the soil, the air, the people. Tecate, California (91980), USA, smaller, dustier, and no magic, lies just across the street. We are divided by an iron gate owned by the Americans who swing it open at six in the morning when two sovereign nations become one. Americans come into Mexico mainly to manage their factories. They buy 7.50 pesos for a dollar. About three dollars buys enough pesos to pay their employees the minimum daily wage. Mexicans must work hard to save up 7.50 pesos to buy a dollar. Then they cross into the United States to go shopping and put it all in the American economy.

American border officers lock the gate at midnight. This is not convenient. Say you're on the American side for a gay evening of wine and dinner and cha-cha-cha. You're having a wonderful time and suddenly you look at your watch and you're obliged to say something like, "I must get home before the clock strikes midnight!" and make a mad dash for the border. If you're a woman, no harm. He'll immediately initiate a search for your glass slipper. In my case she may never go out with me again.

We have been good neighbors since 1894 in spite of the fact that we come from totally different cultures. Thus when you cross the border into my country you may find it necessary to pause briefly for a reality check. You won't see the human flamethrower or the bug eater in your public parks.

You may have a problem that would benefit from ornitho-mancy, but you won't find a charming little bird to offer you his apocalyptic services for a quarter. And I know from personal experience a cucumber Popsicle is out of the question in your country. And if you're in the mood for a calf-eye taco, you're out of luck in the USA.

Because we are a border town, our customs have a tendency to overlap. Our festive piñata is almost standard equipment at your parties. American bartenders serve up more margaritas than martinis. And it is a safe assumption that Americans consume more tortillas than Mexicans do bread. Conversely, the Christmas tree (imported from the Other Side) can now be seen in some Mexican homes where the traditional nativity scene once stood. On America's Thanksgiving Day there is a turkey (imported from the Other Side) browning in nearly every oven in Tecate. This is even more interesting when you consider that the landing of more illegal aliens to the New World was not a great piece of news for Mexicans.

There are a thousand good reasons to live in Tecate. The air is like wine, the smiles are free, there are no strangers, to name the first three. Even if I should list the remaining 997, *convenience* would not appear on the list. In my village the convenience of mail delivery, fire department, and paramedic services is unknown. The joy of the telephone that lets you reach out and touch someone has not yet made an appearance. The lack of telephone and fax can be a source of frustration for publishers, but it is paradise for writers. I gladly forfeit convenience for the privilege of enjoying life among real people rather than computer-enhanced images. We in Tecate have not yet achieved a use-and-throw-away society.

When you place a phone call to a business office here, a real girl answers. You will not spend ten minutes pressing numbers. This is life in the slow lane. I cannot recommend Tecate to the practical mind, but it's a wonderful place for the soul. And if you should opt to remain, forewarned is forearmed. Hold on to your heart. There are no strangers in Tecate. You run the risk of receiving a warm embrace anytime you cross the plaza.

During the preparation of this volume that I am about to offer to my esteemed readers, I thought it might be a good idea to take stock, to see what has changed in Tecate and what has remained the same. I decided that this scholarly research could best be conducted at La Fonda, where our local sages convene every morning at ten in their quest for a caffeine kick-start, as you say in your country, and a Higher Truth. I know I can count on them. They are as dependable as the potholes.

I should explain that these men of wisdom are known locally as Los Cafeteros, the self-appointed Upper Chamber of Deputies. Together, through the democratic process, they draft legislation, pass ordinances, and hand down mandates which are sent to the Palacio Municipal by special messenger where the *presidente* immediately sends them on to the committee, which meets the second Tuesday of every month in the municipal Dumpster.

I have never seen Los Cafeteros at a loss for an agenda. I have seen the discussion change course from the monetary crisis to the ideal way to prepare *carne asada* in the length of time required to pour a cup. I hoped they could stay close to my subject long enough to get an answer.

"Gentlemen, what in your view has changed significantly

in Tecate since the publication of *Enchiladas, Rice, and Beans* in 1994?"

"There is a new sign for the airport," the doctor was quick to observe.

"Yes, but still no airport exists." The dentist shot him down.

"How about the new water reservoir on top of that high hill? That's an important change. And it should solve our water problem." This from the merchant.

"But there's no water in it," the rancher objected.

"Then what about the new freeway?" someone suggested.

"Yes, the new freeway connecting Tijuana to Tecate and thence to Mexicali."

"It was intended to solve some horrendous traffic problems. Tell your readers about that."

"That is certainly a major change and worthy of note," the merchant agreed, refilling his cup.

I thought it was going to be a unanimous decision until the *licenciado* spoke up.

"But they neglected to build the on-ramps at Tecate, so the problem is the same as ever."

"Wait a minute!" our excitable banker shouted. "The North American Free Trade Agreement—that's a new and important change. It involves Canada, Mexico, and Estados Unidos."

"What has changed?" shot back the lawyer. "I cannot enter the United States with an avocado in my car. I cannot come back into Mexico with a television set. And Canada will not allow Barnes & Noble and Borders to open stores in Canada." He drained his cup. "Tell your readers nothing has changed."

"I suppose Alphonse Karr said it best back in 1849," I suggested. " 'The more things change, the more they remain the same.' "

"Never heard of the man, but he certainly knows Tecate!" they all hastened to agree.

"Does anybody here know who will play Los Cowboys at the Super Bowl?" the banker inquired, adding two sugars to his coffee.

I told you it required an agile mind to meet the sudden shift of topics. The Cafeteros could go on like this forever. But enough digression! Let us get to our happy purpose of storytelling before an editor comes flying in here with scissors in hand and demanding a margarita.

The reader must not expect the characters who inhabit these pages to be politically correct. Political correctness is an American concept. Mexicans do not understand it. One more thing: keep in mind that I paint from life. So, if you notice a little wilt on the flowers, a few bruises on the fruit, or if there is a huge crack the full length of the bowl, that is how the subject appeared before me.

Now, make yourself comfortable while I see about getting us another margarita. In the meantime, take a warm tortilla chip from the basket and dip into the salsa.

—D.R.

Tecate, B.C., Mexico

Los Compadres

One of the first questions my visitors to Tecate ask is, where is the entertainment? There is, of course, Rocco's Disco for those physical fitness devotees who prefer the cha-cha-cha and merengué as their cardiovascular discipline. There's always La Fonda for dinner and the gay sound of mariachis. The Diana is popular for a spirited game of backgammon and an honest pour. If, however, it is your intention to have a drink with someone you shouldn't, perhaps in pursuit of some exciting new conquest, I would have to suggest the Cantina Los Cuernos as the only practical venue. The code of ethics at Los Cuernos, though unwritten, forbids clients from mentioning who might have been seen sipping in your company, and the rule has never been violated in the history of Tecate. For my money, however, no one can top the daily entertainment at El Peine de Oro. El Peine de Oro is not a place I could suggest for dinner nor anywhere you would go to enjoy the perfect margarita made with fresh limes. And it really isn't properly set up for dancing. El Peine de Oro, the Golden Comb, is a barbershop across from the plaza on Avenida Juarez. Pelon Garcia, prop.

Some of the most fascinating stories have come to me from this source. The best one I've heard in a long time, and am about to share with you here, deals with a group of *compadres*. You don't have that term on the Other Side so perhaps I should explain it. You become a *compadre*, or *comadre*, if you're a woman, when someone has selected you to be a godparent. You acquire *compadres* when you have done the selecting. The *compadre* relationship is similar to your American old-boy network. But we needn't let a detail like this delay our story.

I first met this colorful group of *compadres* at El Peine de Oro. In those days they assembled at the tonsorial parlor on a daily basis whether any of them needed a haircut or not. Let me introduce the principal four first because you may have a hard time telling them apart. Their handsome brown faces are as similar as tortillas. In truth, if it weren't for their individual mustaches, it would be impossible to distinguish one from the other. In alphabetical order, they are, from left to right; Abel, Bartolo, Clementino, and Dustano. Abel cultivated a narrow row of black bristles closely resembling an Oral-B toothbrush (soft) on his upper lip. Bartolo was vain about his black walrus tusks. Clementino waxed his long *bigotes* thin as a wire all the way to the ends. This, he claimed when inquiry was made, allowed him to estimate the width of an open door before entering. Dustano simply grew an undisciplined clump of black ragweed that covered his entire mouth from view. Sometimes it was hard to tell where the voice was coming from.

Now, the introduction of the protagonist *compadre* requires a little additional explanation. We can assume he was given a name on the day of his baptism at the Church of Our Lady thirty-four years ago. But I have never learned his name nor have I met anyone who could remember it—including his wife. (I know his mother, I'll ask her next time I see her.) He's known to his *compadres* by any number of descriptive sobriquets such as El Chapopote, La Melaza, La Brea, El Chicle, and several other names alluding to his viscosity. It was common knowledge around Tecate that you could get smeared just by walking near enough to him to say *buenos dias*. None of these affectionate nicknames is really translatable without losing some of the color, and we are a very colorful people. For the sake of this story we're obliged to find an English equivalent. Now that the NAFTA treaty has been duly signed, it is a simple matter to import duty free an American neologism that describes this *compadre* to an American T. In a word, a flake. By this I don't mean "a small, thin mass," as *Webster's New World Dictionary* tells us, but in the new sense of the nineties. In short, El Flako.

You would recognize him instantly if you saw him walking across the plaza. His face is as plain as a clay tile, no lines, no ridges, no mustache. He keeps his curly black hair short so that it looks like cut pile. When you first look into his face you might think the poor man has just been goosed with a lemon Popsicle. A reasonable but erroneous conclusion. It was the vast emptiness of the upper lip and the immense ovoid Little Orphan Annie eyes that combined to give him that look of sudden surprise. But when the man smiled at you with all thirty-two teeth, you could be momentarily blinded by the high beams.

I should add that while El Flako's *compadres* were all successful men of business and commerce, he, alas, was not. El Flako's problems probably began the very day he was born,

September thirteenth. A day without an assigned saint. A Friday. He achieved failure early in life. He didn't pass the entrance examination to high school and immediately launched into a long and distinguished career of odd jobs and slippery deals. He was a Virgo by Fate, and maybe there was something wrong with his empathetic earth sign. He didn't have lucky days like the rest of us or lucky numbers or lucky anything, for that matter. And his Nostradamus factor was weak. He couldn't see twenty minutes into the future. And where was his guardian angel? We all have one, right? All Mexicans need a guardian angel. I know in my own case, if I'm about to enter into something that looks like really high entertainment, I can count on the fluttering of golden wings descending to dissuade me from my intention and spoil the fun. But for all these disadvantages inherited at birth, El Flako was a loyal friend. He would give you his blood, his organs (with one exception), or the shirt off his back.

It almost doesn't matter where you begin to relate one of El Flako's adventures. His escapades run in a long concentric spiral. There is no beginning and no end. To get this story under way, a thing editors seem obsessed about, we might as well begin the day Abel's wife was nagging him daily about painting the kitchen. Abel was grumbling about it to his *compadres* at the barbershop when El Flako gladly volunteered to do it for him.

This simple act of kindness from one *compadre* to another gains in significance when, only a few days after Abel's wife was humming in her yellow kitchen with sky-blue cupboards and pink countertops, El Flako sucked Abel into a deal. A week before El Flako began to apply paint, he had been visiting a nearby farm for the purpose of buying a few kilos of acidulated Concord grapes which he intended to press and process into a passable table vinegar which he offered to his friends as wine. In an old decaying barn filled with discarded equipment, El Flako spotted an aging surrey. It was black with yellow wheels. Or I should say, it had been. It had a black leather top and matching seats where pack rats had been living the good life for several generations.

"Why do you keep all this stuff?" he asked. "This old buggy is just going to fall apart."

The farmer shrugged. "What am I going to do, drive it?"

But El Flako knew exactly what he wanted it for. "I'll buy it from you." Then quickly added, "If you don't want too much for a piece of useless junk."

"Hundred dollars. Includes four families of pet mice. For another hundred you get the harness."

El Flako got the thing home in his pickup truck and spent several days sanding and painting. He mended the seats. He washed and polished the harness. Then he brought Abel over to see it.

"It looks brand new, *cabrón*, where did you find it? And what are you going to do with it?" Abel wanted to bite his tongue, but it was too late. He had just walked into another of El Flako's sticky webs.

"You are looking at a gold mine, *compadre*. And I'm taking you in as my partner."

"How can you make money with this thing?" Abel's second question was directed at himself: When am I going to learn to keep my mouth shut?

"Think of it, *compadre*, we will offer elegant horse and carriage service for weddings, birthdays, all festive occasions." He brought out a small notebook. "Look, I already have bookings. The Hernandez wedding, Pablo's *quince* celebration for Carolina, and a baptismal. Three hundred dollars for a short ride. We'll make a fortune!"

One of the dangerous things about El Flako was that his pictures of golden fleeced ovines were flecked with truth. The bookings were a fact. It started to make sense to Abel, and this gave him cause for concern. "You'll need a horse. You don't have a horse."

"That is exactly why I'm taking you in. I need four hundred for a trained driving horse. Once we get started, we'll be doing two or three fiestas a week at three hundred dollars a pop. When did you ever see so much money! You and I split fifty-fifty."

Abel thought about it. Not about the deal he was being offered, but about an effective means of escape without offense. He owed the man a favor. He *did* paint his kitchen, after all. He *was* his *compadre*. And how could he claim he didn't have four hundred? That would be like admitting impotence. It is important to understand that Abel's neural organization of instinctive responses was highly developed. It may have been that the left lobe of his brain was on a short break this morning. Or would it be his right? In any case, he ignored all the strong signals his gut was sending up. Abel reached into his pocket.

A few days later El Flako slipped into Los Cuernos for a nightcap. If I failed to mention it before, I should explain now that the name above the door of the cantina was not Los Cuernos. It simply read, CANTINA TECATE. In our colorful way with language, we say of a husband who fools around that he is putting the horns, or *los cuernos*, on his wife. That is how the establishment earned its name. With that brief footnote out of the way we can follow El Flako through the double doors.

"A Centenario, please." While the bartender poured, El Flako looked around and found his *compadre* Bartolo with a curvacious new challenge in the process of being conquered. She was sitting on his lap. *"Compadre!"* He flashed the high beams. "I didn't see you there. Bartender! Another round for my *compadre* and his guest!"

"Gracias, compadre," Bartolo answered. No introduction was offered and none expected. "What's new?" Bartolo wanted to bite his tongue off. There was no such thing as a rhetorical question when it was directed at El Flako.

"Interesting you should ask. I have invested a large amount of money in a champion driving horse and elegant carriage that I intend to offer for fiestas. I already have bookings."

"Wonderful." It's a hard word to say without sounding sincere. Bartolo hoped he did not.

"I'm short only four hundred to get the project rolling. I'm cutting you in for half. Yes, half, you own fifty percent of the venture."

Bartolo knew from long experience the trap had snapped shut. The implication was that he was loaded with money, and he couldn't dismiss the compromising position of the ripe little mango who presently occupied most of his lap. He could squirm and wiggle and demean himself in front of his prospective conquest or he could look like a high roller, if I can borrow another Americanism. Bartolo slipped into the quicksand when he slipped a hand in his pocket. And he knew it.

A few days later Abel sat in the barbershop with some of his *compadres*. This is one time Abel was actually boasting about his new business venture with El Flako. Much to everyone's surprise, the enterprise was a huge success. Another even bigger surprise came when Abel and Bartolo learned they both owned fifty percent of the deal.

"I never thought I would live to see the day when one of El Flako's business ventures would meet with success," Clementino remarked from the barber's chair where Pelon was trimming up his sideburns. "Maybe he would sell me another fifty percent."

"Should I trim the mustache?"

"Not if you want to live long enough to hear the rest of the story."

Abel continued. "We already have something like thirty reservations with deposits on the books. And next Saturday we have the big wedding for the *comandante*'s daughter's wedding."

"We'll split fifty-fifty, partner, then lynch the *cabrón*!" Bartolo said. "This is one time we're going to see some real profits."

"Then it is your turn to buy the wine!" Dustano's voice came from somewhere behind the ragweed.

Saturday morning awoke with sunshine and birdsong. It was the perfect day for a wedding. At ten o'clock El Flako sat in his surrey holding the reins of an elegant sorrel gelding in the *comandante*'s driveway. The buggy top was fringed with crepe paper roses of lavender and white. White bows adorned the noble animal's luxurious mane. A huge lavender bow held the French braid on the flaxen tail. The front door opened and the glowing bride stepped out in frothy white with her attendants in lavender taffeta. The bride's parents, who were already dressed for the occasion, came out too. The *comandante* helped his daughter into the backseat, with the maid of honor next to her. He sat up front. El Flako picked up the reins, chirped to the steed, and they stepped out smartly and delivered them to the Church of Our Lady de Guadalupe to the rhythm of clip-clopping hooves sprayed with gold lacquer.

Eventually the front doors of the church opened and the bride and groom stood smiling under a blizzard of rice. There was a brief melee of hugs and kisses. They posed for pictures. Then, after another flurry of fizzy embraces, the bride and groom stepped into the carriage for the short three-block ride to La Fonda for the reception.

A young man with a video camera ran up to the buggy and called to El Flako. "Hold it right there for a couple more shots." Quickly the cinematographer turned director. "Bridesmaids here by the front of the horse. Best man over here, ushers fill in over there. Beautiful!" He changed angles. "Now a shot of the bride and groom. Smile. That's nice. Now, give me a wave. A little more enthusiasm." The big sorrel must have been experiencing a minor gastrointestinal discomfort. He lifted his braided tail ever so slightly and, as discreetly as he could manage it, expelled a vast quantity of gas. Both the pretty bride and the handsome groom were furiously waving away the pungent gas with both hands in their effort to save themselves from asphyxiation. "That's more like it. Yes! Great wave. That's a take!" The director seemed pleased.

Relieved of his discomfort, the horse cocked a hind leg and dozed while everyone posed for pictures. It's hard to say just what goes through the equine mind at a moment like this. The noble beast may have been daydreaming about marriage and commitment. Maybe he didn't have time to finish his breakfast that morning. We may never have the answer. But for lack of anything else to do, the restless animal decided to sniff at the maid of honor's corsage of matching lavender roses. Maybe a tiny nibble was all he intended. But as everyone knows, little things always go wrong at weddings. In one big munch he ripped off the corsage and a portion of the young lady's dress.

The maid of honor lost her equanimity. She screamed. The bride followed with a shrill scream of her own. The crowd screamed. Then came another chilling scream when the maid of honor, who apparently felt the cool air on her bare skin, realized she was topless.

Well, of course, these things happen so fast it is almost impossible to know what happened next and in what order. And it probably doesn't matter to the main thrust of the story. The poor horse, frightened by all the screaming, reared up, El Flako reprimanded him with the whip, the animal bolted forward, El Flako fell backward, lost the reins, and there was a runaway horse with a mouthful of roses and a large part of a lavender taffeta gown in his teeth dragging a carriage with screaming passengers through the streets of Tecate. With no one to guide him, the terrified horse ran half a block and made an illegal left into Carranza. He may not have seen the side reading ONE WAY. In making the sharp turn, the surrey sideswiped a slow-moving car, snapped the shafts, and the horse was now headed for home at a full gallop without his passengers.

With the sudden loss of horsepower, the carriage came to a full stop, teetered in slow motion, fell on its side, and dumped the bride and groom on their *nalgas*. But the only damage was to their pride.

Understandably, Abel and Bartolo, equal partners in a total loss, were somewhat resentful about the whole business. In point of fact they went directly to Los Cuernos and took a solemn tequila oath never to put another *centavo* into one of El Flako's schemes again. They would have avoided him altogether, but that's not easy in a little pueblo like Tecate.

A few weeks later the *compadres* were sitting around Pelon's barbershop watching snips of El Flako's black hair coming down to the floor like black snow. The unfortunate business venture was not forgotten but no longer a popular topic.

"You're handsome as the day you got married," Pelon said with the last click of the scissors. He withdrew the sheet and gave it a shake. "Who's next?"

Clementino got in the chair. "Just a quick trim, Pelon, I have to get to Tijuana and pick up some lumber."

"They won't deliver?" a *compadre* asked.

"No, and I still don't know how I'm going to get it back. It won't fit in my car."

"Will it fit in a pickup?" El Flako asked.

"Easily."

"Then take mine, *compadre*." El Flako reached in his pocket and took out his keys. "It's got a full tank of gas."

"But I'll be gone all day. I don't expect to be back until late tonight. You won't have your truck until tomorrow."

"Don't worry, *compa*, what are friends for? I'll manage just fine." El Flako pressed the keys into Clementino's hand, said adios to his *compadres*, and went out the door.

His name came into the conversation as soon as the door closed behind him. "You have to admit it," Clementino said, "the man is sticky as hot tar, but underneath beats a heart of pure gold."

"You speak the truth, *compadre*," Abel answered. "He is not a dishonest man. He's like a child who tells you what he *wishes* were true. Still, I don't intend investing anything over a dime in another one of his schemes."

"No matter how good it looks!" Bartolo finished.

Some days later El Flako was driving south on Highway 3, the main artery to Ensenada and the remainder of the Baja peninsula. Actually, the word "highway" is, if not a misnomer, a plain lie. It is really a narrow strip of buckled asphalt and deep chuckholes where cattle gather to gossip and quench their thirst after a rain. Blind curves and steep grades add to the fun. There is very little shoulder. Most of the nine hundred miles is bordered with a sheer drop, where in fact many motorists often do.

El Flako had just made it to the top of the long climb at kilometer 10 when a terrifying clacking and the hiss of a geothermal geyser of live steam bursting skyward from under the hood gained his attention. The ever-vigilant Flako turned off the ignition, crested the summit, and coasted onto one of the rare shoulders we spoke of earlier.

This quick maneuver probably saved his life, as a semi truck and trailer that was tailgating assumed his place on the road while a car coming in the opposite direction zoomed past at the same moment. El Flako got out, opened the hood to aid the cooling process. In back of the seat he stored the standard equipment every prudent Mexican motorist carries. A spare tire, a jack, and two plastic milk jugs filled with water. He stepped out and sniffed the warm summer air scented with wild lupine and spicy sage. Golden breasted thrushes spoke to him in bright little notes and rolling trills. It was pleasant out here in the country. In half an hour he could pour water in the radiator and continue on his way. He would have to be sure to refill his milk bottles for the journey home.

Not far from where El Flako stood absorbing the bucolic scene, a fine-looking Duroc came snorting and rooting through a cornfield and toward the highway. There is little doubt that pigs appreciate a fine day as much as anyone, and having found a loose board in his shelter, this individual decided to take a walk. He may have noticed that many of his room-mates were being removed and never came back.

El Flako caught sight of the fine-looking pig as the latter stopped to graze on some tender dandelions at the edge of the road. It is possible that at this moment the Duroc decided that the real meaning of Life lay on the other side of the road, and in prosecution of his objective, stepped onto the highway. We can suppose that what followed was simply the result of a bad call. The pig thought he had the right of way. The driver of a beer truck coming from the south thought *he* did.

Well, of course, the confrontation was unavoidable. The beer truck continued roaring toward Tecate while the pig landed not far from where El Flako's pickup was still gasping for air. El Flako ran over to inspect the animal. There was little doubt that his soul had ascended.

"*Tacos . . . ricos tacos de carnitas!*"

"Delicious pork tacos over here!" El Flako sang out while he collected cash and made change as fast as he could. He had two girls preparing tacos, and they too were working as fast as their young hands could move. Cars were lined up two deep. They were only twelve years old but he knew that like all little Mexican girls they'd been doing a woman's job since they were eight. And only a dollar a day. A hot wood fire burned in two steel drums, one for the kettle of pork meat, the other with a scrap of sheet metal over the top to heat tortillas. A row of clay bowls on the tailgate held chile salsa, diced onion, fresh cilantro, and guacamole dip. The customers helped themselves.

"Have you been by there?" Clementino asked the assembled at Pelon's barbershop.

"No, and I'm not getting near there," Abel, who was still smarting, was quick to reply.

"I can't afford another business venture with that *cabrón*," Bartolo grumbled.

"But you have to admit he has a knack for business," Clementino insisted.

"He has a knack for getting into trouble," Abel answered.

Clementino went on. "Of the hundreds of taco places in this town, they are all either beef, calf head, or fish. He *knew* pork tacos was a consumer demand waiting to be met. The man's a genius."

"Strange he didn't approach any of us to get in on it," Bartolo observed.

"Maybe he doesn't need partners," Clementino replied. "I was there. He did three hundred on Saturday and four hundred on Sunday. I'll confess I wouldn't mind owning fifty percent of that deal."

A dusky voice from out of nowhere entered the conversation. "I'm in the deal." Dustano's ragweed barely rustled when he spoke. "I own fifty percent of the *carnitas* business. I'll collect my profits every Monday without doing a thing. I just put up two hundred and fifty dollars for another high-quality pig."

The Monday following his phenomenal success, El Flako headed south on Highway 3 every day in search of another 250-pound porker on the same terms. He was there every day. It was a bad week for roadkill. By Friday the only thing available was a couple of rabbits who probably suffered from night blindness, and a careless German shepherd. And he was on the small side. Twenty pounds tops. El Flako thought this would be an excellent time to head south to Guaymas and visit his relatives. Another failure! El Flako heard his own voice. Here was a chance to win the admiration of my *compadres* and Fate came and dumped on me. How am I going to face my friends? He gassed up his pickup at the Pemex station and set a course for Guaymas.

After three weeks of daily orgies of fresh shrimp, crab-meat burritos, giant lobsters cooked over coals, and all the beer he could drink, El Flako found himself low on funds and friends. He missed his *compadres*. It was time to head back. Everything should have cooled by now. They loved him and they knew he didn't mean to be bad. He headed north.

He only got one flat and overheated twice on the desert. But he was rolling along fine at forty-five with a song in his heart. Up ahead he saw the extortionist's booth at the town of Sonoita. He slowed down. Uniformed officers inspected cars and trucks to be sure no one was carrying anything of value to their families in the south. Radios, microwaves, clothing, all these things were officially forbidden merchandise for Mexicans. But with a couple of twenties you could bring in a nuclear warhead, no problem. This quaint expedient had its beginning shortly after the Spanish conquest and has never lost its popularity. The officers hadn't bothered him on his way down. That trip, he wasn't carrying any more than a load of painful regrets.

As he slowed to a stop, the officer waved him through with a cordial smile, apparently not interested in northbound traffic. El Flako's mind was greatly relieved, and now he realized he would like to offer his bladder the same benefit. A convenient shrub oak welcomed him at the side of the road for a moment of rest and comfort. He pulled over.

While enjoying the hospitality of the shrub oak a southbound station wagon pulled in beside him. He watched a man get out and walk around to the back.

"There is plenty of room here, amigo," El Flako said cordially. "No need to expose yourself."

"*Gracias.* I only stopped to rearrange my load before going through the checkpoint," the traveler acknowledged the courtesy from a distance.

El Flako tucked everything back where it belonged and joined the stranger at the back of the station wagon. "They are very thorough, those *cabrónes.* What are you taking down?"

"Just some old bedroom furniture. A fiver will get that through. That's not my problem. I don't know what to do with this sack full of bulbs."

"Bulbs?"

"Yes, daffodil bulbs. One thousand of them! My crazy *compadre* back home in Durango has this idea that he will plant them in pots and sell them for ten apiece next Mother's Day."

El Flako peered in the big gunnysack. He didn't know a daffodil bulb from a lightbulb. It looked like a bag of dirt clods to him, but the numbers were interesting. "You're right, you'll never get them across. They'll think you're transporting some kind of drug."

"That's exactly what I told my *compadre.*"

"And when you explain to those ignorant *cabrónes* that

they grow into flowers, they'll never believe you. Then you won't get any of this other stuff through."

"I told my *compadre* that too."

"Maybe I can solve your problem."

"How?"

"Look, throw them in the back of my pickup. I'll give you a hundred dollars. At least a hundred dollars is something you can use in Durango."

El Flako had been back from his Guaymas sojourn five days and still hadn't paid a visit to Pelon's barbershop and his *compadres*. The main reason for this was that he got home with a full head of steam and his pickup truck hemorrhaged in his driveway. The aging vehicle was now in Gordo's Garage undergoing a delicate engine block transplant and a radiator bypass. Gordo found a donor in a Tijuana junkyard. In the meantime El Flako used his time wisely. He called on Blanco and Calimax, the two largest *supermercados* in Tecate. A week later he closed his deal and walked the ten blocks to pick up his truck.

"The animal is good for another sixty-four trouble-free miles. Guaranteed," El Gordo teased his client.

"How much?"

"Five hundred."

"I haven't been able to get to the bank. Here's two, I'll be back with the other three this afternoon."

Strict tenets of Mexican etiquette prohibit the use of language that could imply distrust. Without uttering a syllable, Gordo began to kick at the dirt. This body language made it unnecessary to say, "You're dreaming, you flake!" El Flako translated it accurately.

"I know you trust me as far as the bank. I don't keep five hundred dollars in my sock!"

This was intended to fill Gordo with guilt and make him appear mean and petty to the world. The device never fails to succeed when everyone in Tecate follows the same script.

"Of course, *sí, absolutamente!* It's perfectly all right. By the way, you know anybody who wants a Caterpillar D-4?"

"You have one?"

"I have one in perfect condition. El Yones just overhauled it." He meant Jones, an American expert on heavy machinery who was in big demand in Tecate. "Those machines last forever, you know. They're always working. And they charge fifty an hour."

El Flako was well aware that a D-4 was a money machine. He didn't need Gordo to tell him that. "How much?"

"Ten thousand American."

The price was right. "I'll tell you what. I'll be back this afternoon with two thousand, you'll have the balance in sixty days." Gordo hesitated. El Flako saw a dark cloud of doubt cross his face. "If you can find a better deal, take it!" He knew exactly how to look like a fish that was about to get away. The answer came as no surprise.

"Deal!"

They shook hands and El Flako headed for town.

"*Buenos dias,*" El Flako greeted his *compadres* at the barbershop. He carried a large plastic bag in his hand. He withdrew a gallon jug of his homemade Concord vinaigrette.

"*Buenos dias,*" they all replied in unison. No one was getting cropped. Pelon brought out jelly jars, El Flako filled them to the top. They all exchanged *salud* and *provecho* and sipped the wine with appropriate comments from the panel of experts.

"The weather was beautiful in Guaymas," El Flako offered.

No one wanted to reply directly for fear of involvement. Dustano began to discuss yesterday's soccer game. "Gomez is probably the best player Guatemala has right now."

"On the way back from Guaymas I came across a remarkable investment opportunity."

"We play them next week. It's going to be close."

"It's the best investment I've seen in a long time."

"I don't know, I think we look pretty strong."

"It will pay a huge return on investment. Ten thousand American dollars in sixty days."

They weren't ignoring their *compadre* so much as they were trying to avoid getting sucked into another sticky deal.

"We proved formidable against Uruguay."

El Flako pulled a paper from his pocket. "I have a signed purchase order from Calimax. Ten thousand dollars on delivery April twenty-fifth. Sixty days from now."

The conversation stopped. The hum of the electric fan was the only sound in Pelon's barbershop. All the *compadres* gathered around their flaky friend to examine the document. El Pelon, the shortest one in the crowd, climbed up on the barber chair to get a better look.

"This says you have to deliver one thousand potted daffodils fourteen business days prior to El Dia de la Madre on May tenth."

"Where are you going to get one thousand potted flowers by Mother's Day?"

"I already have them. I brought them back from Guaymas." El Flako reached in the shopping bag and brought out a red plastic six-inch pot with a little green spear poking up through the soil. "I have one thousand of these tokens of love that will fill every mother's heart with joy in my back garden. They will be in full flower, ready to exchange for ten thousand dollars in sixty days."

The next afternoon El Flako walked into Gordo's Garage loaded with cash. All his *compadres* wanted in on the deal. He paid his repair bill and put two thousand down on the Caterpillar. El Flako was on top of the world. He spent most of his life looking for the right opportunity to be successful like his *compadres* and now he had it. No more schemes, no more deals. No more digging a hole in order to fill in another. He would never have to run from embarrassment again. The Caterpillar would earn him two or three hundred a day and *dignidad*!

El Flako had no trouble finding work for his Caterpillar. He did one or two jobs and just by word of mouth people came to his house seeking his services. He charged fifty an hour and he always put in four to six hours a day. It cost him fifty to have the machine loaded on a low truck and transported to the job site. He visited the barbershop less frequently now, but when he walked in he could feel the respect of his *compadres* in the air as tangible as the witch hazel. No one avoided him now. Everyone was eager to sit down and have a drink with him. El Flako began to feel good about himself. He was an equal at last. Look out world—El Flako was on a roll!

Time passed swiftly for El Flako. He had a heavy schedule and he worked every day. He was doing a job for the *presidente* this morning. The mayor wanted to enlarge the ranch house, and he hired El Flako to level the adjacent area needed for the addition. El Flako was pouring diesel fuel into his machine when the rancher from across the highway walked over to him.

"*Buenos dias.* Are you available when you get through here? I need to clear some land. My ranch is just over the road."

It was always like this. He would never run out of work. He would never run out of money. The Caterpillar was the best investment he ever made—it was like printing money!

"*Sí,* of course. I should be through here close to noon. Is that your gate with the wagon wheels?"

"*Sí.*"

"I'll be there as soon as I finish here."

El Flako fired up his D-4 and got to work. It was hard ground with solid granite rock just under the surface. He lowered the big rippers in the rear then came back with the blade. Like a tank, the powerful machine clattered on its steel tracks, pushing tons of dirt like a child making a sand pile on a beach. Enormous granite boulders rolled before it like pebbles.

He hadn't seen a soul all morning. There was a Jeep parked near the garage, but the house itself looked quiet, shades drawn, not a sign of life. There was no need to see the *presidente.* He would finish here and present his bill later.

He probably should have been paying closer attention to what he was doing. As he made what he thought would be his last pass, the blade nicked the wall of the house. Ooopa! El Flako was expecting to see a few chips of stucco fly off. He was not expecting the entire wall to collapse. Nor was he expecting to see El Señor Presidente del Municipio de Tecate straddling his pretty secretary in an obvious attempt to conceive a child. He could hear her screams over the rattle of the steel tracks as he gave the machine full throttle and zoomed away as fast as a Caterpillar D-4 could zoom.

This looked like a good time to head across the highway

and get started on the other job. It would take *el presidente* a while to get some clothes on. They could settle up later. He came to the edge of the highway, looked in both directions. What luck! No traffic. He clattered out. El Flako did not look behind him so he didn't see the huge chunks of asphalt his steel tracks were chopping out of the pavement in an interesting design. He also didn't see a Judicial Federal in a black and white squad car that was just coming to the highway out of a dirt road. In his haste to put some distance between himself and the recent disaster, he may have thought it was a large holstein.

God, these Federales are quick, he thought. He just got across the street when the holstein was right next to him flashing red and blue lights. An ugly face in a mismatched uniform was walking toward him.

"*Buenos dias.*" He gave the cop the high beams.

"Save it. Turn off the machine, I'm impounding it. Get in the car, I'm arresting you."

How ungracious these Federales could be! he thought. Didn't even have the manners to return my *buenos dias*. "And the charge?"

"Look at the highway behind you."

"I have barrels of tar at home. I could repair this in a matter of a few minutes. And it's high-quality tar too, not that cheap stuff they put down. I'll have it looking better than ever by the time—"

"Get in the car."

El Flako avoided jail by slipping the *judicial* a gift of a thousand American dollars.

Without his yellow Caterpillar money machine, El Flako had no option other than to stay home and out of sight. He began to make accounts. It didn't balance out well at all. On the twenty-fifth of April he would deliver one thousand bright expressions of love to Mamá and collect the full ten thousand dollars. On the darker side of the ledger he owed Gordo eight thousand on the Caterpillar, which he couldn't return because it now belonged to the federal government, the *presidente* was suing him for five thousand, and he owed a fine of five thousand. Oh, and his *compadres* were now demanding restitution of twenty-five hundred. There was no way he could make ten thousand dollars stretch into twenty.

El Flako sat in hiding at a small table near the swinging kitchen door at La Fonda. Maybe this would be a good time to visit his family in Guaymas. He held a tequila shooter. He shot it down without benefit of lime or a lick of salt. He asked for another. He wanted to get drunk. But he knew he wouldn't. He didn't have enough money. Once more he was humiliated in front of his *compadres*. He fought back the tears. To make matters worse, today was his birthday. "I'm a failure at thirty-five," he thought. He saw the front door open and his heart threw in an extra beat. The list of people who wanted their kilo of flesh was getting longer. He shot down his tequila. He was relieved to see it was only his *compadres*. He liked his *compadres*. He would make it up to them. He really, really would.

Abel took the empty chair at his table. Bartolo and Clementino dragged some chairs over. Dustano preferred to stand.

"A little early, no?" Bartolo said.

"It is my birthday, *muchachos*."

"*Feliz cumpleaños!*"

"*Gracias.*"

El Flako wasn't at all sure what happened next. It all happened so fast. He went to the men's room, his *compadres* followed. Then, without preface, he was wearing someone's raincoat and they all left La Fonda. Together they walked across the street to the plaza. The sun was just going down. They all went up into the kiosk. When his *compadres* took back the raincoat and departed, he was stark naked on the bandstand in the middle of the plaza.

And it was his birthday.

He would not let himself cry. He would show these *cabrones* he was a survivor. He was quick to grasp the fact that a naked man traipsing across the plaza would almost certainly attract attention. The first thing he would do was buy a poncho when the *zarape* man came by. No money. All right, he would borrow a poncho. But the *zarape* man was nowhere in sight. From behind the heavy pillar he surveyed the plaza. It wasn't going to be as hard as he first thought. He saw exactly what he needed. On the street between the plaza and the Cantina Los Cuernos stood an open Dumpster. Once in there, he would be safe. Anybody coming out of Los Cuernos would be somebody he knew. They would bring him something to wear. Perfect plan.

Now, how to get there without risking immediate arrest? He would have to make a run for the big bushy conifer by the fountain. From there, an easy sprint to the monument honoring Lazaro Cardenas. The only risky part was the final leg from the monument to the Dumpster. He scanned the area for something—anything—that would cover that part of him that was illegal. Nothing.

Then he saw the answer. Would it work? It would have

to work. The balloon man was just entering the plaza. He held hundreds of balloons in every shape and size and color. There was Meeky Mouse, El Snoopy, and Porky Peeg. There were balloons in the shape of rockets with fiery red nose cones. Some were shaped like giant sausages, and the man also carried round ones of every size and color. He would cover himself with a few of these for the first leg of his escape from the kiosk to the conifer waiting to conceal him with its dense foliage. Terrific plan. It required money.

El Flako stood concealed behind the pillar of the bandstand, and because he was standing a good six feet above ground level, he could get a pretty good overview of activity. Darkness was coming, traffic was light at this hour. That was one advantage. On the other hand, he needed some activity in order to get his hands on some money. And, above all, he needed the balloon man for his plan to work.

He watched the progress of an old man shuffling toward the bandstand. He carried a long pole festooned with colored paper. Multicolored garlands hung on both arms. He was selling tickets for the Loteria Nacional. He would be loaded with money. The old man came to the edge of the bandstand with the intention of rearranging his burden. He leaned his long pole against the wall. El Flako's bare feet stood inches away from the old man's head.

While El Flako had no saint he could call his very own, his fervor for hagiolatry was undiminished. He invoked the assistance of a stand-in, and San Lorenzo took the call. You can always count on San Lorenzo when the tortilla chips are down. A lean ranchero in Viva Zapata mustache and ten-gallon hat presented himself.

"Give me a strip of ten tickets."

"*Sí*, señor, choose your lucky numbers, señor."

General Zapata chose his numbers and handed the man a fifty-peso note. The lottery man pulled out an old blue sock stuffed with money. He withdrew a roll of money and spread some ones and fives on the floor of the bandstand in order to make change. Neither Emiliano Zapata nor the lottery man was aware that a naked fugitive lurked just behind the pillar where they were conducting business.

The ticket seller handed the man his proper change, stuffed the remainder of his money back in his sock, and trundled off to troll the sidewalk café across the plaza. He never missed the fiver.

"God forgive me," El Flako whispered.

El Flako thought his luck was holding. The balloon man was taking another turn around the kiosk.

"Pssssst, over here!"

The balloon man hesitated. But seeing no one in the immediate vicinity, attributed the hiss to the playful wind and continued on his way.

"PSSSST!"

The startled balloon man looked toward the direction of the onomatopoeic summons only to see a bare hand sticking out through the wrought-iron grille waving a *cinco*. He approached it with the same caution he would employ if he were sneaking up on a snake. The voice seemed to come from behind the pillar.

"The balloons! How much?"

The balloon man still could not see the source of the request, so he spoke to the hand waving the *cinco*. "I have many balloons, many prices. Choose the one you fancy, señor."

"I can't see them. Just give me five pesos' worth of balloons," the phantom hand answered.

A naked man with a blazing rocket in front and Porky Peeg hanging on his back dashed out of the kiosk and disappeared into the waiting conifer. He caught his breath. In a few minutes he resumed normal respiratory function. He waited patiently for what I believe you call a window of opportunity to make a quick run over to President Cardenas's memorial.

Voices!

A young mother and her obstreperous four-year-old walked perilously close. He could hear the little monster whining for cotton candy. He must have seen the front end of the rocket poking through the bushes.

"Mamá, look!" the kid screamed at the top of his lungs, and pointed a sticky finger at the only thing between El Flako and a night in jail.

His mother didn't even turn around. She took his hand and gave him a yank. "Stop that! You want everything you see."

El Flako was grateful for a mother who was not intimidated by petulant behavior even if age-appropriate. He wanted to congratulate her but he didn't think it was a good idea. He buried himself deeper into the foliage to prevent a reoccurrence. It felt prickly.

BANG!

Porky Peeg was dead. He would have to forget the intermediate stop at Lazaro Cardenas and run straight for the Dumpster.

Darkness was closing in on the plaza now. The lights hadn't come on yet. The perfect conditions. All he had to do now was wait. Eventually there would come a moment when there would be no one between his bush and the Dumpster.

He studied the traffic pattern from within the bush. Most of the people were gathered at the other end of the plaza where the food carts were lined up. He waited for some teenagers to pass, an old woman with a string shopping bag in each hand, and a brown dog. Everybody got out of the way with the exception of the brown dog. The inquisitive Airedale, who closely resembled Sandy, sniffed the bush vigorously. He said "Guau!" (Spanish for *arf*) and left a short message for Little Orphan Annie and trotted on his way. It was now or never.

With only the rocket to preserve some decency, he streaked to the edge of the plaza and made a flying leap into the Dumpster. Safe!

About an hour later the doors of Los Cuernos swung open and two men came out into the dark street. Both were bound to a wife by a holy covenant sworn in the presence of a Catholic priest. Love, honor, and the forsaking of all others was an importrant clause in the agreement. But this contract rarely impeded their quest for new adventures.

"We could have taken the girls with us if you had a little more finesse," one of the men grumbled.

"Yours was beautiful."

"And so was yours."

"Yes, but I don't think she liked me."

"Can you blame her?"

"I didn't mean to spill my drink down the front of her dress."

"It wasn't that."

"What, then?"

"When you pressed your ear to her in order to listen to her heart."

"She didn't seem to mind that."

"Until you nipped her!"

"I don't feel too good."

"I don't doubt it, chasing tequila shooters with a beer."

"Where is the car?"

"Right here, *cabrón*."

"I think I'm going to be sick."

"Not in my car!"

In desperation, the man who had been complaining of queasiness ran a few feet, leaned over the Dumpster and began to scream out Mexican street names like a bus driver . . . "CHEE-WA-WA! . . . WAH-HAWCA! . . . KWA-WEE-LA!"

When El Flako didn't drop in to Pelon's barbershop the next day, his *compadres* figured he was still smarting from the ribald prank. But when he didn't put in an appearance on the second day, remorse began to seep into their souls. They decided to call on him at home, take him out for dinner and drinks, and the debt that now burdened their hearts would melt in the heat of much laughter and big *abrazos*. When they arrived, they found no trace of their *compadre* and the house was locked up tight. Then they saw the indictment hanging above the door. The black flag of mourning accused them in deadly silence. Four *compadres* made the cross. They had gone too far.

It was now three o'clock in the afternoon and the barroom at La Fonda was nearly deserted. Nearly deserted. Treenie Contreras was closing a deal with a beautiful young woman interested in meeting an American Prince Charming. Four *compadres* sat around a table, each dipping his mustache in the tequila double in front of him in an effort to drive out the specter of guilt that haunted the chamber where conscience dwells. The *compadres* were on their third round.

Abel lifted his glass. "To El Flako."

"El Flako!" echoed all at table.

"A true friend in the cakes or in the onions."

"Rest in peace."

Four *compadres* picked up their glasses, put them to their lips, and emptied the liquid lightning in one burning gulp. And the big bad machos burst into tears.

"He was both friend and *compadre*," Abel sobbed.

"He didn't have a mean bone in his body," Bartolo managed to say between painful sighs. "A gentle lamb of generous heart and pure soul."

"And now El Señor has called His lamb home."

"And we killed him!" Dustano cried out in pain. His nose was bubbling. He wiped the ragweed mustache with his sleeve. "Bartender—another round of doubles for the murderers!" He yielded to a flood of bitter tears.

"No, no, no." Abel put his arm around his *compadre* in an attempt to comfort him. "It was an accident. Tragic yes, but nobody's fault."

"And what a horrible place to die," Dustano cried as though his heart would break. "A man is supposed to die in his wife's arms, surrounded by his children. But no, El Flako, who never hurt anyone in his life, has—has to—to die like a poisoned rat in a Dumpster filled with garbage!"

"Dear God, dear God, forgive us. Bring Your comfort to our wretched souls—if we have a soul!" Bartolo decanted a torrent of tears. He could not be consoled. Then he took his grief out on the bartender. "Bartender, are you deaf, *cabrón*!"

"When is the funeral?"

"I don't know. I'm going to see Flores Negras at the mortuary and get the details. Does anybody know his proper name? I don't want to call him Black Flowers."

"I think he is Flores-Negrete, but he's been Flores Negras since I can remember."

"Who will go with me?"

"We will *all* go!"

The bartender rushed to the table and put another Centenario double in front of each man. There was nothing wrong with his hearing.

"So young for a heart attack."

"Thirty-five."

"At least he went fast."

"I'm not so sure. He had time to write a note."

"Who found him and the note?"

"Probably the garbage collectors."

"*Ay, ay, ay, por Dios!*" Bartolo wailed and all four *compadres* were again drowning in tears.

Dustano was the first to regain some measure of control. "How did the note get to Father Ruben?" he sniffed.

Abel took a long ragged breath in an effort to regulate his shaky voice. "Father Ruben told me a servant delivered it to him in the rectory." From his pocket he pulled out a dirty envelope imprinted with the Serfin Bank logo. It was creased and smeared with tire marks. "Father Ruben said we should keep it."

Clementino took the envelope. "It smells kind of bad."

Dustano took if from him impatiently and pulled out the paper inside. "Look, poor thing, he scribbled it on a cocktail napkin from the Diana. *Pobrecito!*"

"Read it again."

Dustano's eyes spilled over. "I can't."

Clementino took the cocktail napkin in his hand, and with eyes dim with tears, read. "Forgive them Father for they know not what they do."

Four big bad macho *compadres* broke down in tears. They drained their tequila doubles, set the empty glass down with a bang, and Bartolo burst out, "I'll beat up any *cabrón* in the bar!"

"Sssh, sssh, now, *compadre*. Take it easy. There's nobody here." They managed to find the door, groped their way to somebody's car, and headed for the mortuary.

Tecate's only mortuary is located on a back street wedged between Las Quince Letras—The Fifteen Letters—a small home-style restaurant, and Celeste's Estudio de Ballet. The small room, formerly a piñata shop, had to serve as show-room, office, and chapel. There were a half-dozen caskets on display, a desk in the corner, and a dozen folding metal chairs (courtesy of Tecate Brewery) facing a wooden crate covered in maroon carpet to match the drapes.

Señor Flores-Negrete or Flores Negras, depending on your disposition, came out from behind his desk. He had an unforgettable countenance. Put white sideburns on an eggplant and you pretty much have the idea. He wore a grief-stricken black suit and a dolorous tie dyed in burgundy. "*Señores, mis condolencias*. Please sit down, señores. I stand at your service." He spoke in a low monotonous moan free of all inflection. On an optical sound track his voice would have been a straight line. The eggplant smiled to the gums. It was intended to convey equal parts of courage and comfort. He shook hands with each in alphabetical order, as that is how they had entered. "Can I be of service? Just tell me how." The breathy adverb caused the four *compadres* to retreat a step. Flores Negras reeked of dirty ashtrays and Old Spice.

"We came to see about our *compadre*," Abel answered.

"*Sí*, I know."

"We are his best friends."

"And *compadres*."

"Of course."

"We have decided as his best friends to cover the expenses of our dear departed *compadre*."

"His widow could never afford it."

"We tried to contact her, but she's not at home. The house is locked up tight."

"You señores are the epitome of the meaning of the word *compadre*," Flores Negras moaned.

"And I for one don't care what it costs," Dustano said through the ragweed. His big black eyes filled and once again his nose bubbled.

"Neither do I!" three voices said as one.

"Well, let us see," Flores Negras answered in basso profundo. "I have been preparing some figures."

The pleasant fragrance of browning onions and enchilada sauce seeped into the funeral parlor from Las Quince Letras next door. Somebody's stomach was growling. The sweeping melody of *Swan Lake* could be heard through the back wall along with some heavy thuds as aspiring cygnets made a hard landing.

Señor Flores Negras continued in larghetto. "It comes to only three thousand. I speak in dollars, of course, and this is with a casket *económico*."

"Never! We want nothing *económico* for our *compadre*."

"We want the best."

"And only the best!"

"Let me show you, then, the best casket we have." He led the group of *compadres* to an ornate casket. "Solid mahogany, bronze handles. Fit for a cardinal." He opened the cover. "Pure imported silk interior where he can sleep in everlasting peace."

"We'll take it!"

"It is a wonderful *acta noble* you do, señores. The total is only $5,200."

"You speak in dollars."

"*Sí*, señor."

Four *compadres* made payment of $1,300 each and headed back to La Fonda for another round of comfort.

Emilio Figueroa de Alvarado sat sipping a tall piña colada in the dining room of the luxurious oceanfront Hotel Olas Altas in Acapulco. His table faced the window, providing an unobstructed view of the glistening Pacific. He watched long curls of emerald roll up on the pink beach, then recede, leaving doilies of white foam. Pretty girls frolicked with breasts unveiled like the bronzed nymphs in Greek myths.

Mauricio, maître d'hôtel, materialized at his side with an obsequious bow practiced and perfected for the benefit of heavy tippers.

"Are you ready to order lunch, señor?"

"Mauricio, what would you recommend today?"

"Permit me to bring Alexandro out to you." A subtle movement of the eyebrows, imperceptible to all but the keenest observer, brought the chef de cuisine to the table.

The head chef appeared in bridal white and fluffy marshmallow hat. "*Buenas tardes,* señor. Let me suggest my special chicken Acapulco, succulent breast of chicken stuffed with soft cheese, pasilla chiles, and baby shrimp. I add a touch of tarragon to give it personality. Just a pinch, you know. Any more would be precocious."

"Bring it on!"

"*Sí,* señor." Alexandro bowed, as taught by Mauricio, and withdrew in the direction of his domain.

"Another piña colada, señor?" the maître d'hôtel inquired.

"An excellent suggestion, Mauricio. By the way, who plays in the Flamingo Room tonight?"

"The Sonora Los Guajiros, señor. Direct from Havana. They are *magnífico.* Shall I reserve your table again for tonight? You appeared to enjoy yourself immensely last night. If I may be so bold as to make the observation, señor, you displayed a virtuosity on the dance floor not often seen. You dominated the moves of the cha-cha-cha. The agility of the matador is in your blood, señor. Of course you had many beautiful partners, no?"

"*Sí.* By all means, Mauricio, reserve my table. I intend to dislocate some *nalgas* tonight."

"Very good, señor."

"And after lunch send me something to drink out at my ramada on the beach. I will be selecting dance partners for the merengué."

"I would suggest our popular *coco loco,* señor, a fresh coconut filled with natural tropical fruit juices skillfully blended with volatile spirits. A libation that restores the passion for life."

"You mean it will perk me up?"

"A turbocharger for body and soul, señor. Two of our

coco locos would have Don Porfirio dancing salsa in the plaza, and he's cast of solid bronze."

"I'll take one."

"A prudent decision. Will that be all, señor?"

Emilio Figueroa de Alvarado said it would. He attacked his chicken Acapulco like the legendary *Chupacabras* preys on a goat under a full moon. Through the window he watched an intrepid tourist soaring high above the beach strapped to a paraglider towed by a small motorboat. Copper-plated young boys were diving off eighty-foot cliffs for tips.

Emilio withdrew from the festal board and relocated to the pink beach under the shade of his ramada. He was studying the moves of a pretty young thing in a red two-piece misdemeanor when the waiter, dressed in white pants and a shirt sprayed with yellow hibiscus, delivered the infamous *coco loco.*

"And bring me a *teléfono, sí?*"

"Right away, señor."

Emilio sipped his postprandial cocktail through a straw. Life became more beautiful with each sip. In minutes the waiter returned with a telephone. He dialed a number in Los Angeles.

"*Bueno!*"

He recognized the voice at once. "*Hola, mi amor,* how is everything up there? Good. I'm sorry I had to leave in such a hurry. Important business, you know. No, I'm not sure when I'll get back. But you stay as long as you like."

"My mother thinks it was wonderful of you to give me the money to stay up here for a couple of weeks."

"Anything for my family."

"You got a strange phone call from Flores Negras before I

left. He said he wanted to thank you for your generosity. What was he talking about?"

Emilio answered with congenial laughter. "I gave him five hundred dollars for special services rendered. Have a good time in Los Angeles, *mi amor*. Give your mother my love."

Emilio Figueroa de Alvarado put the phone down and, with full stomach and happy heart, wandered off into a pleasant dream state. He was cavorting in foamy surf in the company of a gaggle of sea nymphs, daughters of Oceanus, and naked as flounders. They were splashing and teasing him mischievously, as these playful little sprites are in the habit of doing. He attributed the happy hallucination to the *coco loco*. He thought he heard the sweet strumming of a guitar in the warm tropical air.

"A song, señor? Fifteen pesos, two dollars, any song."

Emilio looked up. The frisky little fairies of the sea disappeared and a barefoot musician cradling a guitar in his arms assumed their place.

"I have songs to help you remember the woman you lost, songs to help you forget the woman you won."

Emilio thought about it. "Something romantic would be nice."

"*Sí*, señor. What would you like to hear . . . 'Vals Triste' or something even more romantic, like 'God Never Dies'?"

"I was thinking of another old song."

"*Sí?*"

" 'El Flako Never Dies.' "

"I don't think I know that one."

Mexican Folk Dances

There are close to 35,000 faces in Tecate, none alike. You have to wonder how the Great Designer managed it without repeating Himself. Sometimes you see the same face so often you're convinced you know the person and, with frequency, a shy intimacy develops. This was the case with Cecilia Rodriguez. I saw her nearly every day as we passed each other in the plaza. Occasionally I encountered her at Saturday market and I would watch her make her selection among the skinny, naked chickens that hung from baling wire. We always exchanged a smile of recognition, and in time, we added a *buenos dias* and a few cordial words.

Wherever I happened to see her, she always appeared to have just stepped out of that large Diego Rivera mural at the Detroit Institute of Fine Arts. The maestro gave her that typical russet face, the terra-cotta lips, those huge dark eyes that pierce your surface and look straight into your soul. The hair, like a black *rebozo*, fell to the small of her back in one bold brush stroke.

One raw and drizzly morning I found her vigorously sweeping the gutter in front of Casa Monica, a popular bridal shop.

"*Buenos dias*, señora."

"*Buenos dias*." You could warm your hands on her smile that cold morning. "I wonder if I could impose on our long friendship?"

"Of course! *Como no!* What can I do for you?"

"A delivery man left that heavy carton by the door before I got here. I wonder if I could exploit your kindness—"

"*Seguro que si!*" I wrestled the heavy carton all the way into the back of the shop. By the time I turned around she held out a cup of hot chocolate.

"Nothing like a good *chocoláte* on a day like this," she said placing it in my hands.

"*Buenos dias*, Cecilia!" It was the woman from the shoe store next door. "Even in broad daylight that delivery man could blind you with the dazzle of his stupidity. He left a carton in the rain and gave me the packing slip." She handed the soggy bill of lading to Cecilia.

"*Gracias*, Gloria. Will you have a *chocoláte?*"

"Another time. I'm all alone in the shop. You heard Sarita is getting married?"

"No, who's the boy?"

"Arturo Guerra, son of the carpenter."

"You'd better fit her with dancing shoes," Cecilia laughed.

"That's exactly what I told her!"

The friendly neighbor left and as long as Cecilia offered me a second cup, I felt our friendship was now firm enough that I could ask the question. "What was all that about dancing shoes?"

"*La mujer mexicana baila al son que le toque la marimba.*" The Mexican woman dances to the tune of the marimba man.

I couldn't help but laugh. I accepted the second cup, the conversation became easy. While a cold petulant drizzle turned the streets of Tecate to shiny black mirrors, I recorded the human sketch that follows and I can be sponsor for its truth.

Cecilia Rodriguez was a *madre soltera*. In your country you would call her a single mother, but this detail may be somewhat in advance of the story. I suppose her tale really begins the evening she strolled the plaza with her tender fourteen-year-old heart pinned to the sleeve of her summer blouse of pink organdy. Cecilia had fallen in love every day since she turned thirteen, but that day on the plaza was dangerous for young girls with vulnerable fourteen-year-old hearts. It was the annual Romeria Festival staged every August by the church to raise funds, and the plaza was crowded with young girls and boys overflowing with hormones. Dance music blared from the kiosk. Booths were set up with food and refreshments, games of chance, games of skill, and silly games too. One booth sold the traditional Mexican Cupid's Eggs. For twenty-five *centavos* a girl could buy a hollow egg filled with scented confetti. Now all she had to do was crack it over the head of the boy of her choice and he would be obliged to dance with her. The decorated egg has endless possibilities.

Cecilia worked her way toward the kiosk to let the music abuse her eardrums and watch the boys take the girls out to dance. No boys seemed to notice her. She looked around for Hector. There he was, twisting and turning to the savage beat like he was Michael Jackson. When the music stopped he was immediately surrounded by a gaggle of girls who loitered around him between dances like flies on ripe fruit. Cecilia wondered if maybe she shouldn't invest in a Cupid's Egg. She worked her way back to the concession booths and listened to the voices of temptation.

"Try your luck, señorita! Ring around the Coke bottle and win a prize!"

"Hey, *bonita*! Why are you walking alone? Buy a balloon and walk with Meeky Mouse!"

"Capture his heart with one of Cupid's Eggs—that will get his attention!"

Cecilia was tempted. But she was a poor girl, and being poor can teach prudence. If she spent twenty-five *centavos* on an egg and cracked it over Hector's head, she could count on one dance and that would be the end of it. You can't unscramble an egg.

"Señorita! Send the scoundrel to jail. At least you'll know he's not dancing with somebody else!"

There was her answer. Cecilia looked up to see a woman of vast dimensions dressed like a cop. The police department must have loaned her Big Nalgas Machado's uniform. Big Nalgas Machado was the fattest cop on the force. He either had the night off or he was walking his beat in his underwear.

"*Sí*, señorita, have no pity. Put the scoundrel in jail!"

Next to the booth with the imitation cop was a city jail made of red, white, and green crepe paper. The idea appealed to Cecilia, but issuing the warrant was expensive. For a fee equal to three times the price of a Cupid's Egg, the client puts the finger on the boy, the cop rushes out into the plaza and makes the arrest. The suspect is charged and put in the crepe paper slammer. Bail was usually set at one kiss on the plaintiff's lips for misdemeanors. More for felonies.

Definitely more boy for the money. Cecilia paid the fee and fingered Hector. He was dancing an exceptional *quebradita* with a girl she didn't know but found easy to despise on the strength of her beauty alone. The cop pushed through the crowded dance floor, put the arm on Hector, slapped paper handcuffs on him, and took him into custody. The felon was now safe behind crepe paper bars.

"What is the charge, marshal?" Hector demanded.

"You're a *muchacho*."

"That's a crime?"

"Of course! You'll grow up to be a man. Twenty minutes in the hoosegow or three kisses."

Cecilia looked at the prisoner. He was beautiful. This was the Principe Azúl that roams the pages of all the fairy tales. A young crowd gathered to watch the spectacle as Hector was brought forward to face the plaintiff.

"And the court demands real kisses, kisses this girl will not soon forget."

Cecilia was seized by a sudden attack of shyness. Her face glowed in the dark. Hector paid his debt to society and the crowd screamed with delight.

Cecilia would remember those three magic kisses for the rest of her life. On her fifteenth birthday she gave Prince Hector a little princess. They baptized her Anastasia. Prince Hector was obliged to marry her.

And the marimba man began to play. Step point, step jump. Step point, turnaround.

At eighteen Hector, now a husband, was obliged to

apprentice to an uncle. His uncle patiently taught him every-thing there was to know about his trade. He learned to mix mortar, lay brick, and drink mezcal to the point of no return. It took Hector only a few months to earn his macho badge of honor.

Four years later Laura, a second princess, was born. Together the royal family rented a tumbledown three-room villa owned by a vicious landlord known to everyone in Tecate only as the Rodent. By the time Laura blew out the first candle on her birthday cake, Prince Hector emptied the treasury in the coffee can hidden in the dish cupboard and abandoned his family. No one ever heard from him again. Idle gossip had it that he had gone to the Other Side. That's when life got serious. Cecilia left the girls with her grand-mother Pancha or a neighbor while she scoured the town for whatever work she could find to keep food on the table and the Rodent out of her *calzones*.

Even in Mexico time can be said to fly. It seemed to Cecilia that one day Anastasia was bringing home her kindergarten pictures and her biggest problem was scrubbing the paint out of her little dresses. Then came the measles and a variety of fairy folk including the Tooth Fairy, the Easter Bunny, and the Monthly Pixie. Then one day Anastasia came home from school with pink hair and morning sick-ness. Now Cecilia had problems she couldn't solve at the washboard. Cecilia let the boyfriend move in with them even though she didn't approve of him. You couldn't say Cheve was good-looking. He was beautiful! The curve of his vermilion mouth could corrupt a saint. Long black curls cov-ered his ears. He also had a crush on marijuana. Cheve quickly found the coffee can. A year later he left Anastasia with another mouth to feed. They named her Candida. Cecilia looked at Anastasia at fifteen and saw herself. Poor thing, she thought. We are now yoked to the same wagon. I should have baptized her Xerox. Well, God knows best.

Cecilia, now a thirty-two-year-old grandmother, went to work full-time. She put Laura in the convent school. They did without clothes, sometimes without food, but Cecilia wasn't taking any chances. Nothing like this would ever happen to Laura. And it didn't.

It happened to Cecilia.

Cecilia invested what little cash she had in a full line of Jean de Paris Cosmetiques Français made in Tijuana. The profit margin was good but the work was arduous. She pounded the pavements all day long, ringing doorbells, demonstrating, flattering, lying, being as charming as she knew how. She wore her feet down to the bone and didn't move a lot of product.

One dismal day Cecilia decided she had better explore new territory. She took the bus into Colonia Linda Vista. She had never been there before. It was beautiful! Big houses were not shy about flaunting their financial burden on their owners. The shiny cars parked under the arch of the *cochero* appeared to imply that if you were a car, Colonia Linda Vista was *the* place to be seen. The gardens were lavish. Fancy wrought-iron lacework guarded azaleas and prize-winning roses like the children of the rich who must not be allowed to mix with common varieties. She could smell the wealth. These people must bathe with money, she thought.

She let herself into number 22 and rang the bell. She was grateful no dog came out barking an alarm. A young girl in an apron opened the door.

"*Buenas tardes.*" Cecilia smiled. "I have a wonderful collection of La Francia creams and lotions. These are high-quality *productos* you would pay a fortune for at the boutiques, but I offer them today at a special discount." She removed the cap from a jar of pink lotion and offered it to the girl at the door. "Isn't that a delightful fragrance?"

"Oh, indeed it is."

"And now feel this." She took the girl's arm and applied a little dollop of cream and worked it into the skin. "Now feel how soft it leaves your skin."

The girl followed instructions. "Oh, that feels wonderful!"

"And they are on special at only fifteen dollars a jar."

"Only fifteen dollars."

"And with each jar you get a free gift, this little vial of La Francia cologne."

"*Magnífico!*"

Cecilia dipped in her bag and brought out a new jar. "Here, this is a brand-new jar, and here is your free gift."

"Oh, I can't buy anything. I don't have any money and the señora of the house is not here this afternoon."

Cecilia withdrew, disappointed, but not discouraged. She had never been one to admit defeat. She continued down the street with renewed determination. She had a family to support. A dozen or so houses later produced the same disheartening results. This *colonia* had the big houses, and the money, but the señoras were never home and only maids answered the door. She was ready to change neighborhoods. But Cecilia was not quite ready to quit. Feet burning, all sweaty and sticky, she decided to make one last call. Then, if that didn't produce anything, she could retreat with honor.

She brushed away her tears, put on a brave smile, and rang the bell at number 14. A nice man with a fatherly countenance answered the door.

"*Sí?*"

"*Buenas tardes*, señor. I have a complete line of very fine cosmetics *de Francia*. Is the señora at home?" She was looking at a pleasant-looking man, probably fifty something. He had a smooth face, his hair black with tiny silver pinfeathers at the edges.

"No the señora is not home, but maybe I can use some of these things as gifts, no?" He had that authoritative voice all men have. Her father's voice? She couldn't remember. Her father died when she was a girl of nine. But it was the kind of voice she expected God to have when it came time for her final interview. "Please come in."

A hot prospect! Cecilia entered the lobby. She was grateful for the coolness and even more grateful for the chair the señor offered. It felt good to sit. Her feet were killing her, but she couldn't slip out of her shoes. Her feet would swell up like a pair of eggplants and she'd never get them on again. She was satisfied to wiggle her toes inside her cheap plastic shoes to alleviate the stinging. She put her samples on the table.

"I will show you everything I have and that way you can choose what is best for your señora."

"*Magnífico*. I was just going to pour myself a glass of ice-cold lemon water. The *sirvienta* is off on Wednesdays. Would you care for some?"

"*Ay sí, gracias!*" Cecilia looked around. What a palace! I don't smell beans. I wonder what these people eat?

He returned with two tall glasses of icy *limonada*, and she immediately lowered the level in her glass by half. "Now first

I'll demonstrate our skin cream." She took his bare arm and began to apply the cream just above the wrist. "Isn't that a pleasant fragrance? It is a big favorite with the women. Now feel your skin. Isn't it soft and wonderful?"

"Why yes, it's incredible. I definitely want a jar of that."

Cecilia knew she was on a roll. "Now let me show you the cologne." She tipped the vial on her upper arm and rubbed gently. "Now, smell that."

The señor put his nose to her shoulder and inhaled. "Ah sí!" He moved his face to her hair. "Oh, that is so delicate." He sniffed near her ear. "Ah, what a light bouquet, what is that?" He could have been sampling fine varietals in a wine cellar.

"Oh, that is our Shampoo de Paris. It is indeed fresh as a bouquet of spring flowers."

"Sí, I will take one of those too. I know she will like it." He kissed her hair experimentally and awaited response.

Cecilia withheld reaction. What was she going to do? Jump up, scream, take offense? He was a kind and pleasant man and he had just bought close to a hundred dollars of *productos de Francia* made in Tijuana. That was more than she sold in a week! They weren't going to worry about food or rent this month! She left the house light of heart and promised to return the following week. She could have flown all the way home under power of her own wings.

The anonymous señor became her best customer. She could count on a big order. Every Wednesday she rang the bell at number 14 and demonstrated her products while the gentleman demonstrated his affection. It began with harmless little kisses. She couldn't really object to his gentle caresses, he was so courtly, so attentive. She was raised from infancy to be a pleaser, to respect her elders, especially authority figures. And a hundred dollars every Wednesday solved a lot of problems.

One Wednesday, Cecilia was surprised when a maid answered the ring at number 14. "No, there is no one at home," she said. "The señor left in rather a hurry to Mexico City, and the señora is out for the day."

Cecilia retreated. He was a nice man. The gentlest and sweetest she'd ever experienced in her young life. She lost her best customer but she came away with something else. Nine months later Little Jesus was the newest member of the Rodriguez family.

Cecilia was obliged to retire from Jean de Paris and now found herself trying to balance home and a variety of odd jobs. It was tough to make ends meet. She took in washing and ironing. She was also an excellent seamstress. Anastasia offered to take over her sales route, but Cecilia knew they couldn't afford to enlarge on the family. Anastasia was safer at home. She was a good surrogate mother and that allowed Cecilia to go out and bring home the tortillas. By the time Jesus was six months old, Cecilia found full-time employment at the chicken farm. It was still a hand-to-mouth existence but at least she could count on a paycheck every week.

And while Cecilia worked her job, and washed, and ironed, ravenous Time devoured the calendars from Chavez Mini-Mercado that Cecilia hung on the kitchen wall every January. Suddenly Cecilia looked up to see that Anastasia was twenty, little Candida would soon be in kindergarten, Laura was fifteen, and Little Jesus was eighteen months old. Time falls away like young corn before the scythe, she thought.

Cecilia could not take her eyes off the deceitful calendar

this Monday morning. Today was the Day of Circumcision. On your calendar, of course, it says New Year's Day; on the Mexican calendar from Chavez Mini-Mercado it commemorates an important surgical procedure in Christian history. Right after breakfast the girls decided to go down to the park and listen to the band concert. And that was fine with Cecilia. She had special things she had to do today and she preferred to have everybody out of the house.

As soon as they were out the door, Cecilia ripped December from the calendar on the wall with a vengeance. Last year was a disaster. It was time to get a fresh start in life, get the new year started right. She swept her bedroom floor, then did the same with the only other bedroom in the little dwelling where all the others slept. The floors were not dirty. She had just cleaned house yesterday. She was simply following her grandmother Pancha's instructions for the first day of the year.

"You must sweep out any remnants of bad luck from the old year that may still be lurking somewhere in the house." Her ninety-year-old Mamá Pancha knew every spell and charm and incantation practiced by the local *curanderas*. "Remember, blue underwear brings *dinero*, red for a new *novio*."

The kitchen, dining area, and living room were next. But this wasn't as hard as it sounds, as all these were but one room. Cecilia swept the symbolic debris of the previous year out the front door and into the street.

The minute she stepped outside, she felt the first puff of a Santa Ana wind. She saw it as the Evil Wind. It pulled at her hair rudely. She hated the Evil Wind. When she was a child, it brought screaming nightmares. The only thing that changed over the years was that now she didn't scream. It was hardly more than a deceptively gentle easterly breeze at that moment. But when it gathered speed over the snow-covered Rumorosa mountain range to the east, it could roar into Tecate like a freight train. It could blow for a week at a time, bringing ice and dirt, and stacking trash against the front of the house in high drifts. Cecilia knew she would have to put newspaper around the windows to keep them from rattling night and day. She would stuff a Kleenex in the keyhole against the vicious shaft of cold air that chilled the entire house.

She was about to close the door when, just for a moment, she thought she heard organ music. Soft, heavenly. Far away. Impossible! Tricks of the Evil Wind. She listened again. Nothing. A piece of trash fluttered down to her feet. She bent down to retrieve it and as she turned it over she saw it was a color print of her patron saint. Santa Cecilia, in blue gown and scarlet cape, was seated at the organ, her face turned slightly to better see Cecilia. The blessed virgin had black smudges on her blue cloak, a streak of mud ran across her pretty face. Cecilia looked into a face of serenity and felt a brief glow of inner peace. She kissed the ring on Santa Cecilia's hand and brought the print into the house. At the kitchen sink she gently cleaned her up with a damp towel. A corner of the picture was missing but that didn't matter. She took it into her bedroom.

"I think God sent you to me." She kissed the picture again and wedged it into the groove between the mirror of her dresser and the frame. The virgin seemed to smile at her. Cecilia lit a candle for her. Now it was time to continue the removal of all the bad spirits in the house before the family returned from the park.

From the bottom drawer of her dresser she brought out

the special potpourri gathered and prepared for her by Mamá Pancha. It was a mixture of dry leaves, *romero*, *gobernadóra*, and *laurel*. She emptied the contents into a small tin plate and applied a match to it. Almost at once the powerful *santeria* began its work. Thick blue smoke roiled upward. She watched the smoke take the form of hideous faces. Hunger, poverty, and all the other deities of evil floated toward the ceiling and expired. She carried the smoking tray from room to room until all the bad things were expunged from the entire house. Cecilia was now ready to start the new year.

Cecilia could hear her family returning and went to the front door to meet them. Anastasia was recognizable at a distance with her short turquoise hair. The navy blue skirt was intended to conceal the red underwear Cecilia could bet Anastasia had on this morning. God knows she doesn't need a new lover! she thought. Little Candida was walking next to her. Laura held Little Jesus in her arms. Cecilia saw the black skirt and knew that Laura too was wearing red underneath, although she hadn't seen her get dressed this morning. At fifteen, with a body going on twenty, Laura was hanging on to her virginity by a thread. Cecilia didn't want any male over the age of nine anywhere near her.

"Happy New Year!" they all called out as they came in.

"*Feliz Año*," Cecilia answered, and saw that Anastasia was rushing Candida to the bathroom.

"Little Jesus desperately needs a change," Laura said as she hurried into her room.

There was a sudden scratching at the front door. It sounded like a huge rat. And in fact, it was. Cecilia knew who stood on the other side. "It's eleven o'clock in the morning of the first day of the new year and the Rodent is already at the door."

She pulled the door open to reveal the Rodent, a thin, nervous little man with a thin pointy face terminating in a narrow snoot. He had a habit of twitching his mouth when he spoke. Due to the direct connection between the naso-facial muscle group, his nose also had a tendency to quiver when engaged in conversation. These characteristics earned him the appropriate appellation. The similarity was remarkable to the extent that everyone in Tecate was careful not to come near him with a piece of cheese. If he had a Christian name, it fell into disuse years ago.

"*Feliz Año!*" the little rodent squeaked, his small beady eyes twinkling with lascivious curiosity.

"I certainly hope so. I have all your rent money but for ten pesos so we can eat this week. I will have it for you next month." Cecilia handed him 190 pesos.

The Rodent did not put the money in his pocket. He did something to his snoot and the mustache twisted nervously as though sniffing a fine sharp cheddar. "Life is expensive and you want to short me ten pesos. I just can't do that."

Cecilia held no feeling of respect for the little vermin sniffing at her door, but fear filled that vacancy in the seat of her emotions. She could feel the power this man held over her family. He was in a position to put them all out in the street simply to indulge his whim. She decided to be cautious. "Are you going to ask us to leave?"

"Señora, I'm not here to be mean." He put the money away and the voice now oozed out like Karo syrup. "You know, if you paid a little more attention to me now and then, things could be much easier for you."

Cecilia heard this nearly every month. "I have enough troubles as it is."

The Rodent became sociable. "And how are Anastasia

and little Laura these days?" All single mothers were prime prospects for carnal amusement. "*Que bárbaro!* Little Laura is growing up fast!" He licked his quivering lips. "I hardly recognize her!"

Cecilia knew "growing up fast" was intended to mean *what a body*! "The Day of Circumcision will be celebrated again the day anyone gets near my daughters. And I will circumcise at the root." The Rodent's expression did not change, as he did not hear the serrated words. They took form in Cecilia's mind and never escaped her lips. She decided to put an end to the interview. "Your money will be here on the first."

"Happy New Year, señora, I will return then and expect the ten pesos." The repulsive little mouse sniffed, twitched once or twice, and scurried away.

Cecilia went to the kitchen stove and began to prepare dinner. Anastasia returned with Candida and put her in a corner with some toys. Laura carried Little Jesus in one arm and washed his bottle with her free hand.

"*Fuchi!* What's that funny smell?" Laura inquired, taking a bottle of milk from the refrigerator.

Anastasia answered. "Mamá has been exorcising the house for the new year. Grandmother makes her do it every January first, and I'll bet you anything she's wearing blue underneath."

"Blue is intended to bring prosperity, and we can use a little of that," her mother answered.

"Well, I'm wearing red."

"You don't need a new *novio*. We're still paying for the old one."

Tuesday morning Cecilia began the waking process at five-thirty as usual. She drowsed to the pleasant sound of reeds and flutes and sweet recorders. The beautiful music seemed to be in the very room with her. She propped herself up on one arm, now fully awake. The angelic music evaporated. She went first to her mirror to kiss the image of Santa Cecilia. "I know there is a reason why you're here."

She broke her fast on coffee and bread and gave final instructions before leaving for work. "Laura, as soon as you're home from school you wash and iron your uniforms."

"*Sí, Mamá.*"

"And take off that brassiere or mend it before it falls off." She turned to Anastasia. "There are beans in the refrigerator and spaghetti soup for lunch. There is one egg. Scramble it for Candida. We're low on milk. We have to make it to payday."

"If you leave me some money, I'll pick up milk today."

Cecilia felt leaving money with Anastasia was like handing five-year-old Candida a box of matches. She put several coins on the counter. "It is for *milk*." She kissed the little ones and went out the door leaving a trail of instructions behind her. "Remember, I don't want any men in the house—and Laura, come straight home from school and have your homework finished when I get home." Cecilia left for the chicken farm. It paid about 125 pesos a week; twenty-five American dollars.

I suppose at this point I should add the old reliable * and a footnote to explain that what everyone in Tecate called the chicken farm was not the local egg farm where many women of Tecate worked. The sign on the door read OFICINAS MUNICIPALES DE TECATE. A dozen young girls, all in their twenties, staffed the secretarial pool, and like young hens, fluttered about doing their work while doing their best to avoid the big bad rooster, a.k.a. El Gallo, Sr. Enriquez, to his face. After all, he was the department head.

Fortunately for Cecilia, she was buried in the file room. All four walls were lined with file cabinets. If there was a window somewhere, it was impossible to know. As a result she seldom saw the girls in the chicken coop. The only face she saw with any regularity was Dora's, because she was usually the one who brought her files, and they became good friends. On rare occasions El Gallo himself would come in clucking, peck around the files, eye her up and down, then leave.

By seven-thirty Cecilia was in the city offices. She made the coffee, mopped the kitchenette, and went to work. There were stacks of manila folders containing documents and correspondence on her work table, on the floor, and on top of the cabinets. It was her job to return them to the files. She filed all day long. It was a tedious chore, but she was thankful for the paycheck and secure in the knowledge she would never run out of work.

When she came home after work, the two little ones screamed with delight. She played with them for a few minutes and started on dinner. Laura was doing her homework; Anastasia was painting her nails to match her turquoise hair.

Presently the girls fed the little ones, put them to bed, and cleaned up the kitchen. Cecilia went into her bedroom. She could have sworn she heard an organ playing. She went directly to the picture of Santa Cecilia. Once again, that inexplicable warm feeling of peace and serenity came over her. She kissed the picture and lit a small candle. The virgin smiled at her. Cecilia drifted off into a dreamless sleep.

At five-thirty the next morning, Cecilia was on her feet.

She bathed and dressed and sat at the mirror to brush her hair. The little candle was out, of course, but Santa Cecilia was no longer on the mirror. Cecilia found the virgin lying on top of the dresser. She seemed to be smiling. Cecilia picked the picture up gently, placed a soft kiss at the feet of the virgin, and once again tucked it into the mirror frame. As she left the room she thought she heard a choir of angels singing ever so softly.

When Cecilia got to work she found a stack of boxes filled with folders that had to be put away. She was just on her way to the A and B files with both arms loaded when she saw El Gallo come into the file room. The very presence of the boss gave her that same sense of inferiority she experienced in the presence of all men, father, brother, landlord, boss, or priest. She returned the folders to her worktable and gave him her full attention.

"*Buenos dias*, Señor Enriquez."

"*Buenos dias*, Cecilia. I need the Quiróz file back. I think it was brought in to be filed yesterday." He was very abrupt, even his *buenos dias* was without warmth.

Cecilia went to the Q file, which was the bottom-most drawer closest to the floor. She bent at the waist to begin her search while El Gallo took a position behind her. Cecilia became aware that such a position was likely to draw inordinate attention to her *nalgas* and went down on her knees and browsed through the folders. She could feel El Gallo's eyes caressing her body, following her every move. The Q file continued at the top drawer of the next bank of files. She closed the bottom drawer, stood, and pulled out the top drawer. It was high for her and a long reach. She stood on her tiptoes and had to press her breasts tight against the front of the drawer to reach the back. El Gallo continued to watch.

El Gallo rested his hand on her shoulder and peered into

the file over her head. "Maybe I can help you. I'm taller and I would probably recognize the file folder if I saw it." Cecilia could feel his breath near her ear. She felt his helpful hand slide down her back and begin to gently rub her *nalgas*.

Again I must employ the useful *. This incident would have ended up in a courtroom in your country, but not in Mexico. Cecilia was in the presence of omnipotent authority. She couldn't raise a hand to slap him any more than she could pull out a gun and shoot him dead where he stood at the Q file. Like any well-trained and conditioned Mexican girl, the frightened little hen froze in place while El Gallo amused himself. But when the hand worked its way to the front, she gave a sudden involuntary start. Her whole body jumped, her arms flew out, and the file drawer slammed shut. It was unfortunate that El Gallo had neglected to remove his hand.

"*Puta madre!*" El Gallo screamed. He probably would have said more but additional dialogue was restricted by the four fingers stuffed in his mouth.

Cecilia was mortified. She knew it was an accident. "Ay, Señor Enriquez, *perdón!*"

The loudspeaker hanging on the wall saved her from whatever additional attention was to follow.

"Señor Enriquez, *teléfono. Teléfono,* Señor Enriquez, *hablá el presidente.*"

When the mayor upstairs called in those offices, it was customary to run immediately, pick up the phone, salute the state seal, and say "*Sí,* Señor Presidente!" with as much zeal as one could summon. El Gallo removed his throbbing fingers from his mouth and ran to follow this procedure. Cecilia was left alone again.

That evening Cecilia came home too upset to play with

the little ones and too drained to scold the older ones for things left undone. She took refuge in her bedroom. During her absence Santa Cecilia had once again abandoned her position in the mirror frame and was back on top of the dresser. Cecilia was too distracted to think. She kissed the virgin and went to sleep.

Cecilia slept well. As always, as soon as she woke in the morning she went straight to the dresser, only to discover that Santa Cecilia was gone! Her heart stopped beating for a moment. Then she found her lying on the floor not far from the dresser. "I'll have to find a better place for you." She carried her into the kitchen and tacked her to the wall beneath the clock with a pushpin.

Cecilia heard no more from her boss for the remainder of the week. Memories of the embarrassing incident began to fade. Dora came in a couple of times a day with cartons of filing.

"Another load! What a week this has been. I heard what you did to El Gallo. It's all over the office. I congratulate you."

"It was an accident."

"*Felicidades* anyway. I may be leaving the chicken farm soon."

"Oh, I would hate to see you go, Dora. You're the only one I know."

"If you know anyone who wants to buy a house, we're selling ours for four thousand dollars."

"You can't mean it."

"I'm afraid so. The devaluation of the peso has put us all in bad circumstances."

"But where will you go?"

"Both our parents are in Guadalajara. My husband's

people are old and need looking after. We can all help each other."

"If I had four thousand dollars I would buy your house this afternoon. A house of my own would solve all my problems. But of course if I had wings I could fly, no?"

"We'll talk later, I have to get back to work. Oh, by the way, El Gallo says he wants you to drop by his office." And Dora was out the door.

Later that afternoon Cecilia appeared for arraignment. She entered the hallowed office of authority and approached the throne with shaking knees. It was an audience with the pope. She tried not to look at the black fingertips of the pontiff's right hand. Her face blazed with embarrassment.

El Gallo spoke ex cathedra. "Cecilia, I'm afraid I have some bad news. The Presidente Municipal has ordered all the department heads to cut the payroll. I'm afraid it's going to be you."

Cecilia couldn't hold back the tears. "What will I do? My family, my children."

"It is the monetary crisis, there is nothing I can do." Ice formed on the syllables. Then he added a painful lie. "I'm sure you will find something right away." The interview was over. Heel toe, step slide. Heel toe, step jump. The marimba man was at it again.

Cecilia gathered up her few things and stepped into the plaza in a flood of unrestrained tears. She was angry at the world, that miserable man, and herself. She was also terribly frightened. She was holding her last paycheck with that sick feeling her world was coming to an end.

The plaza was busy at that hour. It seemed every citizen of Tecate had to cross the plaza to get wherever it was all these people went. And life went on. Cecilia's grief was hers alone. The hawkers roamed the plaza with merry march and pleas set to music.

"Popsicles . . . ice-cold Popsicles!"

I just lost my job and you imbeciles are peddling Popsicles and tacos as if nothing happened, she fumed to herself. She wanted to scream, a bloodred scream that could be heard throughout Tecate. Doesn't anyone care about Cecilia Rodriguez!

"Don't be seen without roses, sweet roses . . . if he won't buy them for you, buy them for yourself!"

Cecilia ignored them all. She was seething. She had a headache that threatened to split her head open. There was a rancid taste in her mouth. She paid no attention to the human flamethrower who held a small crowd spellbound. Even in good humor Cecilia found the bug eater repulsive. She marched past him with intentional rudeness.

"Spiders for breakfast, snails for lunch. Give me a coin and choose my supper!"

Suddenly Cecilia spun around on her heel and faced him. She slapped a coin in his hand. "Here, eat a cockroach!"

It seems her boss had been right. She found something right away. She walked around the corner to Restaurant La Fonda and offered to wash and iron their tablecloths.

Several times a week someone from La Fonda delivered dirty table linens to her house. Cecilia washed and ironed them for about twenty-five cents American. She averaged about ten a day. She had just finished a stack of fourteen. She folded them neatly and placed them in a clean carton for pickup. That's when she noticed Santa Cecilia was not on the kitchen wall. She was lying faceup on the floor. Cecilia picked her up gently and placed a tender kiss on her ring.

"Oh, you poor thing. What are you doing here on the floor? You didn't want to stay on my dresser, I moved you into the kitchen, and now you're on the floor again. What am I going to do with you?"

Cecilia could only assume some careless person had removed the pin. But when she went to put her back, she saw that the pushpin was still in place. Cecilia couldn't deal with the problem right then. She kissed the saint, then stuck the picture to the refrigerator door with a magnet. The organ music again. Do I really hear it? she wondered. Impossible!

Cecilia looked at the calendar and nearly had a stroke when she saw that tomorrow was the first. The Rodent would be scratching at the door for his rent. And she didn't have it. None of it.

Cecilia slept fitfully that night in the company of one nightmare after another, each competing for the distinction of being recalled in the morning as "most horrible." The next morning she went into the kitchen to put up the coffee and immediately sensed something was wrong. She didn't know what was wrong, but something wasn't right. Something gnawed at her. The silence of the room? It was unnaturally quiet, silent as Saint Luke's tomb. She held her breath to help her listen. Nothing. Not even the soft organ music. Then she realized the refrigerator was silent. She walked over to the appliance and saw the problem in the form of a big puddle of water on the floor in the front of the refrigerator.

"Holy Mary Mother of God!" she whispered. "That's all I need." The refrigerator had been doing its job in that very corner for years. She never gave it a thought. It was something she took for granted. Like the sun or the sky—or even the Rodent. She remembered the day she and Hector bought the aging Whirlpool at a swap meet in San Diego. The color of the exterior finish was undefinable, the wire shelves were red with rust. They gave the man sixty dollars. Then they had to pay the uniformed robbers at the border their last twenty dollars to bring it into the country. Laura was only four. My God, it's been running without attention for eleven years, she realized. She opened the door and the smell was enough to tell her the food was spoiling as she watched.

What do we do now? The tears started. This was too much. She couldn't handle any more. She was willing to let life end right there and then. She decided she would give herself to the Rodent to keep a roof over her family for another month and keep him away from Laura. She would close her eyes and let him have his way with her. I'll offer myself this morning when he scratches at the door, she thought. Cecilia threw a towel on the floor to absorb some of the water. She looked up at Santa Cecilia on the refrigerator door through a blur of tears. How can you smile at a time like this?

She wrestled the refrigerator away from the wall. She had to sit on the wet floor to unplug it at the baseboard. Out of sheer frustration she gave the back panel a furious kick. The panel fell to the floor with a loud clang, a huge gray rat scuttering across her legs. This was the drop that overflowed the glass. Cecilia burst into tears.

Old frayed cables, dirty copper tubing, and other major appliance viscera came spilling out of the unit. An electrical box came loose from the violent impact and fell to the floor. It had the acrid smell of burned wires. It was covered with ten years of thick furry grease an inch thick. Just the thought of touching it gave Cecilia chills. She pushed the filthy thing out of her way with her foot. The lid clattered off. God, another rat! She prepared a scream. Nothing repulsive scurried out. The big rat was already dead and dehydrated and wrapped in spiderwebs. The sight made her shudder all over. Next to the disgusting corpse was a roll of black electrician's tape covered with dead spiders, the remains of a large beetle, and eight thousand dollars.

"A beautiful story," I said, putting down the cup of chocolate Cecilia had brought in to me. I don't know why I was whispering. "You were actually sitting on all that money for years."

"Yes, but it wasn't meant to be found until El Señor sent Santa Cecilia to lead me to where it was hidden. I immediately bought Dora's house and started my bridal shop. The first one was tiny. I've had to enlarge twice. I've been very fortunate."

"And the children? They must be all grown by now."

"Growing like *chamizo*. Candida starts high school this fall. Little Jesus is in second grade."

"And Anastasia and Laura? Married, I suppose."

"Oh yes, Anastasia married a very nice man, a man quite older than herself. He is a widower with a boy of his own." A little laugh escaped. "No more turquoise hair."

"And Laura?"

"Laura married God. She decided to take vows at the convent of Santa Brigida last summer."

I thanked Cecilia Rodriguez for the hot chocolate and the visit. I rose and said adios. As I prepared to leave, my eyes fell on something I hadn't noticed before. Just above the door was a color print of Santa Cecilia in a heavy gold frame. One corner of the picture was missing. She seemed to smile at me as I left. And I *know* I heard an organ playing.

A Matter of Respectability

Alma Silva Fuentes looked like the fairy princess made of spun sugar that stood at the top of the seven-tiered cake. They wore identical gowns. She rose from the head table to be led to the dance floor. The orchestra began to play and Alma swirled across the floor in lavender taffeta the color of a summer cloud at sunset. Her young eyes of Oriental jade, sparkling with veneration, smiled up at her father, her god, her idol, as he proudly held her in his arms for the first waltz. The ballroom filled with the strains of "Cuando Escuches Éste Vals," a waltz so tender it is imprinted on every Mexican heart that ever floated away on the hundred-year-old melody.

> Whenever you hear this waltz
> recall a memory of me
> of the kisses you gave me
> and those I gave to you

At Mass just a few hours earlier Alma walked down the aisle and knelt to accept the Eucharist. The Church of Our Lady of Guadalupe was packed to the walls with family and friends. Alma came to her feet and, leaving behind the ghost of a child, walked up the aisle carrying her mother's rosary and her new rank of Señorita. She was fifteen years old. She now glided over the polished floor, light as a butterfly, her young heart pulsating to the exhilarating three-quarter rhythm of the waltz.

"Ice cream, señorita?"

"Love birds, señorita, blue, green, and yellow. Love birds bring you a serenade every day!"

The presence of vendors in the plaza interrupted the fancy ball. The waltz stopped, and brought Alma back to the present moment. She waved the hawkers away impatiently and resumed the faded memory. What an elegant evening that was! She recalled her father's resonant voice. "You look beautiful, my *princesa*. Be sure you save some dances for Dorian, my dear." God, even then, they were constantly pushing Dorian.

Why am I dwelling on this? That was eight years ago. Quickly Alma found the source of the mnemonic. The lilting three-beat pulse of "Cuando Escuches Éste Vals" was coming to her from the music shop across the plaza. Eight years! All her girlfriends and most of the boys who were present at that ball were married now. With children. Some separated after a few years. Some were still together as man and wife. None of them happy.

It wasn't for lack of opportunity that the beautiful Alma Silva Fuentes was still a señorita. She attracted more suitors than she knew what to do with. No matter who she dated, she got the feeling she was out with the same person with a different face. They all radiated machismo. Beans from the same sack. Dinner, kiss, and grab. And if you didn't provide their pleasure, there were plenty of other flowers in Tecate.

Dorian was still among the single. Dorian! His parents and her parents thought they made darling sweethearts from the time they were three. Alma's mother still kept pictures around of her and Dorian kissing at a birthday party when children are at an age they can be bribed to do anything cute for a bite of cake. Dorian and Alma were twenty-three now and both sets of parents were *still* trying to get them together!

In spite of all their scheming, Alma didn't bother with Dorian. He was always too much in love with himself. And still was, for that matter. Both sets of parents were disappointed. Actually, Alma paid no attention to any of the young men who came buzzing around. She preferred no one. Until one day Mundo asked her out. Mundo was different. He didn't strut, he didn't lie, and he didn't live in mortal fear of being domesticated. Even her own father didn't answer her mother until the third or fourth summons, just to prove he was not to be considered housebroken. When Mundo kissed her for the first time, Alma knew she'd found a treasure. Her life belonged to only one man.

Alma looked at her watch. Six-fifteen. Mundo should be along soon. He said six-thirty. They worked in the same building. He was a lawyer at the Hall of Justice, she was secretary to Judge Valdes. She had to deliver a document to city hall, so she came earlier and was now waiting at the appointed place.

Mundo was like no other young man she'd ever met. Mundo was cut from different cloth. He was raised by his mother, who cleaned houses so he could finish law school. And now he was putting money by for the education of his younger siblings. They were a good family, modest, industrious, and above all, ethical. They'd known each other forever, it seemed. But it wasn't until they began working together at the courthouse where they saw each other every day that the tiny spark ignited the lamp wick and the lights went on in her heart. She knew, even before Mundo asked her out, that it would be Mundo or no one.

"Shoe shine, señorita?"

How absurd! She shooed him away. "Mundo! Mundo, you silly *payaso*, you startled me."

Mundo slipped onto the bench beside her. They exchanged a quick little kiss that did not lack warmth for its brevity.

"Have you been waiting long, *mi amor?*"

"*Una eternidad!*"

"It's only six-thirty."

"Without you, every minute is forever." Alma put her arm through his then cuddled it tight with her other hand.

"Hungry?"

"Faint with hunger!"

Alma still hugging his arm, they strolled across the plaza, crossed the street, and entered La Fonda. A quick survey confirmed that only one table was occupied, all men, all married. Alma wondered why men marry and make a home in order not to be in it. They exchanged a wave of recognition. Beto, the waiter, a young man they knew at school until he dropped out, intercepted the young couple.

"*Hola*, Alma, Mundo, *que tal?*" He showed them directly to "their" table at the back. "*Una margarita?*"

Mundo nodded his ascent and they joined hands across the table. For a few minutes they spoke only with their eyes. They studied each other's faces. Mundo loved her hair, a shimmering runnel of gold that flowed from crown to waist, her smooth cameo skin, and those green eyes that were now whispering silent love poems. Alma adored his smooth doeskin face. Soft, touchable. No macho mustache. She reached across and moved an unruly lock of raven hair out of his face and looked into big brown deer eyes.

"Why so pensive?" she asked.

"Just the Friday release after a hectic week. How about we go to San Diego tomorrow, a movie, a pizza?"

"I would love it. And Mundo, for a lawyer you are a terrible liar. You have that little cross stitch between your eyes." With her fingertips she smoothed away his frown. "What is on your mind?" Alma knew his face as well as she knew her own.

Mundo was on the point of saying something when Beto arrived with margaritas and vanished. Both appreciated his perception. They were also thankful it was too early for mariachis and the Friday night festivities. They wanted to talk. It wasn't the first time they wanted to call a meeting. They saw each other every day, they went out almost every evening. They were *insepárables*. But they could never get past the outer edges of the topic both knew had to be addressed. Both assumed that they would one day marry. That was mutually understood by two hearts that matched each other like two halves of the same orange. But it had yet to be discussed in full. There were problems.

"Alma, *mi amor*, let's finish our drinks. We can talk better in the plaza, then come back for dinner."

"Said and done!" she agreed with an impish little grin. She took a big macho-style gulp and wiped an imaginary mustache. The charming imitation made Mundo laugh, and that's exactly what she had intended.

At this hour it was easy to find a secluded bench between the kiosk and the fountain. Mundo held both of her hands in his, the brown eyes and the green eyes locked. This was a common tableau employed by many couples, designed to inoculate them against pesky vendors. It always worked. They were only vulnerable to flower girls.

Mundo got right to the problem. "I suppose I could steal you."

"Elope? I would do it in a minute."

"Think what you're saying, *mi amor*. It would crush your parents. You're their only daughter. They would be so hurt. It would destroy their lives. I couldn't do that to them—to anybody."

"Then we'll do it according to custom, and Papá and Mamá will be forced to accept my choice for a husband!"

"Oh yes, I can see my mother calling at their grand house to go through the formality of asking for you.

" '*Sí*, señor, I am here to ask for your daughter's hand because Edmundo has no father. My husband ran off when Mundo was eight. We have no pedigree, but I've worked hard all these years so Mundo could amount to something. He is a fine lawyer, and I know he can make your daughter, Alma, very happy.' "

Alma reached out and held his face tenderly between both her hands. "No!" She could see the point Mundo was trying to make. She could feel his pain. "Papá and Mamá can be so impossible! They've known you as long as I have."

"They know me, yes, but they can't accept me. They're not bad people, *mi cielo*, they're just from another world."

"Leave it to me, *corazón*. I'll prepare them. Then we'll face them together."

"Oh, *mi amor*, I've thought about it a thousand times. I honestly don't know what to do. Here we are again with nothing resolved."

And here, as in the past, is where the subject usually ended and the hugs and kisses began. Sweet kisses on the cheek, butterfly kisses on the eyelids, ardent kisses on the mouth. Mundo's hands did not know her. Sometimes Alma ached for his touch. Without ever having spoken, it was understood she would go to the altar a virgin.

It wasn't late when Alma got home. She went through the heavy wrought-iron gates, across the garden, and to the front door. There was a car in the *cochero*. They had company. She recognized the car. Dorian's parents, her parents' best friends. Dorian's mother and father were wonderful people, she loved them dearly, but she just wasn't up to a visit tonight. She applied a smile to her face and walked into the living room.

"There she is! Alma, how lovely you look!"

"Don Julian, Doña Angelita!" Alma greeted them both with warm embraces. They had encouraged her to drop the formal señor and señora form of address when she was but a little thing. She sneaked a quick look around. No Dorian. Now a new dilemma presented itself. She didn't want to ask about him. They will take it to mean I'm interested, she thought. But if I don't, it will appear terribly rude. "And how is Dorian?" *Fuchi!*

"He's fine. Working hard, always asking about you," Doña Angelita gushed.

Alma didn't hear the answer. She greeted her own parents and took a place on the sofa. There was a little silver bell on the coffee table. Her mother gave it a dainty shake and a miniature Oaxaca Indian maid appeared with fresh coffee.

They all made small talk until the company took their leave. It required an extra twenty minutes at the door to repeat everything that was said before. As soon as the door closed, Alma headed for the stairs. She knew what was coming. She also knew it was inescapable.

"Don't leave, my dear, let's talk a minute." Alma's mother was, in her youth, a beautiful woman, and the years had treated her kindly. She retained much of her bloom. Her hair was thick and luxurious, always meticulously coiffed. The only thing that detracted from this exquisite woman was an unfortunate voice, brittle as glass, even when she was in good humor.

Her father moved from the chair where he had been sitting and returned to "his," recently vacated by Don Julian. He had but little hair on his pink head now, but the enormous ram's horns mustache, now the color of snow, could, if redistributed, upholster several threadbare domes. He lit a cigarette to justify a few seconds of delay before speaking.

Here it comes; Alma knew it.

Her father spoke. "We've been invited to a concert in Tijuana. Just the three couples. Julian and Angelita, ourselves, and you and Dorian." He was the undisputed monarch in his house, but still he employed a gentle voice intended to mitigate the eminent authority it implied, and thus give the mandate the appearance of a casual invitation.

"We'll take them someplace nice for dinner," her mother added.

Already they've made us a couple! "When?" Alma asked in a tone that hopefully would imply a full calendar. Maybe I can be out.

"Next Saturday. I accepted for all of us, of course," her father answered.

Alma saw the narrow opportunity of escape slam shut.

There you have it. An edict from above. There was no option, this was a command performance. This was another of the many schemes they implemented in hopes that they could pry her apart from Mundo.

"Look . . ." she began in the voice she used at the office. At this moment Alma did not want to be regarded as their "little girl." "I have nothing against Dorian. He's a fine young man. But I don't feel anything for him, I never have, and I don't want to give anyone the impression that I ever will. I regard him as nothing more than a friend of the family." She put extra emphasis on *family*. This was the most direct speech she had ever dared to make before her father. We might as well separate the whey from the milk right now, she decided.

Señor poured himself a brandy, her mother a coffee. A bad sign. They were getting prepared for a long battle. A battle daughters always lose.

Her mother began trying hard to smooth out her naturally vitreous voice. "But you've known each other since you were babies. Julian and Angelita are our oldest and dearest friends. They've been hoping for you to join their family since you were born. They love you like a daughter."

"And I love Don Julian and Doña Angelita dearly, but—"

The sovereign father cut in. "It's time you begin to consider a serious relationship," he said for the millionth time, and seeing she was about to say something, raised a hand to remind her that daughters do not interrupt. "I know, I know, you and Mundo work together, you go out in the evening. And it's all very nice. But sooner rather than later, you must find someone acceptable you can get serious about."

"I have someone I am serious about."

"I also said acceptable."

"I find Mundo quite acceptable." Alma came close to raising her voice, but one look at her father's face brought her under control. "And I am very serious about him."

"Mundo? You can't mean it. He's a very nice young man, but you can't be serious. He has no real future."

Señora stirred sugar into her coffee as though she were beating egg whites. "He has no connections, no influential family. What can he give you?"

"Love and children."

"Please!" her father roared, then quickly modified his tone and asked the next question with syrup in his mouth because he already knew the answer. "What does his father do?"

"He doesn't have one."

This precipitated a sharp gasp from Alma's mother.

"And his mother?"

"She cleans houses."

Her mother turned her face toward heaven for guidance. "God help us!"

Alma's father didn't need divine assistance. He took a more practical approach. "Be realistic, my child. Dorian's family presides over a business empire that began with their grandparents. And they've given Dorian an important position in the firm. He has his future secured. They know all the right people."

"He can give you everything," Señora repeated.

"Everything but love. I don't mind being poor."

Her mother put down her coffee in a gesture of impatience. "Oh, that's easy to say when you've had everything. You've never washed a dish or mopped a floor in your life. You don't even have to pick up your underwear!"

"You're actually asking me to marry someone I don't love."

"No!" her father lashed out. "We're not arranging your marriage." She had touched a nerve. Dorian as a son-in-law was his dearest dream, and she knew it. "Marry the man of your choice—but at least someone of your own class."

"You're going on twenty-four, my dear. You can't stay single much longer without—without . . ." Her mother left the sordid thought in the air.

"Can't you understand? It's a question of respectability!" Papá crushed out his cigarette.

Respectability, of course! A word Alma learned before she entered kindergarten. "Yes, I can understand that. The more people we reject, the more respectable we become."

"Alma!" A one-word warning that she was standing too close to the fine line that separates opinion from parental respect.

Alma's mother stepped in with what she considered diplomacy. "It's a matter of appearances, *mi amor*."

"Mundo is an honorable man. Why should I care about appearances?"

"Appearances are everything!" the monarch answered. "And so are the right friendships."

Alma was becoming weary. This was not the first time they had this discussion. At that very moment she recalled her conversation with Mundo in the plaza earlier in the evening. *Nothing resolved*. Again, nothing resolved. Well, tonight it would be resolved! "But you've never approved of any man I've ever brought home. It's Dorian, Dorian, Dorian! And now it's time you both recognize that Mundo is the man I have chosen. Appearances or no appearances."

Alma's father's face contorted preparatory to his reply, but her mother's brittle voice cut in. "Well, it's getting late."

Her mother wanted the discussion to end before it grew out of proportion, and before her husband and her daughter revealed tempers which she could see were near the surface.

Papá had the final word. "Well, we already accepted the invitation. We had to. It would have been very bad manners not to."

Dismissal. The discussion was over. Daughters who are properly brought up by the refined do not contradict their fathers. If Papá calls black white, then white it is. Alma was exasperated. My social class lives in glass houses of their own making, she thought. Without another word, she went up the stairs to her room. She was defeated and she knew it.

Señora turned to her husband as soon as she heard Alma's door close. "What are we going to do with her?"

The autocrat swirled his brandy and answered with a weary sigh. "I have never seen her so obstinate. It's useless to order her not to see him." He preferred the impersonal pronoun to using the young man's name, and he would never consider them *novios*. "They're together all day at work." He took a sip. "I'll think of something. We can't let this happen." To himself he thought, What a tragic misalliance. I would probably end up by supporting him. Worse! How humiliating to introduce him into my circle of important friends as my son-in-law. This is the young peasant who lies with my daughter. Never!

Later that same evening, Don Julian and Doña Angelita were in their large *sala* dealing with a dilemma similar to the one in progress in the living room they just left. The main theme was their son, Dorian.

Don Julian rubbed the bridge of his nose and spoke to his wife. "We have to put Dorian in a corner and force him to come to a decision. I rescued him with money from that stupid indiscretion in Tijuana, and it wasn't the first time. And I don't want to go through that again. Apart from the fact that it was expensive, that girl could have cost us a great deal of embarrassment."

"He's young and high-spirited, but I do wish he would settle down before he comes to harm. You're going to have to get very firm with him. He doesn't listen to me."

"Young? Nonsense!" Don Julian answered. "He's a twenty-three-year-old man. He's not your naughty little boy anymore." He stopped here. He recognized thin ice when he heard it cracking beneath his feet. He knew he was guilty of spoiling his Little Prince every bit as much as his wife. They tried to be strict with him when he was young, but severity wasn't easy when dealing with their precious Prince Dorian. Today, severity was beyond their powers.

While Don Julian and Doña Angelita prepared to ambush their son, Dorian was only a few minutes from home. He was helping Consuelo back into her clothes. "Tomorrow night, same time?"

"Yes, yes, *mi amor*. I can't wait!"

Young women were always making themselves available to Dorian. He could affect a manner that imitated charm to a sufficient degree to delude the young. No one could deny that Dorian was beautiful. He was also selfish and demanding and, at times, cruel. It is possible that his dangerous reputation was itself the attraction, much like a thrill ride at the fair.

Dorian started life as a beautiful child, much spoiled, then brought up to believe that God made the world for him and him alone. From that moment on Dorian lived only to please himself. He was given everything he asked for. No, everything Prince Dorian *demanded*. On his eighteenth birthday his father gave him a brand-new Corvette. Dorian quickly realized that the Corvette provided an extension of the self. The girls couldn't wait to take off their *calzones* in exchange for the privilege of being seen cruising down Avenida Juarez in the silver torpedo with him at the wheel.

It was about this time that Dorian cultivated a thin, well-trimmed mustache. His uncles and all the members of the older generation remarked on how he resembled *artista de cine* Don Ameche. Now, Dorian had no idea in the world who Don Ameche might be, but it sounded good and it was enough to nourish an ego already approaching obesity. He chose his clothes from *GQ* and raced to Los Angeles to buy them. He went to the extent of rehearsing a number of affectations he applied to the simple act of lighting a cigarette. In short, Dorian was clinically conceited.

When he reached majority, if not maturity, Dorian lived only for entertainment. Unlike most of the young men of his own age, he was not at all curious about business and commerce. He was visibly annoyed when his father talked to him about "joining the firm" as though he were offering him a double chocolate ice cream cone. The idea of sitting in the confines of an office and moving paper was nothing short of repulsive.

It was after eleven when Dorian came home and found his parents in their drawing room. He was sufficiently intuitive to know what was on the agenda. These people could be so tiresome. When would they give up? He greeted them cordially, and dutifully kissed his mamá. He poured himself a Presidente, took a wing chair, and waited for the scene to begin. *Son, you're going to have to start taking a more serious approach to your life.*

"I'm glad you caught us in, Dorian. We have to talk," the

older man began. "Son, you're going to have to start getting serious about your work and about your life."

I was close, Dorian thought, and sipped his brandy. "Of course, Papá, is it something to do with the office?"

"It's a lot of things, Dorian. I gave you a responsible position in the firm, and I had to hire two assistants to do your job for you."

"It's a heavy load."

"I know, it must be hard to get anything done when you're at the racetrack all afternoon and the dog races every evening."

Doña Angelita spoke for the first time. She wanted to sound stern but she lost her resolve and spoke to him in the same sweet voice she employed when he was four and told him it wasn't nice to kick the maid. "We're thinking only of you, Dorian. Isn't it time you settled down? Wouldn't you like to marry a nice girl like Alma and make a nice home?" She might as well have been saying, Wouldn't you like a nice plate of cookies?

Of course! This is at the bottom of the whole scheme, Dorian thought. They want to marry me off and get respectable. "I'm not even sure if she's available. She has a *novio*, a little lawyer I believe." He could never admit that any woman might reject him.

"Oh, believe me, that's nothing," his mother warranted. "Her parents assured us of that. And you've known her all your life. She's our kind of people. And she loves you, Dorian."

Everybody loves me. Dorian did his trick with the cigarette while he contrived an answer. He never did like going to work. It impeded the pursuit of pleasure. The constant nagging was becoming a pain in the *nalgas* and there was no end in sight. Then, like a bolt of lightning, it came to him all of a sudden. Marrying Alma would solve all his problems. His parents would get off his back, the whole issue of respectability would come to a close. And it needn't interfere with his lifestyle. He would be a free man. *Sí, sí, sí!*

Several days later Señor Silva Fuentes entered his elegant offices on the second floor of the Silva Building, which he owned. He also owned the bank downstairs. His corporations placed their assets in his own bank, of course. His personal bank accounts were safe at Bank of America Mission Valley Branch in San Diego. Señor Silva Fuentes had vast holdings in commercial and industrial real estate. Today he made money like a termite eats wood. It was his nature more than need. Señor Silva Fuentes belonged to Kiwanis, Club de Leones, and attended Rotario meetings in Tijuana. He learned from his father the importance of contacts. And like his father before him, he dedicated himself to meeting all the right people. He was on *abrazo* terms with the *presidentes* of both Tecate and Tijuana past and present. It was his personal ambition to add the governor to his roster. He came within a whisper of meeting the present governor, but it didn't work out. In two years a new *gobernador* would take office, and he was determined to break through the protective curtain of alliances and meet him personally. He would make a substantial donation. The new governor, whoever he might turn out to be, would sit in his living room and sip his brandy. He would have three more years to exploit the contact and expand his financial empire.

In the meantime, Señor Silva Fuentes was going to do everything within his power to bend the bough of his head-strong scion to conform to his design. He picked up the phone and dialed a number in Tijuana.

"*Hola*, Paulo! How are you? When are you and Nena

coming to dinner? It's been a while. Working? You're too old for that. Listen, *cabrón*, we'll take you down to La Paz for a weekend. That's all you need." There was a pause while Señor Silva Fuentes listened to his friend's reply, then he came to the point. "Listen, Paulo, do you know anyone in Mexicali? I need a favor."

When Señor Silva Fuentes put down the phone, he was smiling. His scheme was already in progress. He lit a cigarette, satisfied with himself. *Don't anyone ever tell me that knowing the right people isn't important!*

In less than two weeks Alma was in tears and the old man was rejoicing. Mundo was surprised and a little overwhelmed when he received a job offer in Mexicali. "I never thought a big career opportunity would make me so sad," Mundo whispered. They sat in the darkness of the kiosk, where vendors never ventured. They knew they would be undisturbed here unless another young couple was facing a personal crisis this evening.

"When do you have to go?" Alma asked.

"They want me to start Monday."

"That's less than a week."

"I know. I'll have to move quickly. Judge Valdes said he would drive me to Mexicali Sunday morning." He placed his mouth on hers and held her tight for a long moment. Both faces were wet with their tears. Alma rotated her hips forward and pressed into that part of a man she knew only by rumor. *I am ready to give myself to him right now*, she thought. *Tonight.*

She pressed harder. "Can you feel my love?"

Mundo held her tight, then suddenly sensing the danger of desire, he placed one foot on the step below and broke the spell. "Life is so unfair. Tell me not to go and I'll stay."

"No, *corazón*. I love you and I never want to let you go. But I can't be that selfish. This is the opportunity every young lawyer hopes for. I can't take that away from you."

"I'll write you every week."

"Love never dies." Alma hid her face in his shoulder and sobbed like a child.

"*Ya, ya, mi amor, ya.* Don't cry so." Mundo consoled her with little kisses on her soft neck.

"If I hadn't been such a coward! I should have had the courage to stand up to my parents. I failed—"

"*No, no, mi cielo.* This could be a blessing in disguise. Maybe with this new assignment your parents will see me through different eyes."

"I never thought of it."

"And we'll get married right away."

"And we'll make a pretty home in Mexicali."

They went into a period of denial. Each made up their own fantasy to alleviate the pain. Saturday night, their last night together, they wept in each other's arms. Sunday, Mundo left for Mexicali. The two halves of the same orange were ripped apart and their world came to an end. The old man had achieved his objective.

It only took a few days after Mundo's departure for Dorian's motives to come to ascendancy. He began to call frequently at the home of Silva Fuentes. The call was designed to appear as a family visit. No flowers, no candy. On one of these evenings during the middle of the week, Dorian performed his ritual with a cigarette, and casually suggested they join him for dinner. He addressed the invitation to *ustedes*, thereby including all those present.

"*Gracias*," the head of the family replied, "the señora

and I have a previous engagement or we would accept your hospitality with alacrity." This genial plea to be excused was intended to leave Alma abandoned with no acceptable means of escape.

Alma considered declining as graciously as she could, then realized that the more courteous her decline, the more rude it would appear. To go upstairs and change would give the invitation a measure of importance. Instead, she rose from her chair and said carelessly, "Okay, *vamos*."

Papá and Mama could hardly contain their elation. Alma headed for the door before they could embarrass her with champagne and tumultuous applause.

As Alma entered La Fonda on Dorian's arm, and she couldn't remember when or how her arm got caught up in his, she began to panic. Apart from family and girlfriends, she'd never been in the place with anyone but Mundo. The whole town knew Mundo had moved to Mexicali. Who would be in the restaurant? Who would see them? Everyone! What would they say? Even worse! What would *she* say? Beto met them at the door and, for the moment, speculation ended.

If Beto was startled, he didn't reveal it. "*Hola* Dorian, *hola*, Alma, how nice to see you this evening," he greeted, as though he saw them together every night. He led the way into the dining room. As they followed Beto, they exchanged *saludos* with people they both knew. Alma recognized the look of confusion on the faces as they passed the tables. She knew what they would be saying as soon as she was out of range. Alma saw that by habit Beto was leading them to the table that Alma and Mundo considered "theirs," then recovered his presence of mind, made a sharp right, and put them at a table for four. Dorian could perceive the drooling envy of the men coveting his dinner date.

He held her chair. "*Dos* margaritas, Beto."

"Right away!"

"So," Dorian began, "how do you like working for Judge Valdes?" This is going to be one long boring evening, he thought.

"Oh, I like it fine. I suppose your job carries a lot of responsibility." She wanted to say, Who cares!

"Yes, a great deal of pressure."

The arrival of the margaritas temporarily interrupted the flow of stimulating conversation if not their unspoken parenthetical thoughts.

"*Salud.*"

"*Provecho.*"

They sipped quietly. Neither wanted to be here. Alma was grateful that it was early Thursday evening and they wouldn't have the weekend festivities of mariachis, dancing, singing, and table-hopping. She looked around at the other tables. She could imagine the comments. *Look at that! Mundo is barely out of town and she already has another.* Alma felt she had been caught in a lurid love affair with another man.

A little flower girl, no more than ten, came by with a bright daffodil smile and a handful of corsages. Dorian waved her off, thus infringing on a woman's undisputed prerogative. The transgression annoyed Alma.

Dorian perceived that he was not the center of Alma's universe, and for this reason alone he disliked her sincerely. This whole charade was tedious and repugnant. He was beginning to resent every minute he invested in her. He summoned the waiter.

Beto appeared with his pad and gave Alma a secret smile she understood.

"I'll have the *pescado Veracruzano*," Alma said.

"Bring me the steak ranchero, *sí*?"

"Another margarita?" Beto asked.

"Of course." God, I can hardly wait to get out of here, Dorian muttered in thought. "Well, it looks like winter is finally over."

"Yes, I hate the wind. It will be nice to see summer." I think I would rather be home with cramps, Alma reflected silently.

"We could still get more rain."

"Yes, I suppose we need it."

The second round of margaritas arrived and they expanded the fascinating subject of meteorological phenomena to include barometric readings, cold fronts, and high pressure areas, until dinner arrived.

A wandering musician strolled into the dining room. He was immediately summoned to a table with two couples and began to sing.

Alma listened wistfully. If he comes to our table I'll cry.

That's all I need tonight, Dorian fumed silently, a love song. If he comes to my table, I'll put my foot through his guitar!

Dinner progressed like a requiem mass.

"How's your fish?"

The halibut on my plate has more personality than you do, Alma thought. "Good. How's your steak ranchero?"

Dorian listened to his thoughts. What a dismal evening. I wonder if I should tell her that I remember the day I showed her my *pito* and she covered her face with her hands and ran in the house? Maybe I should offer to show it to her now. He almost smiled. He motioned to the waiter. "Beto, bring us a bottle of Santo Tomás Chardonnay, *sí*?" Then turning to Alma, "You agree?"

"Of course." I wonder what his face would look like if I brought up the day he soiled his pants at Cousin Conchita's birthday party and they had to take him inside to change him?

For nothing better to do, Dorian began to undress her at the table. He had to admit she had a luscious pair of breasts. Does Mundo get to play with those? he wondered. I doubt it. Honorable peasant!

They couldn't wait for the dinner neither wanted, and both resented, to come to an end. Both quickly said no to dessert before Beto could finish reciting the list.

The happy couple on their first date gave secret thanks when Dorian's car pulled up in front of Alma's house. Dorian went around to open the door and help Alma out.

"Won't you come in?"

"*Gracias*, it's late."

Dorian placed a sterile kiss on Alma's cheek only because the absence of the gesture would have appeared rude. Bound by the same statute, Alma was obliged to reciprocate before she fled into the house.

Dorian was irritated when he drove off. What a waste of time! I can have any woman I want and I throw away a perfectly good evening having dinner with precious Alma. Even kissing her is unpleasant. I think I would rather kiss her iron gate post. The lights burning in the house when he pulled into the *cochero* induced thought. His parents were still up. Of course! They were going to ambush him. Suddenly he realized he was losing sight of his objective. His whole scheme could only work if Alma accepted him in marriage. And there was a double reward: pressure to get respectable would cease—and it isn't often you had the opportunity to deflower the most desirable virgin in Tecate. The brief flash of enlightenment brought his purpose back into sharp focus. Dorian's perception of his task began to change. He summoned all the refinements he was taught and rejected years ago and converted them into something he hoped would resemble charm.

Two days after the disastrous dinner at La Fonda, Alma sat reading in the living room in the company of her parents. Señor poured himself a brandy, Señora was busy applying a bit of lace to a handkerchief. The servant girl answered the bell and ushered Dorian to the living room. He came blustering in dressed in formal wear and a swirling black opera cape with high collar and scarlet lining. He looked like the phantom of the opera. He held a violin in one hand, his right hand held a bow.

"*Buenas tardes,*" he greeted the señores, then turned to Alma. "I am come to beg the honor of your presence at the Mainly Mozart concert under the stars on the bay in San Diego." Dorian tucked the instrument under his chin and slashed savagely at the strings. Angry cats leaped out of the pawnshop Stradivarius.

Alma could not contain a paroxysm of giggles. "Only if you take off that ridiculous cape!"

"What about the violin?"

"Oh, you can keep the violin," Alma was still chuckling, "but the bow stays here." It felt good to laugh. She had been walking around with a prickly conscience for the last few days. She had to admit to herself she had been less than charming at dinner. It was hardly fair to abuse Dorian for something he had nothing to do with. Accepting his invitation gave her a feeling of self-redemption. The simple absence of animosity relieved the soreness in her soul. Besides, staying home was no fun, and it was at least someplace to go. Dorian had a brandy with the parents while Alma went upstairs to change.

Behind a Judas smile Dorian became sedulously thoughtful and disarmingly attentive; he offered his arm, held her chair, brought her enormous bouquets of flowers that bordered on the ostentatious. They went out almost every night. Alma was swept away in a whirlwind of concerts, dinners, and parties. She hardly had time to think. Dorian could see he had her thoroughly confused. It was a game of deceit. Now it was fun!

It was Saturday night on the late side when Dorian brought Alma home from a gay fiesta in Playas de Tijuana. He kissed her cheek. She kissed him back just to see if she felt anything. *"Buenas noches,"* she whispered.

In the brief interval between switching out her bedside lamp and touching the pillow, Alma was fast asleep. She dreamt of mariachis, dancing, much hugging and kissing, but the faces were vague and elusive, the kind of dream you want to keep but you can never bring back with you when you wake. The music was achingly romantic. The music? Alma turned over on her back and listened. She was awake now. At least she thought she was because the dream was gone. But the music was still there. To confirm her faculties she looked at the clock. Five-thirty. Her bedroom was black. She was certain she could hear mariachis coming from somewhere.

She even recognized the song. Alma threw off the covers, padded to her window, and looked out. What on earth!

Down below she counted nine musicians gathered in a half circle around her gate, illuminated by the light of the street lamps. They were dressed in burgundy with big silver *conchas* glittering on their short jackets and along the full length of the side seam of their tight trousers. Each wore a fluffy scarlet bow at the collar of a pleated white shirt. Bright little sparks flashed from black felt sombreros bordered with sequins.

Still carrying the melody, the mariachis parted at the center and a white horse with flowing mane appeared prancing proudly with feet high in the air. The horseman, a tall dark *charro* still in shadow, was dressed in black heavily embroidered with silver. She watched the tall horseman remove his sparkling sombrero and salute her window. Dorian!

Four violins in the company of three guitars repeated the refrain. A fat little man raised his trumpet to his lips and unfurled a ribbon of ruffled silver over Alma's window. A rich tenor voice the color of melted gold filled the dawn with the melodic poetry of "Las Mañanítas," the traditional Mexican birthday song.

The serenade drifted up to her like the night-blooming jasmine that laced the garden gate below. Alma stood at her open window with rainy eyes, enfolded in melody and the chaste roseate light of the virgin morning. She was twenty-four.

The following Friday it was close to midnight when Dorian delivered Alma to her door. He did not immediately go around to open her door as he usually did. He was feeling reckless. He put one hand on her arm in such a way that the edge of his hand pressed lightly against her breast, and placed a counterfeit kiss on her mouth. Alma didn't pull away. She may have been reeling, but Dorian was in possession of all his faculties. He studied her like a laboratory technician studies a slide under the microscope. She returned his kiss. He took note that she either was not aware of his hand or she was burning with desire. He watched Alma struggle with her emotions like a butterfly he once trapped in a jar. Flail your pretty wings, Alma, he thought. You don't know what you're feeling, do you? He devoured her mouth and, with a traitor's kiss, took a handful of breast. Oh, yes, my pretty thing, save your struggling, you can never escape. You belong to me now—together we have managed to conserve our respectability!

During the next few days, Alma was forced to do some serious thinking. Dorian's extravagant attention must mean something. Apparently Dorian really did love her. Maybe he loved her all through the years and he was never sure if his feelings would be returned. It could have been his shyness, his fear of rejection, that made him appear so indifferent to her. He must love me or there would be no point to all this courting. And, if he loves me as much as he says, he can't be a bad person. I may have appraised him unfairly. I have to bury the past and marry *somebody* before society begins to wonder what's "wrong" with Alma Silva Fuentes, daughter of a *persona importante*. Her vulnerable soul, seduced by the sorcery of music, sweet whisperings, and erogenous caresses, surrendered with a sigh.

And so the final curtain came down on a stellar performance. Dorian saw he had gained access to a corner of her heart. He succeeded in looting her integrity and decided it was the right moment to propose marriage.

Six months later the *amonestaciónes* were posted and the intended marriage was proclaimed to the citizens of Tecate. Two sets of parents were ecstatic. But as the wedding day approached, Alma grew anxious and began to regret her decision. She thought she had placed Mundo to rest in the crypt of her mind where old memories are buried for eternity. And now he was back. She prayed that someone would come forward and forbid the banns on the grounds that the *novia*'s heart belonged to another. But nothing of the kind happened. The wedding and reception were the most lavish Tecate had ever seen. They booked the entire Rancho Tecate, the posh resort and country club.

They flew to Paris for three weeks on their *luna de miel*. When Dorian took possession of her, Alma pleaded forgiveness and, with eyes full, formally said good-bye to Mundo. She felt more mauled than loved. Together they toured all the places tourists visit when they go to Paris for the first time. While Alma rested, Dorian went off in search of the perfect souvenir. He wanted a conversation piece, something with anecdotal value when he was back among his friends. He found two not far from their hotel who rented out their God-given fixtures by the hour.

Upon their return they were installed in a pretentious house, much too large for a couple, with gardener and servant girl. Alma was determined to be a good wife. She made herself available to his passion although it brought her no reward. She was determined to make her husband a good home. She wanted to know what he liked to eat, and learned to prepare exquisite dishes which later the servant would eat or feed to the dog, as Dorian was never present. Within a few weeks they fell into a predictable routine. Every morning

Alma joined her husband for breakfast coffee and sweet bread. She never saw him again until he appeared in the form of a lump on his side of the bed the following morning.

Dorian also had his routine. He drove to his office in Tijuana right after breakfast. His two assistants briefed him on what had been done yesterday and their plans for today. This usually took until one o'clock. Lunch at the Tijuana Club Campestre in the company of Maribel, an unemployed fashion model. He used Maribel for lunch, dancing at the Pimpollo, and other forms of entertainment. When the racing season wasn't open, he wandered down to his condominium at Rosarito Beach, where Dorita waited with open arms and adult toys. There were several very willing *chamacas* in Tecate that he rotated on off days. This is a great arrangement! His thought thrilled him. I should have done it long ago. No more nagging, no more pressure. I have the best of both worlds—and I have achieved respectability!

Dorian made no effort to conceal his escapades. His girlfriends in Tijuana were known to all who knew him. The infamy was part of the fun. But in a small town like Tecate his conquests were common knowledge to all who were neither deaf nor blind. Alma did not suffer from either of these disadvantages. She only suffered humiliation.

Dorian played the part of the husband for about six months then moved to an apartment in Tijuana. No preamble, no explanation. Alma soon had to accept the fact that they were separated. A confrontation was useless. There was nothing to save. By the time the calendar proclaimed the first anniversary of the debacle, there was a new baby girl in the big house, a new mistress installed at Rosarito Beach, and a very embarrassed set of parents on the husband's side.

Señor and Señora Silva Fuentes were so happy and so proud of their new granddaughter that the maneuvering, the meddling with their daughter's life that eventually led to Magdalena's birth, was conveniently forgotten. They had what they wanted. The damaged lives that could never be restored didn't matter now. Señor Silva Fuentes's only concern now was gossip spreading where his good name might be part of the conversation. Especially among important people.

In the early stages of the farcical marriage, Señor Silva Fuentes tried to console his daughter. "He's young, *mi amor*, he'll get over it. You'll see. A careless indiscretion. He'll make it all up to you."

Alma couldn't believe it. Her own father was consoling his own conscience by defending the man who betrayed her. "I don't see it that way. The first time, maybe an indiscretion; when the whole town knows it, it's treason!"

"You have to learn to take a broad view!"

"While he flaunts his *pito* all over Tecate."

"How vulgar!"

"At last we found something we can agree on."

"I mean your language."

"Oh, it's my language! The disrespect he perpetrates against your daughter, the dishonor, doesn't offend you."

"There can be no divorce, you know."

"Of course, it's a matter of respectability!"

Still running my life, Alma thought. She gathered her things, bundled up baby Magdalena, and without another word to her father headed for the house she could never call a home.

Dorian never put in an appearance. Someone deposited money into her account every month, and the divorce became final. *Sin documentos*. Tradition handed down a life sentence, and the Church made sure there would be no possibility of parole. Another life shattered in the name of respectability.

Alma began to serve out her sentence. She was excommunicated from traditional social functions. Her married friends would not invite her to their parties. A married woman showing up at parties without her husband was not popular. She felt like a leper. Going out to dinner or dancing on her own was "not done" and therefore out of the question. Her only alternative was to go to some restaurant where the old maids, widows, and other castoffs like herself convened to share the bitter cup. She couldn't bring herself to do it. Alma was put into the freezer and frozen while still alive, and she would remain there until the day she grew old and died a natural and more merciful death. She was neither single nor married. Alma was socially dead.

One day soon after Magdalena was born Alma answered the door to find Don Julian and Doña Angelina standing there with nervous smiles on their faces and pain in their eyes. The embarrassment was quickly covered by countless clichés imposed by Mexican tradition. Alma received them with respectful embraces and flowery platitudes spoken verbatim from the scriptures of Mexican etiquette. Alma felt sorry for them. They too were victims. She brought the baby out to them and, by her demeanor, made it easy for them to return as often as they wished to cuddle and coo over their new treasure. Dorian was never mentioned.

Alma called on Judge Valdes, who was delighted to have her back, and this gave her someplace to go. Her servant girl was a reliable woman who watched baby Magdalena until

Alma came home for the day at noon. She never left her house on weekends. She could have joined the ceramics class that all the other nonpersons attended but she preferred to entertain herself at home with the baby.

There came no hint of regret or remorse on behalf of her father. Like most Mexican men, Señor Silva Fuentes was fearless in business yet his courage deserted him when faced with admitting error. He could never admit a mistake even under penalty of death. Señor Silva Fuentes viewed apology as a form of weakness. Resentment built up at a faster rate than his empty smiles could melt the injury, and a glacier formed between daughter and father. Alma's mother, however, came by every day to play with her granddaughter. Once a week, and never on the same day, lest her deed be interpreted as custom, Alma took Magdalena to see her grandfather. Alma was cool and distant. She pretended to read while her father played with the baby. They spoke little. The uncomfortable visit lasted an hour. Never more.

It seemed to Alma that from new sun to cock's first crowing, Magdalena cut her first tooth and clapped her little hands at the sight of a single candle blazing on her birthday cake. By the second shrill clarion, Magdalena was cutting molars and would soon be blowing out two candles. Alma and her mother had just returned from shopping. Grandmother was allowed to put baby down for her nap. She was asleep instantly and the servant brought in a light meal. Alma sensed that her mother had something to say, and it didn't take but a bite of steamed fish before the prophecy was fulfilled.

"It would make your father very happy if we did the birthday party at home."

"This is my home."

"Alma, don't be like that."

"He never calls on me here."

"He's proud, you know that."

"So am I."

"Ay Alma! At least do it out of respect."

There is that word again, Alma thought. How many more human sacrifices do the hungry pagan gods of society demand? I've already mounted the altar and sacrificed my body, my soul, my life! She was about to say something she knew she would later regret, but her mother cut in with a trump card.

"You won't always have your father, you know."

The birthday party was, in fact, a reconciliation party and everyone knew it. There was a cake, of course, and lavish gifts, a mountain of pretty clothes Magdalena would outgrow before she wore, and toys that would require several years to be useful to her. Magdalena was so buzzed it was impossible to settle her down. By four in the afternoon she dropped into an exhausted sleep on top of her Pound-A-Peg. Alma put her down and joined her parents in the drawing room.

The miniature Indian maid served coffee and dainty little pastries from the ovens of the Sisters of Santa Brigida. Alma's mother covered her nervousness with nonstop conversation. Her father now assumed a big voice to hide a weakness conspicuously revealed by substituting extravagance for apology.

"Let me pour you a coffee, *mi amor*, I can see the baby has exhausted you." His exuberant solicitousness deceived no one. He treated Alma like his guest of honor. He was doing his best to regain that hero-father princess-daughter relationship they enjoyed until Alma became a woman. He passed her the pastries. "I know you especially like the apricot filling." He poured himself a brandy and opened several new bottles of fine liqueurs until Alma found one to her liking. Poor man, Alma thought, he's doing everything he couldn't do when I lived here.

After the light repast, Señor Silva Fuentes leaned back in his chair, lighting a cigarette to feign contentment. "Oh, here's something interesting I got in the mail a few days ago," he said as casually as he could, picking up a letter that had been sitting on his side table and had him burning with excitement for over a week; an invitation to the governor's reception. He would have to suffer the long receiving line to shake the governor's hand, but he would find his way to the *secretario*—that was the key. And Señor Silva Fuentes knew from long experience how to peel away the protective layers that shielded his objective from favor-seekers. "It seems the incoming governor is going to address the citizens of Tecate. We're invited to attend. Why don't you join us? It could be a very entertaining evening."

Alma's feelings were still rankled. Her answer was already taking form inside her where it couldn't be seen, but her refusal was clearly written across her face. She had no desire to attend a political twaddle festival that she had absolutely no interest in and was guaranteed to bore her beyond endurance. And she still wasn't ready to forgive all. Then she studied her father's face. He looked old, vulnerable, defeated. A beautiful relationship eroded by pride, she thought. Well, he has only himself to blame!

Then bead by bead little drops of love began to flow into

the well of her heart where resentment is stored. Alma put down her crème de menthe, went over to her father, and put her arms around him. "Of course, Papá, I'll go."

Señor Silva Fuentes surreptitiously dabbed his eyes with the back of a hand. The two women in the room were not required to hide their tears.

The banquet room at the Rancho Tecate resort hummed with the voices of three hundred invited guests, meticulously dressed, coiffed, and scented. They were here to welcome Hilario Cornejo, governor-elect of Baja California Norte. The head table was raised on a platform to allow guests a better view of its distinguished occupants. A labyrinth of banquet tables under glimmering chandeliers spread out from the main table to the back wall. Seating was arranged according to social rank. A glance at the place cards revealed the importance of the invited. First row from the head table, the governor's best friends, followed by several rows of important guests, and against the back wall, those who knew someone who could get them in.

Decorators had arranged the Mexican tricolor ensign behind and above where Don Hilario, as he wanted to be known during the campaign, would make his first public address to the citizens of Tecate. The tables were set with green tablecloths and exotic bird of paradise centerpieces.

Señor and Señora Silva Fuentes, along with daughter, Alma, whose only reason for her presence was to make her father happy, were busy circulating, shaking hands, exchanging *abrazos* and flyaway kisses and gushing the prescribed social banalities to everyone they knew. "Alma, how lovely you look!" Exchange greetings. "How nice to see you again, Señor and Señora, what a pleasure to greet you." And thus Señor and Señora Silva Fuentes and daughter moved through the throng to see and be seen.

Alma felt out of place, an espoused widow on display, the subject of comments whispered out of hearing. The function hadn't even begun and she was ready to leave. As they turned to change direction, the three of them nearly collided with Mundo. There was an awkward moment of recognition.

Alma felt her heart do a cartwheel.

Señor Silva Fuentes jumped back as though a thousand volts had been shot through him. "*Buenas noches,* Mundo, nice to see you," the señor lied.

"*Buenas noches.*" The four jagged syllables fell from señora's lips like shattered stemware.

Alma felt herself go faint. The banquet hall began to spin around her. The droning of three hundred people made her dizzy. The two erstwhile lovers held a silent conversation with their eyes.

Alma, how beautiful you look!

I have never stopped thinking of you.

Neither have I.

Sometimes it still hurts.

I've kept you in a little corner of my soul.

Why did you stop writing?

You no longer answered.

Alma's and Mundo's eyes alighted on Señor Fuentes's face at the same instant. The answer was there written.

Love never dies.

Mundo remembered he had someone at his side. "May I present my wife. Rosamaria. Rosamaria, my dear, these are old friends from Tecate. Señor Silva Fuentes, his señora, and their daughter, Alma."

"*Mucho gusto,*" Rosamaria replied courteously and offered her hand.

Alma didn't know whether to embrace Mundo or shake his hand. It had to be a quick decision. She extended her hand to both of them in turn. She fought back an incredible impulse to throw her arms around him; she wanted to reach out and move that unruly strand of raven hair off his forehead. She struggled for self-control.

Señor prepared for a quick escape. "You will excuse us, I think we better find our table. It looks as though things are going to get started."

"Yes, and we are all way at the back of the room," Alma said innocently. Her father would have elbowed her but she was beyond his reach. "Where are you sitting?" Alma gushed before her father could stop her. "Maybe we can get together afterward."

"*Magnífico!*" Rosamaria ejaculated.

Mundo answered. "I'll look for you at the end of the program. We'll be at the head table."

Señor Silva Fuentes's elegant Ionic mustache nearly fell to the floor. Señora's elaborate coiffure seemed to wilt like wet hay.

Alma watched Rosamaria cuddle Mundo's arm in both hands like she used to do in a gesture of adoration. "The *gobernador* has appointed Mundo to be his Secretario de Gobierno. The governor will announce it this evening. We're so proud of him!"

Treenie

_H_ere on the ranch we have a big red rooster on the payroll whose job it is to tiptoe on the fence, flap his wings, and, with shrill clarion, command the sun to rise and shed its golden light across the valley of Tanama.

This morning the cock of the walk overslept.

But with Chemo also on the payroll, it hardly mattered. Chemo was as dependable as our resident herald of the morn. "Just look at this beautiful morning God has been so generous to offer us, Don. The _calandria_ is on the wing, the worm is on the _nopal_." It was not unusual for Chemo to sound a bit like the poet Browning, though he'd never heard of him.

"And today is the first day of the month, Don, I have everything ready," he announced like a talking calendar. Chemo came into the barn carrying a carton of anthelmintics.

We wormed all our bovine guests at the ranch on a regular basis. The mystery here was, how did Chemo always know the date? He didn't own a calendar, and even if he did, he couldn't read it. If life is a tragedy for those who read,

Chemo lived in paradise. He was spared the futility of struggling against life forces he didn't understand. He couldn't even sign his name. And yet I've seen him weather the vicissitudes of life better than I have. Chemo is the quintessential ranch manager. "The paragon of rancheros" would not be overstating the case.

"The morning is full of promise, Don." Chemo was also a philosopher. He gave me this forecast with a grin that exposed his few remaining candy corn teeth. He was in his seventies, I suppose. He wasn't sure himself. He was skinny as a cornstalk. I can't tell you much about his hair. He could be gray, or black, or bald as an oyster. In all the years I've been lucky to have him, I have never seen him without his beach umbrella sombrero.

"Look, Don!" The cause of his excitement was a snow-white dove that had fluttered down near where we stood and began pecking and crooning. "A white *paloma* is the messenger of good news, Don. You'll see soon enough." Chemo was an encyclopedia of omens good and bad. He also knew every legend, every superstition in the book. I suppose I should have said his empirical book authored by experience.

I looked up at that moment to see a car I didn't recognize zipping its way up the winding drive toward the villa. It appeared to be in some haste and it was towing a long coil of thick yellow dust. A big, red Ford Expedition. Nobody I know, I thought. Probably a lost tourist who took a wrong turn and is now admitting to his wife that he needs to ask directions.

I squinted the naked optics to bring the image into focus, but I did not meet with a great deal of success. "I better go up and see who that is before we get started," I said to Chemo, and headed in that direction.

The driver's door opened, and you can imagine my total astonishment when I saw Sydney Greenstreet come lumbering out of the vehicle. And then I recognized Chuck Eastman. An understandable error on my part when you consider Chuck resembled the great actor both in volume and gait. Chuck is probably the most talented cinematographer in Hollywood. We've worked together for many years.

"What kind of operation are you running down here? Just look at this!" he ranted even prior to his salutation. "Hi." He led me around to the rear of his car. I was prepared to see the rear end smashed in. I saw nothing unusual, personalized license plate, a trailer hitch.

"I don't see anything."

"Of course you don't! Twenty minutes ago there was a forty-thousand-dollar cabin cruiser back there that I towed down here with the intention of taking it down to the Bahía for a few days of fun, frolic, and fishing."

"Where is it?"

"I'll tell you where it is. I'll tell you where it is!" Chuck spoke in doublets when he got excited. "It's sitting under lock and key at the Mexican port of entry. It was impounded! Impounded!"

"Impounded!" I made it a triad. "But why? I'm sure you have all your papers in order."

"Everything is in order, vehicle, boat registration, ownership papers, the works."

"Then why are they holding it?"

"Because—get this . . ." Here he paused long enough to grind his teeth. "Because the license plate is missing from the trailer! The man said I could bring the boat in, but the trailer could not come in without a license plate. Is that stupid or what?"

"Where's the license plate?"

"Who knows? It probably got scraped off the last time I went down a launching ramp. They usually always do get scraped off. And you can't see the damn thing when the boat is on the trailer."

"That's ridiculous. Who did you talk to?"

"A little fat-assed squid with a wart on his nose and probably on his tallywhacker—if he has one!"

"My! A vivid description. I think you have just rendered a faithful portrait of Big Caca."

I should explain here that Chuck is not ordinarily an excitable individual. He is usually cool as the proverbial *pepino*. He is an ace cameraman. Together on film assignments we have faced death and danger all over the world. And while I made what I thought were sensible suggestions about returning to the hotel for a shooter, Chuck remained composed of mind and nerve. He never came away without his shot. We have lain hidden deep in the rain forests of South America to get a forbidden shot of secret tribal rituals, and never a complaint from Chuck. We had to fly aboard a papier-mâché airplane with no doors into the jungles of Tikal. He showed nerves of steel. In Guatemala we were filming an erupting volcano. Hot ashes were falling on us like burning snowflakes, soldiers were evacuating the village, lava was flowing inexorably toward us. Instant cremation was imminent. I began to give some serious thought as to the final destination of the soul. But Chuck never took his eye off the lens. That's the unperturbable Chuck Eastman I've always known. So to see him so hysterical was cause for concern.

"I may never see my boat again!"

"Calm yourself. This is not something to get so upset about. Keep that up and your gallbladder will release copious amounts of bile and soon you will be complaining of headache, constipation, and lassitude."

"You mean you can get my boat back?"

"No, no. I don't have that kind of *palanca*, leverage, you know. But I know who can."

"Who?"

"We refer to him as *el chingapaleta*."

"What does it mean?"

"An obscene sobriquet that, while original and colorful, does not easily yield to translation. But basically it alludes to someone who can come out of a sticky situation a winner. His actual name is Trinidad Contreras. He is also known as Treenie."

"Good?"

"It is said here in Tecate that the man can walk on water. I have never seen him perform this particular feat myself, but I have seen him perform what can only be described as miracles."

"Let's go find this dude right now."

Chuck drove. We walked into the plaza and took a pleasant table under a yellow umbrella at a sidewalk café. Almost immediately a pigeon and a waiter came nodding toward us. He placed a bowl of salsa and a basket of chips in front of us. The waiter, not the pigeon.

"Bring us two margaritas and menus. Have you seen Treenie?"

"Not since yesterday."

"You know," Chuck said, "if it wasn't for my problem, this could be very pleasant."

"We owe the pleasure to Treenie."

"Huh?"

"Just a few years ago we couldn't have been sitting here."

"Why not?"

"We would have been flattened by a car most likely. We're sitting right in the middle of what until recently was a busy east-west artery."

"And Treenie is responsible?"

"You could say Treenie Contreras has made his mark in this town. All over this town."

I thought it would do Chuck good to get his mind off his forty-thousand-dollar boat condemned to purgatory. A brief history of the sidewalk café could be an interesting distraction. And how Treenie rerouted the streets, redesigned the plaza, and thus changed the face of Tecate.

It was about ten years ago, as I recall. In those days the plaza was surrounded by streets on all four sides. Across the street on the south side where we now sat were a few government offices and Vicente's, a small café renowned for congenial service and perilous fare. Next to the café was Banco de Mexico. Treenie sat with Vicente in a small booth working on a pair of polyurethane eggs sunny side up.

"You know, Treenie," Vicente said, "if I could expand, I could make it big in this business."

Treenie and Vicente were the only people in the café. "To what end? You have a dozen empty tables right now."

Vicente ignored reality. "I have big plans. If we had a sidewalk, I could put out tables and umbrellas and I would pack them in. We have a long season here. I would double my volume."

Treenie looked around. "That would give you a total of four customers, if you count yourself."

Vicente wasn't listening. "If I could get the *presidente* to close off this street and extend the plaza all the way to my front door, I would be a millionaire in less than a year!"

"Have you talked to him?"

"He hates me. He found a frog in his taco."

"Alive?"

"Of course not. But he made a big scene. I told him if he'd been in a fine restaurant on the Other Side, he would have paid a fortune for that frog."

"But that didn't seem to placate him."

"No. He hasn't spoken to me since. But you know something, Treenie? You have a way with people. I've seen you do the impossible. You could probably get him to approve such a project." Vicente could see that he had lost his audience. "I could make it worth your while—very worth your while."

He regained his audience. A sly smile came into Treenie's face, his eyes grew larger, whiter, indicating to those who knew him that his attention had been gained. He studied his fingernails.

"Two thousand American dollars, Treenie. You have my word on it. The day the project is finished, I'll hand you two thousand American dollars."

"What you propose is close to impossible, Vicente."

"Make it three thousand."

Treenie gave his fingernails further study.

"A thousand when the city breaks ground, two thousand when it's finished."

Treenie gave no sign that he was listening.

"And one thousand in advance."

Treenie came to life. He walked out of Vicente's with heartburn and one thousand American dollars in his pocket.

This would be a good time to render a thumbnail sketch of Treenie Contreras. Treenie did not resemble most Mexicans. The voice was not the usual melodic Gay Caballero type. It was more of a hiss, a raspy whisper often associated with laryngitis. The face, a dark Eastern Mediterranean with a serpentine smile, hinted at international intrigue, secret cartels, and other dubious endeavors. His passport was probably forged. The heavy eyelids gave him a deceptively sleepy look. But when interested in the subject of conversation, Treenie could pull them back to full open, and it put you in mind of two black olives in a saucer of milk.

Two days after his memorable breakfast at Vicente's, Treenie walked into the Palacio Municipal and asked for the *presidente*. This, of course, caused all the pretty little señoritas in the mayor's concubine to burst into peals of what sounded like insiders' giggles. No one ever walked in and asked for an audience with the *presidente*. It was like seeking an audience with the Wizard of Oz. But much of Treenie's efficacy lay in his intimate knowledge of the food chain in Mexican government waters.

Treenie could assume the visage of a hungry barracuda with incredible fidelity. He assumed this role now. "The *presidente* will be quite upset if he doesn't receive the information I bring him. But of course, that's his *problema*, not mine." He turned to go. The señoritas realized at once that it would also be *their* problem.

Predictably, all the little minnows scurried in all directions. Two shapely young things led him into the office of the appointments secretary. On first sight Treenie thought they were stabling a horse in the office. The horse behind the desk rose on his hind legs and exposed a row of equine incisors.

"*Buenas tardes,*" the equine whinnied, and extended his hand. "Sylvestre Ochoa, your *servidor*. What can I do for you?"

"Trinidad Contreras. I wish to make an appointment to see the *presidente*."

The horse reared back, filling the room with a loud nicker that seemed to Treenie to contain more sarcasm than mirth. "I am afraid, señor, that the *presidente* has a very full calendar." He took a huge volume resembling *Webster's Unabridged* seventh edition from a side table and began to turn the pages. "I would like to accommodate you, señor, but I see there is nothing available." He advanced another dozen pages. "The *presidente* is a very busy man, you can understand. How long do you need to see him?"

"Less than ten minutes."

"Oh, I think I can squeeze you in. Yes! I have a ten-minute segment available . . . let's see . . . yes, you can have three-thirty to three-forty."

"When?"

"On Thursday, February twelve."

"That's nine months from now."

"I wish I could do more for you. If you would be kind enough to fill out this application for an appointment, I'll put it in his book." The phone rang at that moment. "It was nice to make your acquaintance. See you in February." The horse picked up the phone with his ears up. "Put her on! *Sí, corazón,* yes darling. Mmmm, I can hardly wait . . ."

While the man was gushing treacle into the phone, Treenie filled in his name and handed it back with one hundred American dollars adhered with a paper clip.

The horse laid his ears back. "I've told you not to call me at the office. I'm in conference!" The secretary slammed down the phone. "How about this afternoon at four-thirty?"

The horse escorted Treenie into the *presidente's* office at the appointed hour, introduced him, and withdrew.

"It is a pleasure to make your acquaintance, Señor Presidente. What I have to say will take less than ten minutes, but I felt you should hear it from me."

El presidente grabbed a pen and dashed off a note, a brief reminder to be sure to have his appointments secretary executed in the courtyard first thing in the morning. All he ever got were complaints, the potholes in the streets, the faulty traffic lights, the extortionists dressed as cops. The complaints never ended. And now this man with the shifty eyes was allowed to come in here with more. *El presidente* turned off his auditory process and looked at his watch.

"I represent a group of citizens who admire everything you have accomplished here in Tecate in such a short time," Treenie began. "We have taken up a collection, in fact I have already collected over a thousand dollars." One of the things that has contributed to Treenie's success over the years is his flair for showmanship. Treenie withdrew an untidy bundle of bank notes that overflowed both hands, and allowed them to flutter to the floor. "It is our intention, you see, to erect a monument in your honor."

El presidente reamed his ear out with a paper clip.

"We thought bronze would be appropriate."

"Can I pour you a brandy?"

Treenie glanced at his watch. "Our time is almost up."

"Time is meaningless in the service of our community. It is my duty as *presidente* to listen to the citizens." By the time he had said this the mayor had poured two fingers of Presidente brandy in glasses and handed one to his guest. "Bronze?"

"The ideal material for this kind of tribute. I visualize a great block of granite as a base. Or perhaps something vertical. Yes! An obelisk to carry the plaque below the bronze figure."

"Granite block . . . obelisk, you say . . . bronze figure?"

"Maybe a facia plate of pink marble would be more suitable."

"And where would we, uh, you place this, uh, this structure?"

"That seems to me the only problem. I have a couple of locations in mind, but they may not be available."

"Like where?"

"Well, there seems to be a small space near the municipal landfill. We would have to landscape a little to screen the piles of burning trash. But of course, my first choice, the most elegant site for this important monument, is probably not available."

"Try me."

Treenie put down his brandy and walked to an aerial view of the plaza and Palacio Municipal that hung on the wall. He tapped it with his long index finger. "The south end of the plaza is ideal for such a tribute. The low slanting rays of the early morning sun would illuminate the profile with a shot of light, producing a dramatic effect. In the afternoon the setting sun would seem to transform the entire figure to gold."

"Let me pour you another brandy."

"I'm afraid I'm keeping you from your business."

"I am a servant of the people. Nothing is more important than attending to a citizen of Tecate. A light of burnished gold, you were saying?"

"Of course we would plant flowering trees, jacaranda would lend a touch of color and dignity. And of course, some dramatic lighting for the evening. Soft colors. Nothing too harsh, you understand."

"I understand, I understand! Yes, of course!"

"But we have a space problem."

"Explain."

Treenie picked up a colored thumbtack from the mayor's desk. "May I?"

"By all means. Take several."

"This is the ideal site." Treenie returned to the print on the wall and pushed the red pin into the middle of the street. "In this location the great piece can be viewed from all directions. The multitudes who cross the plaza every day must pass through its shadow. But of course, as you can see, it would require paving over the avenue and expanding the plaza. And that may not be possible."

"Everything is possible."

"It would be ideal if we could assemble the military band for an unveiling on Independence Day, but then—"

"Work begins in the morning. Are you disposed to some dinner, Treenie?"

It was pleasant sitting out under the umbrella. It was nearly noon and there wasn't a vacant table. Chuck had already emptied three goblets, and I thought it would be wise to order some lunch. I handed Chuck a menu.

"Am I going to get a frog in my taco?"

"I'm afraid not. Vicente sold out and went to the Other Side. This place is now called Café de Paris."

"And where is the monument?"

"By the time the work was completed on the expansion of the plaza, *el presidente* was out of office and the whole business was forgotten."

The sweet strains of a thousand angels singing floated across the plaza.

"Ave Ma-ree-ee-ah . . . gra-tee-a plena . . ."

"Am I hearing things?" my guest asked.

"You are listening to Gounod's Ave Maria which announces twelve meridian. Every radio station in Mexico broadcasts the music at noon every day, as it is believed that it was at this hour that the Angel Gabriel explained to the astonished Virgin Mary that she was to be a mother.

"Ave Ma-ree-ee-ah . . . BLAAAAAT!"

"What the hell was that?"

"The steam whistle at the Tecate Brewery also announces noon. I think we better order lunch."

"I wish your man Treenie would show up. I'm getting worried. Maybe I should just go to the U.S. Consulate."

"Your case would take weeks to resolve through channels. Leave it to Treenie."

"I know Treenie is a miracle worker, but what is his real profession?"

"Lawyer, doctor, embalmer, civil engineer, land management, accountant, import-export agent, and matchmaker."

The waiter appeared and took our lunch order.

"But what does he do for a living?"

"All of the above. Although, I suppose I should have omitted *lawyer*. He's only tried one case that I know of. But he won that. Another stinger while we wait for lunch?"

Chuck agreed to the suggestion, and I distracted him from his problems with some details about Treenie's first litigation.

Treenie had just arrived at Tecate from somewhere in the south. He's never been too definite about that. He is of unknown provenance. He was carrying a black briefcase containing everything he owned when he got off the bus. He wandered over toward the courthouse as though he understood the reason for it. It was noon, court was closed until later in the afternoon. Treenie entered the patio, took possession of a small bench, and began to eavesdrop to gain a basic understanding of how the game was played. He listened to *licenciados* discussing their cases with their clients, planning their strategy, or discussing lunch plans.

In a few minutes Treenie was the only one remaining, with the exception of the small urchin with a runny nose who shined shoes. The gate creaked opened and a young woman entered the patio. It didn't take her but a moment to ascertain that Treenie and the urchin with the runny nose who shined shoes were the only inhabitants. Her clothes alleged her rather modest place on the socioeconomic scale, clean though they showed a lot of mileage. But she had a shape that reminded Treenie of a classical guitar. The face, Treenie conjectured, would be beautiful were it not burdened with a serious problem. Her large dark eyes caught Treenie and she approached him tentatively.

"Excuse me, señor, where is everybody?"

"Court has adjourned until three o'clock."

The pretty girl burst into tears.

Treenie made room for one more on the bench. "Tsk tsk, nothing can be so serious for someone so young. Sit down and tell me what is wrong. There exists a solution for every problem."

"God bless your kindness and attentive ear, señor. I have a case before the judge this afternoon, and I don't see my lawyer. I'll lose my case by default!" A torrent of tears followed. She searched the depths of her purse, probably for a tissue, Treenie surmised, but she was not successful.

Treenie handed her a handkerchief. "Give me the details of your case. Maybe I can render some assistance."

"*Gracias*," she sniffed, accepting the handkerchief and

sopping up the rainfall. "My name is Maria Martínez. I loaned my car to my *novio*. He drove it to Mexicali to see another woman. On the way back the car overheated. The repairs came to five hundred dollars and he's determined to squirm his way out of it."

"Five hundred American dollars is no small sum, Maria."

"I know and I don't have it. I'm a poor girl. I work cleaning houses and I need that car to get to my jobs." Maria yielded to another spasm of sobs.

I should add here that Treenie was down to his last few dollars himself. But he recognized opportunity when it was sitting next to him on a little bench in the shape of a classical guitar in the patio of the Tecate courthouse.

"Dry your tears, señorita, by this afternoon you shall have your money."

"You mean it?"

"All of it."

Maria Martínez set aside all the things her mother and her grandmother had taught her as a girl. She threw her arms around her benefactor and put a soggy kiss on his cheek. "What do I need to do?"

"Very little." What Treenie did next was not an act of charity or human kindness. It was the gesture of a man who had a keen understanding of Mexico and the Mexican mind-set. Treenie reached in his pocket, withdrew his last twenty, and pressed it into Maria's delicate hand. "First, you will go into town and buy yourself something to wear. Something black, plain, but elegant. You understand?"

"*Sí, sí!*"

"And perhaps a little makeup to repair the damage. Meet me back here at two-thirty."

"I'm terrified to go before the judge."

"You have nothing to fear. Your *servidor* will take care of everything."

Maria looked like she was going to cry again. "I don't have your fee."

"Please, do not worry yourself unnecessarily. Two-thirty."

His new client left in the direction of town, and Treenie entered the nearly empty courthouse. He stepped up to the counter and addressed a señorita of tender age who was trying to manage three jobs at once. She was feeding pages into a fax machine and a French roll into her mouth while applying a coat of Revlon's Lilac Shimmer to her fingernails with her free hand.

Treenie put the timbre of authority into his voice. "I must speak to the judge at once!" Treenie knew his delivery was perfect when the girl behind the desk began to tremble. "You mean, Judge Cayetano Godoy?"

"Of course!" He affected impatience.

"He is out to lunch, señor, and won't be back until court resumes at three," the girl whimpered, and began to quiver like a sapling is said to quiver.

"So, I will find him at home?"

"No, señor, he didn't go home today. He went to La Fonda."

Treenie thanked her with a cool formality. Twenty minutes later he pushed through the door at La Fonda. He could see every head rise up from the viands to take in the stranger who just walked in the door. Treenie walked in slow motion, allowing everyone ample time to make assessment. His big black olives scanned the dining room. Every table was occupied by men, with the exception of the one against the wall, where three women chattered over their meal. They took note of him with greater subtlety than the men. Treenie found an empty table, settled in, and let his eyes do the walking. Two tables had four men, the rest had three. Which one was the judge? He counted seventeen candidates.

The only waiter in service arrived. *"Buenas tardes, solamente usted?"*

"*Sí*, I am alone. Bring me a glass of red wine while I look at the menu, *sí*?" Treenie sensed more than saw several men from other tables sneaking a look at him. He couldn't possibly ask the waiter who the judge might be. The man could be sitting at the next table.

The waiter returned with a glass of a fine full-bodied turpentine with a deep ruby color and an aromatic bouquet of questionable character. Now, it has probably become apparent to the reader that one of Treenie's most valuable skills was his profound understanding of Mexican custom. The veneration of titles is endemic to Mexico. When titles of nobility were abandoned the day the Revolution of 1910 ended, they were replaced with academic titles the very next day. No self-respecting Mexican would leave his house without his title, any more than he would without his clothes, and Treenie knew this. He sipped his alleged cabernet sauvignon leisurely, allowing time and custom to take its course and eventually identify the judge. He set his ears in the on position.

He listened to the waiter addressing the men at the next table. "Is everything all right here? Another *cerveza*, Doctor? Right away."

This was going to be easier than he thought.

"Are we ready to order, Señor Licenciado?" The waiter caught sight of a man nodding from another table. "Right away, Señor Ingeniero."

It would only be a matter of time. Mexicans wore their

titles like trophies. And Treenie knew that at least half of these, like his own, were probably self-conferred.

"*Profesór*, nice to see you again!"

The waiter returned to Treenie's side. "Ready, señor?"

"Bring me the *chile relleno*, please."

The waiter took a few steps toward the kitchen then a sharp left to answer a summons from another table. "Your *carne asada* will take only a tiny bit longer. I told the cook to leave it on the charcoals until the edges were just slightly crisped. Just the way you like it, Señor Juez."

Bingo! Treenie had his man identified without calling attention to himself. The man wasn't tall, but, of course, he was sitting. He had thick glasses with black frames heavy enough to serve as scaffolds. His hair was abundant and white as an onion. Treenie felt he had every right to be vain about it if he was so disposed.

Treenie finished his meal and ordered coffee. The next phase of the operation was critical. It would require perfect timing, a challenge anywhere but highly more speculative in Tecate. He followed the waiter with his eyes. He watched him go to the coffee urn at the end of the dining room. He poured coffee into a cup. He put down the coffeepot and turned in his direction. Now!

Treenie got up from the table, left a tip, picked up his check and walked toward the cashier.

The waiter caught up with him just as they came alongside the judge's table. "Señor! You have not had your coffee."

"I'm afraid I let the time get away from me. I come all the way from the state capital just to represent a client in court this afternoon. Such a nuisance! The governor's niece, you know, I couldn't refuse. Thank you, anyway."

Treenie did not have to look around to see the effect of his conversation with the waiter on the judge's face. He could feel the judge's eyes making positive identification. Treenie could have recited every word in the conversation that followed the moment he was out the door and out of earshot.

At half past two Treenie again occupied the small bench in the courtyard of the courthouse. Men, women, some with briefcases, some with strained faces, began to filter into the patio. They gathered in groups of twos and threes huddled in whispered conferences. Treenie hardly recognized his client when she came shimmering toward him. Maria Martínez arrived in clingy black leggings, and a matching black top that conformed to every contour of the matrix like wax in a mold. Her makeup was slightly understated. She looked important.

"Excelente!" Treenie was pleased. "Let us go in now and see that justice is done." They walked into the waiting room to be called.

Maria Martínez was nervous. "Oh my God, he's here. He just walked in the door!"

"Who?"

"My ex, the man I'm suing."

"Don't look at him. Look at me and nowhere else."

A young man in Levi's jeans and green cowboy shirt, apparently the bailiff, came into the waiting room. "Martínez versus Correa," he said and returned into chambers. He carried a legal file in his hand and a *Captain Marvel* comic book in his hip pocket.

"What do I say?" Maria was beginning to panic.

"Do not be nervous. I will do all the talking. When we are all through, the judge will ask you about your legal fees. You simply say two hundred dollars."

There was no more time to be nervous. Suddenly Maria Martínez found herself standing before the robeless judge. Treenie was next to her. Her ex *novio*, a handsome young rooster in stovepipe jeans and pointy boots, was standing to the right of him.

"Please explain your case," the judge crooned to the plaintiff.

Maria gulped, and Treenie took over in a voice freighted with impatience. "Señor Juez, we will not waste your valuable time. My client was generous enough to loan her car to the defendant. The defendant drove it to Mexicali. It overheated over the mountain pass. It cost the plaintiff five hundred dollars to repair the damage. It is a simple case of negligence, and my client simply wants reimbursement. Nothing more. That, Señor Juez, is the sum total of our case."

No questions. The judge reacted exactly as Treenie had programmed him. He turned to face the ex *novio*, who looked like he wanted to bolt. "Are these *datos* correct?"

"*Sí*, señor." It was a squeak.

At this juncture, Maria nearly sent the whole case down the *tubos*. "And I need my car to get to my—"

Treenie finished her sentence. "Her uncle's office in Mexicali."

His Honor appeared to deduce that the governor allowed his pretty little niece to play office with her favorite uncle. "The court orders you to pay Señorita Martínez the full amount." He gently caressed Maria's breasts with his eyes, and wondered if he could make points with the governor via his attractive niece who now sat before him. "And your legal fees, señorita?"

"Two hundred dollars," she sniffed.

The judge glanced at the *licenciado* who "had come all

the way from the state capital" to represent the governor's niece. "The court orders total restitution. Now. Case closed."

Treenie thought the judge was about to throw his client a kiss. But the scrunching of the mouth could have been a bit of *carne asada* caught between the teeth. He was ready to make his exit when the judge continued to gush.

"And be sure, señorita, to convey my warmest *saludos* to your uncle."

Treenie pulled Maria out of there before the judge could invite them to stay for cocktails and dinner. Cash disbursement of funds was made in the lobby. Treenie said adios to his client and took his leave with two hundred dollars tucked in his pocket. He returned to La Fonda to sample the product of the local brewery, approved, and decided to stay. The citizens of Tecate need a specialist like Treenie. Always available. No job too big, no job too small.

Chuck appeared to be chilling out, as I believe you express a mellowing condition in the argot of your country. This was due mostly to four margaritas and a heavy meal of fresh guacamole dip, *carne asada*, refried beans snowy with white cheese, and a mound of fluffy rice. He also worked his way through two baskets of tortillas. Nothing impaired Chuck's appetite. Chuck now began one of his favorite pursuits. He began to people-watch.

"You have some really good-looking women here, you know that?"

"I agree."

"What's the story on that guy on the other end of the plaza? He's got a big huge crowd of people around him. It looks like he has a bird in a cage."

Chuck was born with a 12 to 120 zoom lens in his head, while my gene pool supplied me with optical equipment of lesser quality. He could focus sharply on things I couldn't even see, and yet I knew exactly what he was talking about. "That's the local fortune teller."

"Geez! I just saw a guy blow a big huge flame out of his mouth."

I did not call attention to Chuck's favorite redundancy. I did not need 20/20 to know all the colorful denizens of the plaza were out in full force this pleasant afternoon. It wasn't necessary for me to see them while I had Chuck to provide the voice-over.

"This is like watching a movie. Hey, you're not going to believe this, but there's a guy walking by the fountain that looks like he just stepped out of an old Bogart film. Wilted white suit, a shifty look in his eyes. He could pass for Peter Lorre's double. Do you know him? He's coming this way."

"*Hola*, Treenie, sit down. I want you to meet an old friend of mine, Chuck Eastman."

Treenie offered his hand and spoke in a raspy whisper. "How do you do Meester Eessman." The inability of the Hispanic tongue to form three consecutive consonants is widely known and recognized by the most progressive researchers of the medical profession.

"Have a drink with us, Treenie. My friend here has a little problem with Big Caca. I told him the word *problema* has no meaning to Treenie Contreras."

"Thank you for your confidence," he hissed. He then turned to Chuck and spoke in his laryngeal whisper. "Tell me about your problem, Meester Eessman, perhaps your *servidor* can be of some service."

I snagged the waiter at that moment. "Bring Treenie a José Cuervo double and a dozen limes, *sí*?"

Treenie listened to Chuck's story attentively, and when

he was through giving his deposition, Treenie blotted his lips with a napkin and his eyes seemed to widen. He lit a cigarette, exhaled with a *sssss* and spoke. "I believe this is something with remedy, Meester Eessman. I will call on the *comandante* immediately. Perhaps I can do something to convince him to adopt a more congenial point of view." He almost laughed, but it was really an evil chuckle in the company of a smile. One of his sardonic ones.

Chuck appeared to have been hypnotized, not an uncommon reaction to an interview with Treenie. He sat motionless, goggling at the man in front of him. It appeared to me that Chuck had momentarily lost his ability to form words. I think this is known within the medical community as an aphasic condition. Anyway, I turned to Treenie.

"Shall we summon the paramedics for another tequila?"

"Thank you, Don, but I better put in an appearance at the port of entry before it gets any later. I wouldn't want the *comandante* to decide to spend the rest of the afternoon with his mistress." He rose and shook hands with Chuck. "I will report to you as soon as I have concluded the business at hand, Meester Eessman. I should be back before too long."

We watched Treenie leave in the direction of the fountain, the same way he came. We were quiet for a moment, then Chuck spoke. "And I'm leaving the safe return of my forty-thousand-dollar boat in the hands of Peter Lorre?"

"You've lost confidence?"

"He looks shifty to me."

I thought another page out of Treenie's résumé would restore Chuck's confidence. It happened only a few years ago. It was a year of firsts for Tecate.

It was the first time a member of PAN, the opposition

party, won the seat of Presidente Municipal. We got our first motorcycle cops, our first woman judge, and our first woman Director of Public Works. We want the world to know that here in Mexico we do not have a glass ceiling. Ours is made of baked adobe. But I'm getting away from the main thrust of my story. Sandra Quiróz was not only the first woman to hold the post of Director of Public Works, she was also the youngest. Twenty-eight, brainy, and gorgeous.

One afternoon pretty Sandra Quiróz sat in the *presidente*'s office with a list of projects she wanted to accomplish during her tenure. She was dressed in camel pants and a tailored mustard blazer. *El presidente* listened attentively while he speculated whether she had anything on under the jacket other than the gifts God gave her in a moment of generosity.

"And one of the projects that I think deserves high priority is the installation of a new monument at the very entrance of our border with the United States. It will be seen by every visitor that enters our country."

"Ah yes, I'm in total agreement, wonderful. Maybe a national hero or maybe a monument to fathers. We don't have a monument to fathers, you know."

"A national heroine is more what I had in mind."

"You can't mean *heroine*."

"That's exactly what I mean. Every civilized country in the world honors its women except Mexico. Think of it. There was Athena, Venus, Helen of Troy, Aphrodite . . ."

"But that was a long time ago."

". . . Cleopatra, Joan of Arc, Madam Curie . . ."

"You're still talking ancient history."

". . . Queen Elizabeth, Indira Gandhi, Harriet Beecher Stowe, Helen Keller. Susan B. Anthony even made it onto a silver dollar. Do you realize Mexico has never honored a woman? We weren't even considered smart enough to vote until 1953. It's a disgrace!"

"We don't have a woman in our history! Where are you going to find one?"

"I've already found her."

"Who!"

"Juana de Asbaje."

"Who?"

"Juana de Asbaje, 1651 to 1695, the first feminist in the New World! A young and brilliant woman who wanted to study medicine. She was not allowed into the University of Mexico because she was a woman! She turned to writing. She has bequeathed to us numerous essays, and several volumes of poetry. When her macho guardians ordered her to stop writing, she ran off to the convent and took the veil. That's who we are going to commemorate. That's the statement we want to make to our liberated visitors from the north!"

"And who's going to do the sculpture?"

"I have also learned that right here in Tecate we have a man who might very well be a genius who works in stone and marble."

"Who?"

Sandra was beginning to think *el presidente* was sounding very much like an owl. "Lazarus."

"The man is insane."

"Genius is often misunderstood."

"I wish you the best of luck."

There lived in Tecate at that time an eccentric young sculptor who lived and worked in a large ramshackle barn of corrugated iron perched like some predator bird on a rock pile appropriately known as Vista del Aguila. Sandra followed the dirt track over ruts and craters until she realized she would require a Caterpillar D-4 to make it the rest of the way. She abandoned her car and continued on foot to the entrance of Lazarus's studio.

It was unnaturally quiet, deserted. She strolled through the enormous building admiring works in various stages of completion. Massive statues of heroic figures looked down at her. She recognized busts of Padre Hidalgo and Juarez and a frieze of Don Porfirio Diaz. There was a full-size granite of Cuauthemoc getting his feet roasted over an open fire while the *conquistadores* made inquiry as to the location of a chest of gold. Scattered about the studio were clay heads and plaster molds of people she didn't recognize. Huge blocks of quarried stone and marble waited for the master to give them life. Lost in her self-conducted tour, Sandra felt herself being drawn to a smooth pillar of creamy alabaster. Two small spheres formed the base. The surface was smooth, polished to a glossy sheen. Almost without prior intention she realized her hand had gone out to touch it and she was gently caressing the imposing cylinder. It felt like she was stroking silk.

Sandra came out of her reverie. It was too quiet. She walked toward the back of the studio in search of the artist. "Maestro?" she whispered. "Maestro?" Only a faint echo answered. It was impossible to be here without gaping. She paused to admire a grouping hewn of gray stone. A masterpiece if ever she saw one. There stood Artemis, goddess of the moon and wild life, in a full-length gown ingeniously modeled to suggest a breeze in the forest. Artemis was resting her hand gently on the back of a timid fawn.

Behind her and slightly to the side stood Pan; his handsome smooth face and tangled curls looked almost real. He held a wooden flute to his lips. Sandra nearly wet her pants when Pan played a sweet diatonic B flat scale, first up then down, then smiled.

"I am so sorry. I did not mean to frighten you." Pan stepped down from the pedestal, leaving Artemis to her fawn. "I often join my friends. We often share the sweet banquet of the heart together. Were you looking for me?"

Sandra would have leaped for the door but her limbs were inoperative at the moment. It took her a few more seconds to compose herself. Like everything else in the studio, every inch of the man's surface from locks to sandals was covered with a thin layer of white stone dust. He appeared to be made of solid granite. The man was real, all right. She could see white teeth and a pink tongue when he talked. On closer examination she saw that he was shirtless. He was wearing a pair of shredded pants and huaraches.

"If you are Lazarus, I am looking for you."

"I am Lazarus, your *servidor*, son of the beggar. Sit down, Señorita . . . ?"

"Pardon! I am Sandra Quiróz, your *servidora*."

"Diminutive of Alexandra, the defender. How beautiful." His voice was soft, ethereal. He led her to a pair of tall bar stools by the window, blew the dust off one of them like a good host should, and perched on the other. "I'm sorry about the mess. Everything here is covered with dust, stone, plaster, marble. Including myself. I wish I could make you more comfortable. As you have seen, I live alone among my works and don't often get visitors. Some coffee perhaps, cinnamon tea, or maybe a cup of chocolate?"

How thoughtful! Sandra was touched by his simple and innocent graciousness. "*Gracias*, I am just fine." He was impossible to age. He had the muscular upper body of a strong, healthy man. The face, smooth and serene, was that of a child. Even his voice was pure and crystalline. A boy soprano. His hair was longer than her own and held back with a braided diadem that tied at the back of his head. "You do beautiful work." She found she was whispering.

"*Gracias*. Come, I will show you my life's work." Lazarus placed her arm through his own and, holding her hand in both of his, guided her safely over the expensive debris scattered about the floor.

"Recognize them?"

"Only the figure of Jesus. Who are the rest of them?"

"The Six Prophets."

"Six?"

"*Sí*, according to the Koran there were over two hundred thousand prophets, but only six brought new laws. And there they are. Adam, of course, followed by Noah, Abraham, Moses, Jesus, and Mohammed."

Sandra gazed at six life-size figures that appeared to rise from the marbled floor of Heaven. She was overcome with an inexpressible emotion so intense it robbed her of speech. Lazarus did not disturb her communion.

"It required eight years of my life and a passion for three-dimensional space."

"Who could afford to order such work?"

"It was commissioned by God. It is my final statement as a sculptor. I plan to die when I finish it."

He was smiling when he said this, as though it was the most natural thing in the world. Maybe death was natural, but the theme made Sandra uncomfortable. She sought to draw attention to another work and they returned to the bar stools where they had been sitting. "What is that contemporary piece, the tall marble shaft with the two spheres at the base?"

"Exquisite, no? I saw you fondling it earlier. Everyone who sees it experiences the same impulse to touch."

Sandra understood. "It is a strange sensation to discover that a material as hard as marble can feel so silky. It is irresistible to touch. What does it represent?"

"It is titled Manhood. It was to be a monument to fathers for the city of Ensenada."

Sandra blushed to the roots of her hair.

"Pure form and symbol. But of course, the ignorant cannot understand that."

"Yes, of course." She was sorry she'd asked.

"Over in the back corner I have another abstract titled Womanhood. We missed it on the tour. Would you like to see it?"

"Perhaps on another occasion." Sandra perched herself on the stool. She was no longer concerned with dust.

Lazarus took the other one, propping one foot on the high rung. "What can I do for you, Señorita Alexandra?"

It was impossible not to notice that her host's wardrobe did not include underwear. She locked her eyes on his. "I represent the municipality and I'm here to commission a statue of Juana de Asbaje. I brought photographs."

"Let me see them."

Sandra handed him the only two photos she could find. Both were head shots, but at different angles.

"Yes! Look at those eyes. There is a spirituality about her, no? You can see peace and beauty within her. It is said Truth has such a face. I can hardly wait to let her live again!"

"You have divined her correctly." Sandra was delighted at his enthusiasm for the work. And *el presidente* said the man was crazy. He was lovely. "I want her full length, maybe with an open book in her hands. I leave that to you."

"Size?"

"Three-quarter."

"Material?"

"What would you suggest, Maestro?" Sandra glanced over to the abstract recently under discussion. "Alabaster?"

"Excellent choice. Alabaster has an inner light of its own. When do you want the work?"

"June fourteenth. There will be a grand dedication cere-mony. She will be placed at the entrance of the town to wel-come visitors from foreign lands. That gives you six months. How much should we expect to pay you?"

"I find economics a dismal science, Señorita Alexandra. Whatever you think my work is worth."

Everyone must cheat this poor genius, she thought. He's much too fragile for the real world. "How about fifty thou-sand now and another fifty thousand pesos when we pick up the work? Does that sound fair?"

"I know so little about these things. I leave the entire matter in your hands. But it will be ready the day before your dedication."

"*Magnífico!*"

"I only insist on one thing."

"And what might that be?"

"I must not be disturbed. No visitors. No one may view the work until completed."

"That's more than fair. I'll have your money this afternoon." Sandra left the sculptor in his shredded pants and braided diadem, and hiked back down the mountain, her bosom swelling with joy and pride. The first woman to be so honored in Tecate and it took Sandra Quiróz to do it!

On the morning of June thirteen Sandra was too excited to go to her office at the Palacio Municipal. She gulped a cup of coffee and a piece of sweet bread and headed directly for Lazarus's studio. She already had the ceremony organized. At ten tomorrow morning every schoolteacher in Tecate would bring their classroom to witness the event. She had arranged for the military band to play. They weren't very good, but it was all she could get. *El presidente* would unveil the work of art, and Sandra herself would deliver an inspirational address, and Mexican womanhood could hold their heads high with pride!

Sandra was almost giddy with anticipation when she entered Lazarus's studio. There in the corner was a canvas tarpaulin draped over a figure nearly life-size. She stood before it in reverent silence.

"Unveil your work, Maestro."

Lazarus pulled away the canvas.

"My masterpiece, Señorita Alexandra. It was a moment of cosmic influence. I will never again do anything so inspired."

"I don't know what to say." Sandra was overcome with emotion and not afraid to show it. Big tears came to her eyes and began to roll down her pale cheeks. *"Ave Maria!"* she whispered.

"I understand. I cannot look at her with dry eyes either."

"Holy Mary Mother of God!"

"That is exactly how I feel. This is as close as I will ever come to touching Heaven." His eyes were wet now. "She's alive. I strove to achieve a smooth three-dimensional fluidity. I feel I have conquered the material. Notice the distribution of weight, the rhythm of the figure, the almost sublime expression on her face. Look at the detail, every hair, every pore . . . Juana de Asbaje lives!"

"I'm looking at every detail, every pore, and I also see she's stark naked, YOU IDIOT!"

Lazarus looked crestfallen.

Both of Sandra's hands flew into her mouth in horror. She felt like she had just struck a defenseless child. "Oh, I'm so sorry. I had no right—" Pretty Sandra Quiróz gave way to a *chubasco* of tears. "Please, forgive me!" she sobbed.

"Please. Save your tears for a grief more deserving. You may be right. I am the one who is sorry. I have disappointed you."

"Everyone in this town will be at the ceremony tomorrow. It's all been arranged. They expect a monument to be dedicated. What do I do now?" The flood of tears was renewed.

"Perhaps something else here would solve your problem." She realized Lazarus was just trying his best to be accommodating. "Choose anything here you like. The abstract figure of Manhood makes a rather honest statement."

"Too honest. Please!" Sandra did what every woman wants to do when she knows she has a serious problem and no ready solution. She began to tear her hair out. "Nothing here is appropriate!"

"Then accept the nude. I'm sure the people of Tecate will admire this great work."

"I would sooner have myself gilded and stand out there naked myself before I let that go out of here."

"I have a quart of gold paint. I should think that would be enough. And we could have it done in time. I would use a very soft brush, of course."

"Aaauuugh!"

By the time Sandra got back to town her nerves were in shreds and her hair was a mess. She returned to her office. But the phone never stopped ringing. Everyone was calling with some last-minute question or detail about tomorrow's unveiling. She sequestered herself at her mother's house and searched every cell in her brain for a solution. She looked at her watch. Suddenly it was eight o'clock in the evening. Tomorrow morning five thousand people will be gathered to watch the unveiling of their new momument. Bands will play. Even XEWT Channel 12 from Tijuana will be covering the event. And Sandra Quiróz will die of humiliation. She would join Lazarus at the base of the Six Prophets in sweet painless death.

Sandra thought of drowning herself in the treacherous Tecate River in disgrace. But throwing yourself into a dry riverbed would lack style. She thought maybe the Reverend Mother would let her hide out in the convent of Santa Brigida. She considered the evening flight to Tegucigalpa.

Then she thought of Treenie.

But how could she approach this? Sandra knew where she could find him at this hour. That wasn't the problem. She didn't want to walk into the Diana, the all-macho cantina across from the plaza. That was the problem. She found a place to park, a good omen, she thought, and stood before the dark narrow entrance with the word DIANA written out in pink neon. She drew the sign of the cross in the air, stepped inside, and waited for her eyes to adjust.

"Good evening, Señorita Sandra," the sandpaper voice rasped in the darkness. His elbow rested on a small table. His hand, bent at the wrist, held a smoldering cigarette between the fingers. "I cannot imagine what a young lady would be doing in the Diana, but sit down and let me order you something to drink."

"Treenie, I have to talk to you!"

"I assumed that much, but wouldn't you rather talk sitting down?"

"Not here, Treenie."

"The men's room is the only other place here, and there are several men standing in there at the moment."

"Outside, Treenie!"

"Of course, I will only be too happy to join you." Treenie took his drink with him and walked Sandra out into the small courtyard in the rear, where a stone-carved Diana was the sole witness to this conversation. "You seem anxious, Señorita Sandra, what seems to be so urgent?"

Sandra filled him in on all the events leading up to the present crisis and summed it up. "So you see, there will be five thousand people out here tomorrow morning at ten, a band, television crews, and when the *presidente* pulls the drapery, something has to be there."

"You're right, Señorita Sandra, the problem is far from simple. Very critical, actually."

"Tell me about it! That's why I'm talking to you."

"I'm going to assume you want me to search the world for something appropriate during the course of the night and have it in place for tomorrow morning's ceremony."

"Very perceptive, Treenie, that's exactly what I want."

"It sounds almost impossible to accomplish."

Sandra could see they were wasting valuable time. She

spoke the only words Treenie understood. "I don't care what it costs, Treenie, it's coming straight out of the municipal budget."

"I'm on my way. What do you want me to provide?"

"I don't really care, provided it has clothes on."

"Put away your worries, Señorita Sandra, the problem will be solved," Treenie hissed, and evaporated into the night.

I interrupted this fascinating account because Chuck saw Treenie coming toward us with the awaited verdict. The figure was not yet in focus for me.

Treenie fell into a chair and answered our question before it was asked. "Your problem is solved, Meester Eessman," he whispered. "The *comandante* asked me to convey his heartfelt apologies for the inconvenience, and that he would be honored if you would be his guest for cocktails and dinner. You can pick up your boat and be on your way any time."

Chuck's face was the image of frozen ecstasy. Then, when the cranial nerves finally carried the information up to headquarters, I thought he was going to leap up on the table and do "La Bamba." But good old Chuck regained his composure and pulled out his wallet. "I cannot thank you enough, Treenie."

Treenie waved a hand toward his overture and spoke. "Please, put away your money, Meester Eessman. I have been amply remunerated by the *comandante*."

"The *comandante*!"

"What exactly did you do, Treenie?" I have never known Treenie to waive a fee.

"Actually, it required little effort on my part. I simply

arrived at his office with a tow truck from Gordo's Towing Service and had Gordo park behind his brand-new Thunderbird. Have you seen his new Thunderbird?"

"Yes."

"A beautiful *automóvil*, no?"

"Yes, yes, get on with it!"

"The *comandante* can see the car from his window. So naturally he came storming out. 'What do you think you're doing!' he screamed at me.

"Gordo said nothing, but I asked the *comandante*, 'Oh is this yours, Comandante? I didn't know.' I withdrew an envelope from my inner pocket. 'This is a court order from the Judicial Federal to impound this car. It seems it is stolen.'

" 'Stolen! *Imposible!*'

" 'Perhaps you would like to look at the court order.'

" 'No, I don't want to see it!' Then there was a sudden voice change. 'What are we doing out here in the hot sun? Come up to my office. I have some very good brandy.' "

"And what happened in his office?" I think Chuck and I said this at the same time.

"We exchanged favors like two gentlemen."

"But how did you get a signed court order so fast?"

"I didn't have a court order in the envelope."

"My God, what guts. How did you know the car was stolen?"

"A safe conjecture." Treenie's twisted mind obviously understood how the convoluted Mexican system worked.

"And on top of all that you were remunerated?"

"Yes, you see, I agreed to lose the court order and he agreed to forget about the license plate. As to remuneration,

I have been retained by Meester Keety, an American with an unpronounceable last name. He is coming to Tecate to manage a *maquiladora*. He wants to bring things into Mexico without a problem. And the *comandante* was in a generous mood. It ends well when everybody wins, no?"

I saw Chuck look around for the check. "Chuck, I'll get this. You better get over there and retrieve your vessel. They close customs at three and it's twenty of."

"I will drive over with you, Meester Eessman."

Chuck looked at me. "But how are you going to get home?"

"Oh, that is not a problem. I'm quite resourceful. Move along, you should be able to make it as far as El Rosario before dark."

"Hey, you didn't finish the story! What the hell happened at the unveiling of the monument?"

"Go! You'll see it when you drive back into Mexico with your boat."

I watched as Sydney Greenstreet and Peter Lorre walked side by side across the plaza and disappeared behind the fountain. They appeared to be on their way to Casablanca to talk to the Maltese Falcon about the acquisition of an original Rembrandt.

Suddenly alone, I thought one for the stirrup would be a good idea and I signaled my intention to the waiter. That's when I saw a life-size candy cane coming in my direction. I made an unsuccessful attempt to focus the old corneal apparatus. The candy cane waved. I wasn't at all sure it was intended for me but I continued to strain all the optical equipment in hopes of getting a sharper image on the old retinas and thus make positive identification. I

have been known to hold conversations with store man-
nequins. I have given my best smile and a friendly wave to
trash barrels, when they are standing at some distance, and
also when they are painted the same colors as jogging suits,
which are very popular down here. The people who know
me intimately are aware of this deficiency and are quick to
identify themselves as friendly craft before entering my
space.

"*Hola!* What are you doing here all by yourself?" the
candy cane inquired.

Sandra was dressed in a crisp summer sundress, sleeve-
less, backless, and nearly frontless, with swirling red and
white alternate stripes.

"What a pleasant surprise!"

"Please! Don't get up," she said, bending down to kiss my
cheek.

"Join me in a *copa?*"

"*Gracias*, I will. I walked by the plaza earlier, but I
saw you in heavy conversation with a stranger, *un ameri-
cano*, so I didn't want to interrupt. Of course, you couldn't
see me!"

I knew Sandra liked her margaritas king-size, and I
instructed the waiter to bring us two margaritas *gigantes*.

"I wish you had stopped by. You would have enjoyed
meeting him. We had some business with Treenie."

"Your friend had a problem?"

"Nothing Treenie couldn't solve. He's a miracle worker.
But then, who knows better than you?" The waiter appeared
with two enormous deep-dish margaritas. We said *salud* and
tilted our cups. "I'll bet you still think about the unveiling."

"Please don't remind me! I've been trying to forget about

it all these years. But erasing the memory seems impossible. I may have to submit to therapy."

"You have to admit you handed Treenie a 'Mission Impossible' kind of task."

"I admit it."

"What could you expect? He only had a few hours to slip over to the Other Side and have something in place for you to unveil."

"And at least it had clothes on!" She appeared to be thirsty. Her goblet was at low tide. "Every time I cross the border I see the thing and relive the whole painful fiasco."

And then Sandra burst out laughing. "Just imagine how many Americans come in and see the bronze, then wonder why they are being welcomed into Mexico by John F. Kennedy."

Beeg Mac

***

$\mathcal{H}$ere in the valley of Tanama, a few kilometers south of Tecate, winter and summer campaigned against each other like two bitter political candidates. Spring had already lost in the early primaries. Everyone predicted a close race. On Tuesday incumbent winter held a slight lead. Dormant fields and sullen hills shivered under a crunchy frost. A vindictive wind with icy breath flailed trees until they trembled, and nagged at the cattle, causing them to become sulky. On Wednesday summer came from behind unfurling lavender bunting of ruffled lilacs, rolling out a yellow carpet of buttercups and dandelions. Swallows, golden tanagers, and wild canaries arrived in time to cast the deciding votes. The Divine Electorate declared summer the winner. And Thursday, Carlos and Amador and Francisco along with Father Ruben were seated in Café Los Alamos doing damage to huge plates of sausage and eggs and refried beans.

In outward appearance Carlos and Amador and Francisco were as similar as potatoes, lean, handsome adobe faces, bushy black mustachios. A tall sombrero added height and authenticated their vocation. Father Ruben, on the other hand, struggled against a lusty palate that refused to be appeased, and the sharp angles of his form now had beveled edges. He never wore a hat and his face was as smooth as a girl's.

Carlos was reading a letter, Amador and Francisco were sharing the sports page of the *San Diego Union*. Father Ruben was concealed behind the front page of *El Mexicano*. He wasn't interested in the news of the day so much as he was interested in a golden nugget of fried potato sitting unattended on Amador's plate, and the newspaper provided excellent cover for his spurious intention. Father Ruben directed the tines of his fork in that direction.

Amador put down his newspaper at that moment and the fork was quickly called home. "What kind of letter could absorb a man through an entire breakfast?" Amador asked the table in general. "It can only be a love letter."

Francisco and Father Ruben also put down their newspapers and looked at Carlos while he satisfied their curiosity. "It seems I'm going to have company."

"Is she pretty?"

"Nothing like that. A fellow I roomed with at school. I haven't seen him in twenty years. He married one of our classmates, a Mexican girl, Lupita Hernandez. I've never heard from him directly, but Lupita sends a letter every Christmas with all the news. He signs 'Hoss' at the bottom."

"Strange name."

"No, no, his name is Graham McGuffies. We called him Hoss because he resembled that big giant of a man on 'Bonanza.' You remember, Dan Blocker played the role."

"I remember that man," Francisco said. "He can always help us push the pickup next time we get stuck in the river."

"Interesting man," Carlos went on. "Ten years after we were out of college, he's a millionaire."

"*Dios mío!* What does he raise, ostriches?"

"He's not a rancher. He's a building contractor. Poor man, though."

"I thought you said he was a millionaire."

"He just had open heart surgery."

"And this man is coming here to Tanama where we have no *teléfono* and no doctor and we use an old UPS truck for an ambulance?"

"I'm to pick him up at the San Diego airport this afternoon. Listen to this." Carlos read from the letter. " 'I'm terrified of his going down there. He is in no condition to do anything but stay at home. But he says he's not going to hang around here waiting to die. He wants to see you again before he dies—and get this—he wants to catch a marlin! That has been his dream for twenty-five years. The man is clearly crazy but I love him anyway. I'm counting on you to keep an eye on him and send him back to me alive. . . .' "

"I can understand that," Father Ruben said. "We all have things we want to see or do before we're called away."

Francisco never talked back to fate. "If you have to go you have to go. And a heart attack is probably the best choice. Bam! It's over. You don't even know it."

"Yes, but we're talking about *when* not *how*," Amador cut in. "How would you like to die when you've worked in the fields all day, you come to the table with a hungry tiger growling inside you, your wife serves you a big steak ranchero with rice and beans and a stack of freshly made tortillas— and *zas!* the lights go out!"

"To die hungry . . . you're right," Father Ruben agreed. "That would be sad."

"That's nothing. Just imagine if you died on your way to cash your winning lottery ticket."

"But there is worse," Amador shot back at Francisco. "How would you like to die with a stiff *pito*?"

The philosophizing was quickly buried in shards of masculine laughter. Ribald conversations like this did not offend Father Ruben in the least, as they dealt with each other no differently now than when they were in grade school together. Father Ruben seized the opportunity offered as a consequence of inattention and was now savoring that long coveted fried potato from Amador's plate. "It doesn't matter how you die, it only matters how you live."

"Well," Francisco said, getting up, "I've got men in the fields. I better get back. At least if I die now, it will be on a full stomach."

It was close to three in the afternoon when Carlos pulled into Rancho Las Tunas with his houseguest. Graham McGuffies stepped out of the pickup, stretched voluptuously and inhaled profoundly, drawing every sweet fragment of summer deep into his lungs. Graham could see only wandering fields watched over by guardian hills under a cloak of blue. It could have been the day the earth was born. The holy stillness was sheared by the sudden grating of metal against metal followed by a painful wheeze, and a dust-colored burro strolled into the scene.

"This is Poncho. He's a better watchdog than El Capitán." The beast nuzzled at Carlos's shirtfront as he scratched the enormous furry ears. The dog recently mentioned recognized his name and trotted over to answer the summons. He was the color of toast with a white vest. He waved a feathery tail, quickly lost interest, then collapsed in a heap in the shade of the pickup and applied himself to the business of licking his genitals.

The house was a typical Mexican rural ranch house, one long adobe building with a red tile roof and a covered porch that ran the full length of the house. Carlos was quick to grab Graham's heavy bag out of the truck and show him to his room. "Siesta time. I'll meet you out here on the porch for a little shooter—ah, refreshment this afternoon."

"I'm not an invalid, you know."

"The siesta is for me."

The sun was just kissing the tops of the hills when the two old friends met on the porch and eased themselves into leather chairs with a glass of watered-down homemade wine from one of Father Ruben's barrels.

"You don't have to give me church punch, you know. I can handle a beer."

"What do I tell Lupita if you check out?"

"Okay, okay, we'll save the good stuff for later." Graham sat quietly devouring the serenity with hungry eyes. At last he spoke. "This is your work? You've been ranching right here in this valley since we left school?"

"Twenty years."

"I remember, you always made the right decisions."

"You haven't done badly yourself, Hoss."

"No, you don't understand. Look at you, you're strong and healthy. You don't look a whole lot different from when we were up at Davis. You have everything. Me, I have only the things money can buy."

"Well, come on, then, I'll give you something your money can't buy. You can help me with the chores."

Early next morning Carlos and Graham pulled up to

Café Los Alamos, an adobe walk-in closet dozing under the tall poplars that gave the little café its name. Blue smoke curled out from the rusty cap on the exposed stovepipe, the seductive smell of a mesquite fire burning in the old iron stove arousing their appetites. A half-dozen pickup trucks loitered out front, two of them head-to-head with the hoods open. A Ford Bronco appeared to be administering mouth-to-mouth resuscitation to a Jeep Cherokee. Two bay geldings contemplated the equine condition in the Third World at a hitching rail. There were squawks and cackles and a flurry of red and white feathers as the two men stepped around the chickens and into the diminutive café.

The security and convenience of a fire department does not exist in Tanama, thus there was no advisory on the wall specifying the total number of occupants the café could legally accommodate. Seating capacity was determined by the twelve chairs and three tables covered with an atrocious oilcloth. Two of these crude tables suffered a serious limp. One chair concealed a vicious crack in the seat and deservedly earned a reputation for nipping the occupant. When Carlos walked in with Graham, all ten occupants turned at once to witness the total eclipse of the sun as the stranger filled the space where the door had been. Graham was a huge man, well over six feet and broad as a barn. He wore his shirt, a ferocious green-on-green plaid, on the outside of his kelly green pants, which now hung loose where they had recently been filled with corporeal substance. The Jolly Green Giant had come to Mexico. His face was the color of unbaked biscuits and yielded to gravitational influence. The smile was pleasant, though too weak to light up the room. Twenty-five watts at best.

Carlos found Amador and Francisco and Father Ruben

with their noses in cups of coffee at their usual table near the only window.

"Señores, this is my old college roommate, Graham McGuffies."

The three men at the table came to their feet at once and extended their hands. It took several minutes for each man to recite his family tree, omitting none in the long list of maternal and paternal surnames associated with his ancestry.

"Glad to meet you fellas, sit down, please." Father Ruben pulled up the only available chair for the guest. "*Gracias*. Now, let's see if I got this right. You're Amador, you're Francisco, and I didn't get all of yours."

"This is Father Ruben, our local padre who manages that big vineyard down the road."

"Pleased to meet ya, Padre. I know priests are allowed to wear civilian clothes up in the States, but I figured down here would be different."

"It is just the opposite. We must, by law, be in civilian clothes. We are not allowed to wear our habits outside our store."

The men appeared to be avoiding the use of Graham McGuffie's name, as they recognized a high risk of labial cramps. Eventually someone was bold enough to ask Graham how he pronounced it, and they all experimented with an interesting variety of pronunciations. Beeg Mac was the unanimous choice. As so often happens in cases where two languages must be managed simultaneously, their conversations were richly textured. All the men could read English and understand it from long exposure to American television, but speaking the language required labial dexterity beyond their skills. Francisco couldn't negotiate the hurdles over the steel-reinforced consonants and ended up by biting the inside of his cheek. On the other hand, Beeg Mac, being married to a Mexican girl, understood them perfectly. But sliding in and out of those slippery diphthongs was more than his leathery Anglo-Saxon tongue could manage.

When all the breakfasts arrived, Chola served Beeg Mac a platter laden with fresh mangos, cantaloupe, orange segments, and bananas.

Father Ruben turned to Beeg Mac. "I hope you will be staying long enough to visit our vineyard."

"The door is always open at your rancho," Amador said, politely offering the guest proprietary rights to his rancho.

Francisco quickly followed. "Your home is Rancho Santa Gertrudes at kilometer fourteen."

Beeg Mac was familiar with these statutory courtesies from exposure to his wife's relatives. "*Gracias*. I'll be here for at least a week if Carlos can handle it. Then I want to go down to La Paz and catch me a big ol' marlin."

"This is certainly the right time," Amador answered. "You are a sports fisherman, *sí*?"

"I've never done it in my life. I've got this big ol' fireplace in my house with a big ol' mantel and I've always wanted to put a marlin up there."

Chola trotted by and refilled all the coffee cups. Francisco looked to Amador. "Is your baler working? I may need to borrow it for a few days. Mine is down."

"It's yours any time you need it. I thought you had Eulenspritz out there working on it."

"Every day for the past month he's been telling me he will be there to fix it. He comes by, tinkers with it, then never comes back. I would really like to strangle the man, but Father doesn't approve of things like that." He turned to

Beeg Mac. "You see, we have problems here you do not have in your country."

"We solve our problems with money."

Everyone got a chuckle from the honest remark. "That would not work down here."

"Sure it would. I don't care what the problem is, throw enough money at it and it'll go away."

"Again, please?"

The mumbled contraction of *it will* baffled the ears of the listeners. Carlos translated and Francisco came back. "You can solve *everything* with money?"

"Sure. Hey, you could solve the whole mess in the Middle East if you could write a check big enough."

It took the men a couple of minutes to absorb this concept. Francisco was still fascinated with the idea. "Then you must come to your rancho and get Eulenspritz to fix my baler."

"You say when, I'll show you how it's done."

"How about right now? He said he would be there this morning about this time."

"That doesn't mean he'll be there," Carlos said. "But I'd like to see this too. We'll follow you over."

All the men came to their feet. Beeg Mac reached into his pocket. "The breakfast is on me this morning, *muchachos*."

Carlos quickly put a hand over his in an effort to prevent his friend from committing an innocent but disastrous social error. But the generous offer was spoken too fast, the words run together, for immediate comprehension, and in the meantime Beeg Mac got the point. Each paid for his own breakfast as was their custom, and they filed out the door.

Francisco led them to a low shed where he kept his farm

equipment. They could hear the metallic clink of a wrench and the clickety-click of a ratchet. "We are in luck, Beeg Mac, Eulenspritz is here. I can hear him working on something." When they walked in they saw a jolly little man with merry eyes of delft blue inspecting the ailing baler.

"Ah, I see you showed up. Well, when will you have it running?" Francisco called out.

Eulenspritz turned to face the voice that greeted him and adjusted the bright red knitted ski cap he wore winter or summer. He was a short little man and put one in mind of those miniature Hümmel figurines with dimpled knees and dressed in lederhosen who are always so jolly. He answered in Spanish under a thick slice of brat-wurst. "*Yah, sí,* I found the problem. It is in the knotter. I go into town right now and buy the part. I be back this afternoon, put it in, you be in business, hah?"

"We know it's the knotter. You have been telling me this for two weeks!"

"I have been so very busy. But I promise you. I go right now, buy the part, and come straight back."

"What time?" Francisco knew all this man's clever evasions of specifics.

"Two, three o'clock. Maybe four. You be here?" Eulenspritz did not own a chronometer, and it was rumored around Tanama that the only calendar he consulted was the Aztec calendar. "Once I have the part it will only take me an hour to install it."

This was the moment Beeg Mac was waiting for to prove his theory. He reached in his pocket and pulled out a bale of American bank notes the size of a small head of cabbage. "Tell you what, fella." He removed the outside leaf. "You see this here C-note? If this here thing is running at five o'clock this afternoon, it's yours."

A merry twinkle came into Eulenspritz's blue eyes. He could have been looking at a Viennese Sacher torte. Francisco and Carlos were expecting him to dance a little schottische with a yip and a yodel and a slap upon his thigh.

"Your problem is solved," Beeg Mac boomed at Francisco, who looked like any man would when he sees the new day is off to a good start.

"We have to be on our way," Carlos said. "I promised the nuns I would seed their fields for them. I'll go over this morning and see just what it is they're going to need."

"You have a convent here?" Beeg Mac asked as they got in the pickup.

"Our neighbors, the Order of Santa Brigida. They're only two doors down from me. Poor things, they work harder than some men. Francisco and Amador and I take turns with the tractor work."

"And while we're talking about your neighbors, where does Eulenspritz fit in?"

Carlos laughed. You couldn't mention Eulenspritz without laughing. "The man came over from Bavaria years ago, maybe twenty or twenty-five. He lives about four or five kilometers back into those hills over there. He has re-created the Black Forest and his house looks like the gingerbread house in Hansel and Gretel."

Carlos made a right turn onto a road nearly hidden by a thicket of eucalyptus trees, stopped, got out, and opened a heavy iron gate.

"I'll close," Beeg Mac said as they drove through. He looked in all directions as he closed the gate and saw nothing but woods. Presently they came to the moat. "I don't believe this!" Carlos got out, removed the heavy crossbar at the bridge, and the truck rumbled across. "I'll close," Beeg Mac offered again, and this time as he slid the heavy timber back in place, he saw a low adobe building cloistered under ancient oaks.

Beeg Mac followed Carlos on foot to a decorative wrought-iron gate separating them from a small enclosed garden. Carlos pulled on the rope and somewhere far, far away they heard a timid silvery tinkle.

Neither spoke. After several long minutes a door opened and through the iron lacework they could see a tiny figure wrapped in bolts of gray muslin come floating silently toward them. A tight black veil closely framed the top and sides of the head, and the white bib completed the enclosure right up to the chin. A radiant smile appeared as Sister Anamaria recognized her neighbor.

"Don Carlos, *buenos dias!*" She could have been singing.

"*Buenos dias, Madre.*" Carlos took the proffered hand gently into his own. "I would like to present you to a very dear and old friend."

"*Buenos dias,*" she sang again, and put her hand out to Beeg Mac, who couldn't take his eyes off the white crown and cross on the headpiece, with large scarlet stigmata at each intersection representing the five nail wounds sustained by the Savior. "Let me unlock for you and tell La Superior that you are here." Sister Anamaria stepped out through the iron gate and with her big key unlocked the door of the adjacent building.

The two men stepped into a nearly empty reception room. It held a few chairs for visitors and a long counter at the far end. In a few minutes a rear door opened and Madre

Superior Macrina stood smiling behind the divider. A sweet brown face, soft and serene, peered out from within the black and white cocoon, Sister Anamaria behind her. They looked like a pair of mission doves in mourning garments.

Beeg Mac began to feel uncomfortable. Nuns did not evoke pleasant memories. The only nun he ever liked was Sister Sally Field, and she had the habit of flying. But then he heard the Reverend Mother begin to sing. "Carlos, our wonderful neighbor! *Buenos dias*."

Carlos replied and introduced his friend. Madre Macrina welcomed him like a friend of long standing. "I thought this would be a good time to see what kind of tractor work is needed."

"God bless you, Carlos, you are so thoughtful. Let me finish with our study group for my novices and I will be right out."

"Can we tour the grounds, Madre?"

"But of course!" The two nuns retreated and the two men stepped outside.

"There are about ten nuns here, I believe, two are novices. Come on, I'll show you the grounds." Carlos led his guest up a small rise. "They have close to fifteen hectares here. I usually come in and prepare the ground, and do the seeding. Then either Amador or Francisco come in later with the rake and baler."

They walked back down toward a plank barn with a Dutch door. "As long as we're here I should introduce you to two more sisters, Elva and Mariquita." Hearing voices, Elva and Mariquita, appareled in black robe and white wimple, poked their heads out. They studied the stranger with big inquisitive eyes, then the two holsteins resumed munching their hay. "Well," Carlos chuckled. "They really are sisters. A gift from Francisco. They provide milk for their meals and for the making of *rompópe*, their ninety-proof eggnog. No, you can't have any."

"They actually milk these two locomotives?"

"Twice a day." They also keep Naná, a big milk goat. I believe one of the sisters can only tolerate goat's milk. I'm surprised that crazy goat isn't back there eating with them."

"This is a pretty big spread. Who works this place?"

"Come on, I'll show you."

They followed a winding dirt track behind the barn and entered a large garden. At one end was a flowering fruit orchard covered with pink and white foam. In the vegetable garden the rows were black and long and straight. The sweet smell of rich fertile soil rose from the newly turned earth. Two nuns were stooped over the furrows, planting beans, tomato, and squash. Radishes and cilantro were already breaking through the dark loam. Another two sisters were bent over long-handled hoes, reshaping the dirt bowl around the base of the fruit trees. Glossy black crows screamed above the fields in search of opportunity.

All the sisters were busy chirping among themselves until they recognized their neighbor. "*Buenos dias*, Don Carlos," they called. Morning greetings were interrupted when sister saw that Naná was eating the paper seed packets. Quickly, three sisters carefully gathered their skirts and skipped over rows toward where the brindle goat was munching. They looked like children playing in the dirt, leaping between furrows in pursuit of Naná. "Shoo shoo, *andele*," they laughed. Naná rolled her yellow eyes and trotted away with no real sense of urgency.

"Ah, there you are! Come, we have coffee and pastries for you gentlemen in the kitchen." It was Madre Superior.

She led them back along the chicken pens where red and white chickens scratched and clucked. A nun walked along the boxes filling a basket with fresh eggs.

"How is the harvest this morning, sister?"

"Beautiful, Mother, a dozen white and six brown."

None of this was new to Carlos. He was here to help with something on a regular basis. Likewise, his presence on the grounds was familiar to all the sisters. But Beeg Mac was gobbling up the scene with eyes the size of canning rings.

La Superior led them to the back of a building. An enormous mountain of firewood, assorted logs and branches, reached nearly to the eaves. At the foot of the heap a nun no bigger than a sparrow was swinging a small ax in an effort to reduce it to firewood small enough to fit into the woodstove. She placed a log flat on the ground, held it steady with her foot, and attacked it with the ax. She gathered the small pieces and loaded them into a wheelbarrow. Beeg Mac calculated she would have it finished by the turn of the century. He could not stand to watch another minute. He ran over, took the wheelbarrow in his hands and delivered it to the back door.

"*Gracias*," the aged woodcutter said with a saintly smile.

Mother Macrina turned her face, glowing with inner peace, to Beeg Mac. He could feel the heat of her smile. "We are not afraid of hard work, but you are very kind." She led them through a side door into a large kitchen. The six-burner iron dragon with an insatiable appetite for wood stood against the far wall and appeared to be groaning for more. "Sit down, please."

She served them big cups of fresh coffee and flaky *empanadas* filled with fresh apples and dusted with glistening sugar and cinnamon.

Like a child secure in the feeling that his guardian would hardly correct him in this holy environment, Beeg Mac devoured a plate of *empanadas* while Carlos ate one. Beeg Mac made no effort to conceal his pleasure and his smugness as La Superior refilled his plate with a look of admiration. She and Carlos began a conversation about the tractor work that was to be done in the fields. In the meantime Beeg Mac let his eyes roam around the room. He found a hole in the wall near the ceiling with a tangle of colored wires hanging into the room. He saw the same thing above the door.

"Ask her what that mess of wires is all about."

Carlos put the question to Madre Macrina then explained to his friend. "It is rumored that the power company will be coming in this direction with electricity rather soon. So they want to be ready for the day. Problem is, the electrician left before finishing his work and never returned."

"That's kind of standard down here, isn't it?"

"I'm afraid so."

"Tell sister I'll finish the wiring."

"But you wanted me to take you to La Paz to bring in your marlin."

"My marlin can enjoy swimming around for a little while longer. I can finish this in a few days if you can put up with me a little longer."

Carlos explained it to Madre Macrina, who could not contain her happiness and gratitude. She threw out her arms as though to embrace the spoken deed. An aurora of gold lights radiated around her veil. "God bless you, God bless you and repay your kindness." The song of her voice could have been written on the five lines of the staff. She fluttered to him and filled his plate again. Beeg Mac got that old feeling he was being pampered in his grandma's kitchen.

Beeg Mac ignored the worried look on Carlos's face and ate contentedly. "Ask her how the convent supports itself."

Carlos did so and translated. "They are not affiliated with a school or hospital. Their sole means of support is the sale of their eggnog and baked goods—if you haven't eaten them into bankruptcy."

"You've got to be kidding."

The Reverend Mother addressed Carlos. "Ask your friend if he would like to see our dream."

Beeg Mac popped an *empanada* in his mouth and the two of them followed La Superior out the door.

On the other side of the complex La Superior led them to a pile of bricks on a gentle knoll. On closer examination Beeg Mac could see it was a chapel under very tentative construction. It was little more than a shell. The back wall where the altar would one day be was about four feet high. There were no side walls and no front wall. The roof was blue sky crossed with rough beams.

"We are in the process of building this chapel, as you can see. We, of course, have a small sanctuary inside. But it has long been our dream to see a chapel standing on this knoll." She brought her hands to her bosom in rapture.

"How long ago did you begin to build?"

"It will be nine years this summer. Every time we sell a kilo of our baked goods, we buy another ten bricks. You can see it will one day be very beautiful." She clapped her hands together like a schoolgirl. "In the meantime Heaven is our ceiling."

Beeg Mac looked into the incomplete shell. He contemplated the sky through the rafters and the floor still covered in brown winter rye and dandelions. He saw Naná, the brindle goat, eating the paper from a bag of lime. Even the novices won't live long enough to see it finished, he thought.

Beeg Mac conveyed that he would start the electrical work in the morning and stay on it until it was finished. Madre Macrina blessed them both and nearly skipped back to her cloister. The two men headed out along Highway 3 back to Rancho Las Tunas.

Early the next morning all three tables at Los Alamos were surrounded with hungry men putting away eggs and beans and thick slices of ham. The table by the window was one man short. Francisco was not present.

"Francisco has not yet made his appearance," Father Ruben commented. "Most unusual for him."

Amador placed the wire napkin holder between his plate and the padre's as a deterrent. "He might be out baling. He was anxious to get started, you know."

"You may be right," Carlos agreed. "We saw Eulenspritz over there yesterday and he promised to have it fixed."

"A promise from Eulenspritz is like a guitar with no strings," Amador chuckled in reply.

"It only means I proved my point," Beeg Mac said.

"What?"

"The power of money, remember? I dangled a hundred-dollar bill in his face yesterday and told him it was his if he fixed the machine by five o'clock yesterday."

"That's got to be it," Father Ruben agreed.

The men finished their breakfast and Francisco failed to make his appearance.

"We better go check on Francisco, then get over to the convent." Carlos and Beeg Mac got up together, paid for their meals, downed a quick auxiliary swallow of coffee, and left.

It was quiet when they pulled into Francisco's ranch to see if Beeg Mac's tractor repair theory had worked. "It's unusually quiet," Carlos observed. "I don't hear the tractor either."

"Maybe he's in the house."

"Not at this hour. Let's go back and check the machine shed."

They could hear the clanging of tools as they approached and that familiar salsa and liverwurst voice. "Almost finished. I going to need about two feet of hydraulic line. I can get it in town. You be running in an hour."

"Then use one off your car, but you're not moving from under there until this thing is running!"

Carlos and Beeg Mac saw a pair of feet under the baler and Francisco seated on a stump with a loaded shotgun across his lap. "The American system fails as soon as it's imported. Now we try the Mexican system."

"You mean the promise of a C-note didn't bring him back yesterday?" Beeg Mac asked incredulously. His system never failed him before.

"Of course not. I went over this morning, got him out of bed, brought him down here, and put him to work. I have every confidence I'll be baling in a little while. Right Eulenspritz?"

"*Yah sí*, Francisco, *absolutamente*! I be through here and you be baling as soon as I connect this hose."

Carlos was still laughing as he headed his big Massey Ferguson down Highway 3 in the direction of the Convent of Santa Brigida. Beeg Mac followed behind in Carlos's pickup with flashers on. They were warmly received by La Superior, declined an offer of breakfast, and each man went in the direction of his task.

Beeg Mac was led into a small sanctuary. The votive candles did not provide adequate lighting beyond that needed for contemplation, but there was a flashlight in Carlos's toolbox. Mother Macrina walked to a Hammond electric organ at one side. She spoke to Beeg Mac in Spanish as though there was no doubt that everyone in the world, at least in her world, was fluent in this important language. "This beautiful organ was given to us by a wonderful lady friend and neighbor, God rest her. But we have never had the pleasure of its music. The electrician left a skein of wires behind it. You may want to have a look."

Beeg Mac nodded, somewhat amazed at himself that he understood, if not every word she used, certainly the general idea of what she said. He began to pull the organ away from the wall.

"We will leave you now to your work you offer us with such kindness."

Beeg Mac inspected the existing wiring, clicked his tongue in disapproval, and began to install a double wall plug where it had been begun. He heard the muted tinkle of a tiny bell from somewhere within the labyrinth, then nothing. The silence and the semidarkness were all-consuming and yet not oppressive. Aromatic incense gave him a feeling he was in another world. Right now, Los Angeles, his home, his business, his problems, did not exist. That was another world, another time zone almost beyond recall. Was he really here, or did he die on the operating table and was now having an out-of-body experience?

Beeg Mac finished the installation, picked up his toolbox. On his return to the reception room he could hear a chorus of angels in the company of a lute. Maybe I *have* gone to the Other World, he thought. When he reached the reception room, he saw two novitiates through the window. They wore pure white veils and they sat side by side on a rustic bench, like nature's handmaids, weaving sacred songs for the angels. One cradled a lute across her lap.

The sight of colored wires wrapped in friction tape poking out of the baseboard and the ceiling convinced Beeg Mac he was still in the real world and reminded him why he was here.

By the middle of the afternoon, both men, conscious that they were interrupting the sisters' routine, left the convent. They stopped in Tecate for Beeg Mac to pick up some electrical hardware and plead a beer. The following morning the entire cast was present and accounted for at Los Alamos. The smell of sausage and eggs, the hiss of beans in a skillet, the clatter of dishes, provided the continuo for the men's voices. The sound was turned off the small television set on a high perch. The faces on "Good Morning America" mouthed like a silent movie.

"I'm going to assume your baler is working," Carlos said.

"Better than ever. I've got to admit that man Eulenspritz sure knows how to fix things right."

"Getting him to do it is the problem," Amador said. "But I guess it proves what Beeg Mac said—you can solve any problem with money."

Beeg Mac burst out laughing. "Not quite. It turns out Francisco had to sit next to him with a shotgun." Now they all laughed. "I still don't know why it didn't work. I could never get away with your shotgun trick in the States."

"How are you coming along at the convent?" Father Ruben asked. It was a simple ruse. His target was a tortilla that Amador seemed to be neglecting.

"Just fine. The wiring is kind of funny, but I'll have it

licked in a few days. Then I'll just wire the main panel and they're in business."

Carlos translated the idiomatic expressions.

"I'm just amazed how ten women can work such a big farm, chopping, hoeing, planting. Hey, men in labor camps don't work as hard as those sisters."

Father Ruben enjoyed a moment of triumph. He succeeded in acquiring the tortilla. He covered his move with a bit of narration. "They are not afraid of hard work. If these good men didn't offer to go help with their machinery, the sisters would do it all with mule and muscle."

Beeg Mac sighed. "I wish I could do something for them."

"You are."

"No, I mean something of real value. I just admire them, I guess, they work like field hands and yet they smile, and sing, and talk, and laugh the whole time. They're always cheerful, I've never seen anything like it in my life. They act like they've got the world on a string."

"They are convinced they do," Father Ruben explained after a quick translation of the metaphor.

"What is their mission, Father?"

"They are dedicated to prayer. Their daily dream is to buy another brick for that little chapel you saw there."

"That's another thing. They'll never see it finished at the rate they're going. It'll take an eternity."

"They have an eternity to do it. In the meantime they enjoy the dream. It is the whole purpose of their existence."

"I guess. What's that little bell I hear all during the day?"

"They pray to the Eucharist in teams. They take thirty-minute turns. The bell announces the change of each shift."

"I suppose we better get over there or we'll find the Superior behind the wheel of a Massey Ferguson and the rest of the sisters installing wire," Carlos said.

Beeg Mac could hear the distant rumble of Carlos's tractor as he pulled wires and installed receptacles and light switches. He was at the top of a ladder this morning working in the big kitchen. Down below he watched a group of sisters bustling about. A little nun not much taller than the counter was rolling out pastry dough. Two others were working over a steaming kettle on the massive iron stove. One of the novitiates seemed to be preparing fruit preserves in a large earthenware bowl. They laughed and chattered like schoolgirls. He heard the tinkle of the bell somewhere in the cloister where he had never been. In a moment four nuns walked briskly into the kitchen and took over the chores at the stove and pastry board. The four sisters who had been preparing pastries gathered up their skirts and rustled out the door. He was witnessing the changing of the guard.

The aroma of fruit and spices and *empanadas* baking in the oven was nothing less than delicious agony.

When Beeg Mac at last came down the ladder, one of the sisters put a plate of warm *empanadas* on the table and a thimble of their ninety-proof *rompópe*. The crinkled smile and the wave of the hand left no doubt that it was intended for him. He conveyed his thanks and indulged hungrily. He was tempted to hold out his thimble in an appeal for seconds but thought better of it. He went out the door with the ladder under his arm before the sisters could grab it and struggle under its weight in their effort to help him.

Beeg Mac didn't approve of the wiring in the main panel. In addition, the breakers were all wrong. He would go into Tecate later and get what he needed. He was almost sorry the job was nearly finished.

When he got down the ladder he found Naná, the brindle goat, eagerly attempting to eat a roll of black electrician's tape. "Give me that! You eat that stuff and it'll never come out the other end." He pulled it away from her and put it in his pocket. This did not hurt Naná's feelings in the least. She rolled her yellow eyes at him and loped off in search of new mischief.

Beeg Mac discovered a wire suspended overhead from a metal pole. He followed it and once again stood facing the little chapel on the knoll. The wire stopped there. It was obviously intended for the chapel. It made his fragile heart ache just to see an impotent wire coming from a dead box and connecting to nothing, waiting forever to light the chapel that would never be, and bring life to the organ that would never be heard. The pile of bricks intended for the completion of the chapel seemed to have a few more. They must have sold a kilo of *empanadas* yesterday. They'll never get it done, he thought, they'll never live long enough to see it finished.

"A beautiful dream, no?"

Beeg Mac wheeled around to see Mother Macrina standing behind him, serene and full of inner light. "Yes, a beautiful dream," he agreed in principle.

"Every day we come here and give our thanks to El Señor for His blessing and the work we do for love of Him. The products of our little kitchen keep us moving toward our beauteous and worthy goal. Every day is another brick. By the end of summer we hope to have enough to lay another course on the wall. It only takes a willing imagination to see the pews full, the altar ablaze with candles, to hear Father's Mass and receive His blessing."

Beeg Mac's imagination just wasn't that agile. He was the only one who felt empty. Mother Macrina's voice was sweet as a flute, warm, confident, and colored with faith. "Come into the kitchen and take a little something."

Pastries! Beeg Mac followed like a puppy. There might even be another thimble of *rompópe*.

Mother Superior answered his prayer.

Early the next morning Los Alamos was filled with hungry men. They talked about barley, and cows, and baseball, the price of hogs, and every man's failure to comprehend the mysteries of feminine logic. Then the subject veered in another direction.

"How is the work progressing at the convent?" Amador asked.

"I've just about got 'er licked. Another day, maybe."

Carlos saw the perplexity on Amador's face. The men had no trouble understanding Dan Rather and Daniel Shore, but casual contractions of mumbled words and colloquialisms were hard to catch. "He should be through with all the electrical work in another day or so, and I expect to be through seeding this afternoon," Carlos said.

"What did you put down?"

"Alfalfa mostly, some oats. The other half under corn."

"I would really like to do something for those ladies," Beeg Mac remarked. "They work as hard as we do and yet you'll never see a frown or hear a sigh. There is always joy in their faces."

"Believe me, they are grateful for everything you have done already," Father Ruben replied.

"Hell, that was nothin'. I thought somethin' more'n that."

"I'm sure they would appreciate some small gift," Amador said after the translation.

"I was thinkin' more along the lines of gettin' their chapel finished. Fifty, sixty grand is all it should take. It'd be done in a week to ten days."

Carlos quickly recognized the need for another translation.

"But you would be stealing their dream," Francisco said.

Amador was more dramatic. "Sixty thousand dollars!"

"Hell, my wife throws more'n that away on wedding presents for people we don't even know. This here is something worthwhile."

"Put the idea away, Hoss," Carlos said. "And we better be on our way. We ought to finish up today, and we can bring the tractor back. We can be trolling for marlin in a couple of days."

Carlos and Beeg Mac went out the door. Francisco moved over into the chair recently vacated by Beeg Mac and flew three feet toward the ceiling with a yip. "The thing bit me! Chola, you are going to have to use this chair for firewood." Then he turned to Amador and Father Ruben. "You don't suppose Beeg Mac would actually do what he is thinking, do you?"

"I was wondering the same thing," Amador replied. "He is very impulsive, no? Did you hear how he talks about sixty thousand dollars? Like it was his candy money! He will shatter all their illusions."

"Maybe he's just a millionaire who wants to show off," Francisco said.

Father Ruben answered. "The man is not a showoff. He

takes his money for granted in the same way we regard our livestock. The man has a generous heart, but yes, he would be very hard to control. We are going to have to think of some way to dissuade him from a noble but misplaced deed, and yet spare the good man's feelings."

"But how do we stop him?"

"Steal his checkbook."

"I'm serious."

"Me too," Father Ruben said. "I wish I knew, I wish I knew. You left half your beans!"

"Help yourself, Father."

"Just a little taco. It should help me get my brain into a lower gear."

Amador and Francisco emptied two more cups of coffee while Father Ruben put away his taco. "Well, did the beans feed the brain and did the brain respond with an idea?"

"As a matter of fact, yes. Stop by the vineyard and tell Luis he's in charge until I get back."

"Of course," Amador answered. "Where are you going?"

"I must make a quick trip to Ensenada. I'll probably be gone most of the day." He downed the rest of his coffee on his feet and almost ran out the door.

"Unusual behavior for the padre," Francisco whispered.

"Most unusual," Amador agreed.

Next morning all four friends gathered at Los Alamos. Francisco hung back and let everyone get seated. Carlos made a vertical leap, clearing the chair by several inches.

"At least now we know where the beast is and it's safe to sit down," Francisco observed.

Breakfast arrived and the men fell quiet as they abandoned themselves to their appetites.

Father Ruben was the first to break the silence. He spoke to Beeg Mac. "I'll tell you a problem I've never been able to solve, maybe you can show me how to solve it with money."

"What's that?" Beeg Mac asked.

"Getting these three men to attend Mass."

Amador quickly introduced a new theme. "Soon you will go to La Paz and catch your marlin, no?"

"Whenever Carlos thinks he can get away," Beeg Mac answered, then turned his attention to Father Ruben. "I respect your position, Father, but that little bit of sausage you're eyeballing is spoken for." He stabbed the spicy morsel and popped it in his mouth.

Father Ruben was obliged to suffer their laughter.

"As a matter of fact," Carlos said, "we can leave the day after tomorrow."

"I've thought about this for years. In a couple of days I'll be on a boat with a two-hundred-pound marlin on my line. I can hardly wait!" Beeg Mac slapped his stomach. "Damn, that was a good breakfast!" He was feeling good and he was letting it show.

The assessment of the breakfast was unanimous. The five men paid and strolled out the door, scattering chickens as they went to their respective vehicles.

Father Ruben put a hand on Beeg Mac's shoulder. "Oh, Beeg Mac, step over to my truck a minute. We have a little present for you."

Everyone saw the perplexity on Beeg Mac's pale face and the embarrassed little smile he was helpless to control. Then they looked into the padre's angelic countenance, which shed no light on his intentions. All the men walked over to Father Ruben's Ford.

An oily, plastic tarp covered the entire bed of the pickup. Father Ruben took up a corner. "Just a little something for you to remember us, and to show you how we appreciate everything you've done here." He pulled back the tarp to reveal a huge marlin, stuffed, lacquered, and mounted. A small brass plaque read 1979, doubtless commemorating the year the big fish failed to see the hook hidden in his lunch, and this would help explain the startled look on the marlin's face.

Father Ruben announced, "To our good amigo Beeg Mac, from all of us."

Silence.

Every man was stunned. Even the chickens suspended their clucking. Big Graham McGuffies felt his recently overhauled heart drop into his shoes. Bitter disappointment misted his eyes. He could feel a bone in his throat. Father Ruben began to regret his cleverness.

Then Beeg Mac threw his head back and a giant rumble of laughter came thundering out, quickly infecting the others. They laughed until they were close to collapse. Every time their guffaws subsided, someone caught sight of the marlin's startled glass eye and the spasms would begin all over again.

Beeg Mac began to cough. He wiped the streaks from his face with a handkerchief and slowly regained his breath. "You all knew what catching that marlin myself meant to me. You knew just thinkin' about it made me feel good all day. Gave me somethin' to look forward to." He came down to a chuckle. "You pulled my dream right out from under my feet. I don't know why I couldn't see it for myself."

The chickens resumed their happy clucking.

"Your intentions were laudable," Father Ruben said. "We are all your friends. No harm done."

"I'm afraid the harm is already done," Beeg Mac groaned.

"What do you mean?" This was said by all four men. They sounded like a barbershop quartet.

"I left a check for sixty thousand dollars in the music bench of the organ," Beeg Mac confessed.

Three big macho rancheros and a servant of God nearly swooned like señoritas on a divan. A profound silence returned to the side of the road as each man visualized a negotiable instrument worth sixty thousand dollars sitting in the music bench in the sanctuary in the middle of a cloistered convent where no one had access.

Father Ruben was the first to speak. "This is going to be a tough mango to peel."

"We're going to have to move fast," Carlos added.

"I have it," Father Ruben exclaimed. "I will go right now with Francisco. I will see the Mother Superior and discuss the details of tomorrow's Mass."

"What good am I doing there?" If there was a way out, it was plain Francisco was desperate to find it.

"You will explain to the Superior that Beeg Mac has asked you to collect some tools he left in the vicinity of the organ. You go straight to the music bench and retrieve the check for sixty thousand dollars before anyone finds it."

Francisco looked uncomfortable. "Is it a sin to lie to the Mother Superior?"

"Don't worry yourself. I'll make it right with El Señor."

"Then we better get moving before someone decides to bring out the hymn books. We'll take my truck and leave the marlin here."

Carlos, Beeg Mac, and Amador watched the two men

pull out in a jet stream of dirt and gravel. "What if Father Ruben and Francisco are too late?" Beeg Mac inquired.

"We need an alternate plan," Carlos suggested.

"I agree," Amador replied.

"Are you thinking what I'm thinking?" Carlos asked.

"It worked before," Amador pointed out.

"Then let us away!"

The three men crowded into the front seat of Carlos's pickup and rumbled off in the direction of Canyon de la Cueva. Beeg Mac knew this mission somehow concerned him, but he didn't know how. And he was starting to show signs of anxiety.

Carlos turned left into the canyon and set the Ford into four-wheel drive. They lurched and bounced over jagged chunks of granite and treacherous gullies that promised to snap an axle. Carlos decided to proceed on foot in exchange for whiplash and body bruises. In a few minutes the trio arrived at Doña Lala's pretentious gate. Carlos stared at the fence made of rusted bedsprings and looked over to Amador, who seemed to confirm his thoughts. It wasn't that long ago that both men stood here on an urgent mission now nearly faded in memory. Carlos gave Amador a subtle toss of the chin. A big black rooster, cold and quite dead, hung upside down just inside the gate. Carlos reached for the carriage bolt tied to a rope and struck the blue enamel dishpan. *Ding ding ding!*

Beeg Mac felt it was time he made inquiry. "Where are we?" he whispered. "What are we doin' here?"

Carlos thought it was time to explain. "Doña Lala is a . . . a . . ."

"A witch." Amador supplied the missing word.

"See ya later, fellas."

"No, no, wait a minute. She's harmless. But she can perform great miracles."

"*Buenos dias.*" It was too late to explain further. Doña Lala suddenly took form before them.

She looked no different to Carlos and Amador than she did six years ago when they consulted her regarding the mystery of "The Miracle," an event familiar to readers of these chronicles. Doña Lala stood in a long and shapeless black sack. Probably the same one. The face, dark with deep creases like a walnut shell. Hair white as gypsum covered her back and shoulders like a shawl.

"Don Carlos, Don Amador, it has been a long time, no?" Her dewlap flapped when she spoke.

"A long time," Carlos agreed. "Let me present to you a very old and dear friend of mine."

"Doña Lala extended a gnarled black hand. "*Bienvenido,* señor."

Beeg Mac took a step back. "I feel like I'm at Universal Studios."

"Watch it," Carlos muttered, "she can read minds."

Beeg Mac believed she could too. He could feel the faded yellow eyes drilling holes straight into the very core of his being. He was obliged to receive the old spook's claw. It felt rough, and brittle, and weightless.

Doña Lala dipped a bony hand into a bowl of water on a table nearby, sprinkled all three of her visitors, and pulled back the rope that separated them. "Come into your house." She ushered them into her surgery, a small yard shaded by an aged *pirúl.* An old bureau held a skull with a frozen grin. An assortment of glass jars filled with colored solutions suspended things that are best left undescribed. Amador gave Carlos a little nudge. In the corner stood the same old maroon restaurant booth that looked like it had been pulled out of a Denny's. A young girl sat stroking a black cat.

Carlos began the consultation. "We have a very unusual problem, Doña Lala."

"A most difficult situation," Amador added to the *sopa*.

"It may even be beyond your powers."

Doña Lala let out a long blood-chilling cackle that almost sent Beeg Mac loping back toward the gate. Carlos restrained him. "Nothing is beyond my powers—nobody fools Doña Lala!" She gave them an unsolicited encore of the hyena cackle.

"You know, guys, I think I ought to be heading back to L.A. right away. We can catch a marlin some other time." Once again Beeg Mac was about to head in the direction of the gate.

Carlos detained him with a hand on his arm. "Trust me."

"Why?"

"Because I am your best friend."

"Then why are we here?"

"Look, Doña Lala is a little creepy maybe, but she's infallible."

"She has worked wonders for us before," Amador reassured.

"Tell your friend to sit down in this chair and relax." Doña Lala instructed. "No harm can come to him."

Carlos relayed the information. Beeg Mac took the chair without noticeable enthusiasm. Carlos began to translate for Doña Lala.

"You come from very far away."

Beeg Mac was not impressed. "A six-foot gringo in the middle of la-la land—what else is new?"

"You have a very long life ahead of you."

"There's a joke for ya, it's all bullshit, guys."

"Yes, a very long life. Someone has repaired a damaged heart. . . ."

"Whoa! Tell her I'll do whatever she says."

"Now explain to your friend that before anything we must cleanse his soul." Doña Lala went to the dresser and returned with her wand, a nosegay of fragrant leaves. She laid it on Beeg Mac's head, his heart, then both shoulders. She chanted some unintelligible words in the language of the spirit world. Then she spoke to Carlos.

Carlos translated. "She says for you to take three deep breaths and relax." Beeg Mac shrugged to indicate he was indeed relaxed.

Doña Lala made a journey to the black rooster who hung out by the front gate. She plucked a long tail feather and returned to her patient. She placed it first on his head, over his heart, then over his diaphragm. Carlos repeated her words in English.

"You seem to have misplaced something—something of great value."

All three men were visibly startled by the remark.

"Didn't we tell you she was fantastic?" Amador whispered.

"Hey, ask her if she'd like to come and work for me. I could make a fortune with her."

"Quiet!" Carlos warned.

"But I don't understand," Doña Lala continued, "there seems to be some confusion—you want to lose it again?"

"This is unreal," Beeg Mac gasped. "Yes, yes!"

"Very well."

Carlos thought, This is where she sends the girl for eggs. But he was wrong.

"Bring me the goat," she croaked.

The young girl abandoned the cat and disappeared behind the wall of wild honeysuckle that covered a little shack at the rear of the yard. Carlos and Amador exchanged a secret smile. Beeg Mac was over his fear and seemed to be enjoying the performance.

In a few minutes the girl was back with a sable goat on a short length of plastic clothesline. Doña Lala tethered the animal to the tree and continued her ritual. She poured what appeared to be some colored water into a small glass and lit a candle. She held the candle over Beeg Mac's head and Carlos translated. "Drink this tea."

Beeg Mac's suspicion returned. He sniffed into the glass, and finding it rather pleasant, drank the alleged tea. Doña Lala took the glass and blew out the candle. She poured liquid from another pitcher and lit a new candle. She held this candle over his heart.

"Drink," came the translation.

Beeg Mac cooperated. He drank it down, and again Doña Lala blew out the candle.

"Now we wait."

No one knew what they were waiting for and no one said a word. A few chickens could be heard scuffling and clucking at the rear of the yard. Flies were humming in the vicinity of the dead black rooster. Doña Lala stared at the ground with her wrinkled black hands in the lap of her black dress. The old witch appeared to have dozed off. Carlos and Amador exchanged a look of consternation. Beeg Mac looked like he wanted the game to end so he could go home. What were they waiting for?

The goat that had been browsing the whole time raised

her head, stretched out her hind legs, and released an amber stream. In an instant Doña Lala leaped to her feet, held a glass under the flow, and came up with nearly a full glass. She faced Beeg Mac with a lighted candle in one hand, the glass with the amber liquid in the other.

"That's it, I'm outta here." Beeg Mac started to get to his feet. "Adios, guys, it's been fun, but I'm not gonna drink goat piss. No way!"

Carlos and Amador ran to Beeg Mac's side to reassure him, although they weren't sure of what. Doña Lala handed Beeg Mac a lighted candle, and Carlos translated the instructions just in time to keep Beeg Mac from taking flight through the canyon.

"Extinguish the candle in the glass."

Beeg Mac shoved the candle upside down into the specimen so generously provided by the goat. It expired with a loud hiss and a puff of white smoke. Doña Lala placed the glass on the table and returned with a pair of scissors in her hand. She clipped a few hairs from the animal's withers.

"Take the animal away."

The young girl led the goat back into the darkness of the yard while Doña Lala went to Beeg Mac and snipped a corner of material from his shirttail. Everyone watched with some degree of horror as she dipped the goat hair in the urine then wrapped it within the swatch of cloth. She bound it tight with a red ribbon then attached it to a leather thong. Now she faced Beeg Mac and placed the necklace over his head.

"Do not remove the amulet until Tanama Peak is in full sun."

"But what about the—" Carlos began.

"Your problem has been solved."

"But—but the—"

"Your problem has been solved!" the old witch repeated a little louder, in case Don Carlos had gone deaf.

Carlos made payment, the equivalent of ten American dollars, which he considered could be either a bargain or a waste of money. They wouldn't know until tomorrow. The three men said adios and headed down the hill. They were followed by the wild laughter of a hyena.

When Carlos, Amador, and Beeg Mac returned and found no trace of Father Ruben and Francisco, they decided to check at the convent on Sunday morning. They found Father Ruben waiting by the moat already dressed in sacerdotal attire. Francisco was at his side. They all exchanged a hushed *buenos dias*.

Carlos whispered. "Did you find it?"

"When I looked in the music bench, it wasn't there!" Francisco confessed in another whisper.

"That means somebody found it and they know," Carlos said. "Has anybody said anything?"

"Not a word. But there is a melancholy in the air and their smiles are the color of February."

"We looked for you late yesterday and couldn't find you," Father Ruben said.

"We went to consult Doña Lala."

"Don't tell me about it."

"What do we do now?"

"Right now we do nothing. In a few minutes I will say Mass in the little half chapel on the hill. When it's over, we can see which way would be best to proceed."

They walked in silence to the unfinished chapel on the knoll. All the sisters were already seated on the two front benches. They recognized the Mother Superior at the end of the second row. The men took the only remaining bench at the back and Father Ruben proceeded to a makeshift altar. The sky poured in from above and bathed them all in soft morning sunlight. Father Ruben said the Mass.

When the last of the sisters had taken communion, everyone rose and assembled at the open entrance of the chapel where one day there would be doors. Father Ruben joined them. No one spoke. The morning seemed to be holding its breath. A pair of ground squirrels scurried up the unfinished wall. Doves murmured softly in the rafters.

After a long interval, Mother Superior Macrina allowed her thoughts to become speech. Her voice was small and frail and empty of its customary melody. "I would like to make a short announcement."

All turned to give her their full attention.

"I want to take this opportunity to thank our friends and neighbors for all their help. Don Carlos has disked and seeded all our fields so that next year the barn will be filled with hay and corn. We thank him, and ask God's blessing upon him." She paused as though trying to clear the cobwebs out of her throat. "A new face has come to Tanama, the face of a man who comes from far away to offer us his kindness."

Everyone saw her reach in the voluminous folds of her gray habit. Beeg Mac recognized his check in her hand. She held it in both hands behind her back. Beeg Mac would have run at this point but there was no place to hide. He wanted to disappear through a hole in the ground.

Mother Superior continued. "Our new friend has made us a most generous gift. . . ."

Beeg Mac winced. Here it comes, he thought. She's gonna say some big gringo blowhard came down here and took away their dream.

Reverend Mother interrupted herself as she could feel someone kissing her hands, which she still held behind her as she spoke. The little kisses became nibbles. She turned around in time to see a pair of flippy lips and Naná's pink muzzle rotating contentedly as the last corner of sixty thousand dollars disappeared down the animal's gullet.

"*Ay Dios mío!*" the startled Reverend Mother squeaked as she took a leap forward. But it was too late. Naná rolled her yellow eyes and sprang away before anyone could reach her. Mother Macrina quickly regained her composure and the flute tones were back in her voice. "Our visitor has worked for several days preparing all our buildings for electric power. I want to convey our thanks on the part of all the sisters and myself for his generosity. God bless you, Don Beeg Mac, and repay your kindness."

A loud hiss followed. It sounded like a big tractor tire losing air, but in reality it was five huge, simultaneous sighs.

"You are all invited to coffee," Reverend Mother concluded.

After coffee and *empanadas*, all the men gathered at the side of the road in front of Café Los Alamos. "Well, amigos," Beeg Mac said, "it was great fun meetin' ya. Me an' Carlos are headed for La Paz."

"Oh, but we will see you on your way back with your marlin," Father Ruben said.

" 'Fraid not. I'm catching a plane in La Paz straight to L.A. So I'll say so long right here."

Amador took Beeg Mac's hand firmly in his own, then pulled him closer and embraced him. "Good-bye, my friend. Come back to see us soon."

Francisco too put his arms around the big man. "I hope you catch the marlin that will make *el record de Guinness*!"

Father Ruben stepped up with a macho embrace. "Beeg Mac, we expect to see you back here in Tanama. I am only sorry you had to make the acquaintance of Doña Lala."

"Hey, that reminds me, is Tanama Peak in full sun?"

"Oh yes, look."

"Good." Beeg Mac removed the amulet from around his neck.

"*Fuchi!*" Father Ruben exclaimed. "So that smell was coming from you! I could smell it all during Mass. What are you going to do with it?"

"Are you kidding, Padre? I'm gonna keep it. You couldn't buy this here thing for all the money in the world."

Beeg Mac and Carlos got into the pickup. Father Ruben stepped up to the driver's side and spoke to Carlos. "Tell Doña Lala I owe her one."

The men remaining at the side of the highway drew themselves closer together in the warmth of a long friendship to watch Carlos and his guest head in a southerly direction.

"You have to say this for him," Amador said. "The man is all heart and he proved the power of money."

"I have never met such a generous man, but remember, he was wrong about the power of money," Francisco answered.

"Ah, but he accomplished something much greater," Father Ruben said.

"What do you mean?" Amador and Francisco asked in one voice.

"All three of you *cabrones* attended Mass, didn't you?"

Candelaria

"I seeng for you, señorita, a berry romantic song ees called 'Los Dos.' "

José Machuca was speaking to my American companion, who shared my corner table at La Fonda. Maybe José's English wasn't sufficiently symmetrical (or brittle) to provide the American ear quick and easy acoustic orientation, but it hardly mattered. His normal speaking voice was a song in itself, and when he sang, every heart within range was vulnerable. José could kindle a dangerous fire. I could see that he had Pat's heart melting like the candle on our table. He was by far the most popular balladeer in Tecate and he held Pat in a trance. Pat Harrison was my houseguest, and she had expressed hopes that she could come away with an article on Mexican Womanhood for her magazine up in San Francisco. But she was enraptured with José and the music right now. I doubt she was even thinking about work. Her eyes glistened. Language was unimportant, for José sang to her in the universal language of the soul. When the song ended with the last strumming of heartstrings and a sigh, the entire dining room at La Fonda burst into applause.

"*Gracias,*" Pat whispered to José as he bowed to her and left our table. Then she turned to me. I know I saw stars in her eyes. "I'm sorry I have to leave tomorrow. I could stay here forever."

"Stay an extra day and I promise to introduce you to someone who can give you what you need for your magazine article."

"It's a temptation. I feel like I'm in a movie. And you live like this every day?"

Before I could answer her, the front door opened, and when the figure was within my range, I recognized Lucila, whom I've known since her college days.

"*Hola, chulo!*" she trilled, kissing me first on one cheek then the other.

Chulo is a hard word to translate. It falls somewhere between *precious* and *darling.* "Sit down and join us." I introduced the two young women of about the same age. Thirty something.

"I can only stay a few minutes," she said to me. "I'm meeting Magi. She's giving Candelaria a baby shower, but we're doing it at my house so more people can come."

"Candelaria from the Deposito Corona?"

"The same."

"I didn't know. I guess that's why I haven't seen her in the store for a while." I felt someone grab a handful of flesh on my left thigh, and because Pat was the only living creature residing in that vicinity, it was child's play to deduce she was trying to gain my attention. When I gave it to her, I noticed her eyes kept darting toward Lucila, and being a highly perceptive individual, I caught her subtlety and spoke to Lucila. "My friend Pat is working on an article for a woman's magazine. And I know she's dying to ask you some questions. Do you mind?"

"Of course not, *chulo*, but you'll have to translate. I don't know *papa* in English. What does she want to know?"

I took this opportunity to order a margarita for Lucila and replacements for Pat and myself, and translated between interviewer and respondent.

"The first thing I'm curious about is this," Pat began. "Is the Mexican woman equal in the workplace?"

"Equal? No, no, no! In the workplace the Mexican woman is superior. She is in greater demand. Most supervisory jobs are held by women. We work better, we don't fool around, and we show up for work every day."

"God, that's wonderful! I'll confess that is not what I was expecting to hear." Pat reached for her purse and pulled out a notebook. I could see Pat felt she'd rolled a seven on her first throw. "And is she equal in the home?"

"In the home we are equal to the broom and second only to the kitchen sink."

"What!" Pat was bristling visibly. "Excuse me, but American husbands and wives consider themselves a team." She seemed to be searching for an example. "The American husband does laundry!"

"The Mexican husband *provides* it!"

"I don't want to believe this. The American husband even helps with the housework—and he irons!"

"If you ever see a man down here pushing a vacuum, he's a vacuum cleaner salesman. And if he's got an iron in his hands, it's probably a nine."

I was laughing even before I translated.

I thought Pat was going to choke on a tortilla chip. She

put it down and began to scribble furiously. "Tell her, then, that what I'd like to know is why do they put up with it? No American woman would!"

"What may be hard for the American woman to understand is that as soon as we have children, we are out of the workforce, and we become dependent on a man for our economic survival."

"But then you are forever under a man's control!"

"Exactly. You could say we are like stray cats. As soon as we leave our box under the porch, we go from house to house in our perpetual search for food and shelter for our kittens. And believe me, there will be kittens!"

Pat ignored her drink. She was burning up pages in her little notebook. "Then you are not your own person!!" As long as I have known Pat, she punctuates everything she says with exclamation points.

Lucila released a long sigh. "I'm afraid God made the Mexican woman with a cookie cutter. Let me tell you the story of Candelaria, the girl whose baby shower is this evening."

Lucila poured out the whole story from beginning to end. But of course, I couldn't translate it as it came off the press, so to speak, so it would have to wait until we got back to the villa.

When we got home, Pat would not let me forget that I still hadn't told her the story of Candelaria as told to us by Lucila. Pat left for the Bay Area the next day and I haven't heard from her since. I don't know if she got her article, but this is the story she left with.

Candelaria stretched every muscle in her body to its limit in an effort to reach the farthest depth of the wall refrigerator. She withdrew a cold six-pack of Corona and put it on the counter in front of her customer, a young macho type in Levi's 501 slims, cowboy hat, and honey-colored boots. His friend, a Xerox facsimile, stood at his side.

"Will there be anything else?" Of course there would be something else. These young studs always wanted a bottle of orange Fanta. It was a standard ruse in Tecate.

"Yes, a bottle of orange Fanta, please." Every young rooster in Tecate knew the bottles of Fanta were kept deep in the back on the lowest shelf. The long reach was impossible to manage without standing on your head, bottom high in the air in full display, providing live entertainment for anyone in the store.

Candelaria was used to it. She was careful to dress modestly for her job at the Corona Deposito on Calle Revolución. She made sure her pants weren't too tight, and wore baggy sweatshirts most of the time. She groped for a bottle of Fanta, endeavoring as much as possible to restrict gluteal gyration to a minimum. Her customers were predictable. The *piropo* would come next, spoken to his companion, of course, but intended for her.

"Hombre! What curves—and my brakes are bad!"

The Xerox added his observation, "So much to see, and me with only two eyes!"

Candelaria ignored them both, rang up the sale, and watched them sniggering like adolescents as they went out the door. They were her age. Twenty-one, tops. Another pair of gamecocks strutted in as they walked out. She noticed a third right behind them, a man she knew she'd never seen before. The stranger went directly to the back wall and began to browse as the two regulars stepped up to the counter.

"*Hola,* Candi, what's new, *chiquita?*"

"*Hola,* Pancho. Nothing new, working as always. What can I get you?"

"Give me two sixes of Corona and a bottle of José Cuervo."

Candelaria put everything on the counter. She was prepared for the orange Fanta. "Anything else?"

"Yes, when are you going out with me?"

"When three Thursdays come together."

"Go ahead, trample my heart. A package of Montanas."

Candelaria took the cigarettes from a drawer and rang up the sale. She prepared for the *piropo.*

"And convey my gratitude to your mother."

"Whatever for?"

"For having given you life!" He put his hand over his heart. "And bringing beauty to a troubled world."

His companion followed quickly. "Blessed is the cloud that watered the tree that gave its life to produce the cradle where you were rocked."

At least it was a *piropo* she hadn't heard before. Candelaria couldn't help herself. She had to laugh with them. They left and she turned her attention to the stranger who had walked in with them. He was still studying the vast selection of estate-bottled vinifera vinegars labeled as wines.

"Can I help you, señor?"

The young man turned toward her and she felt her heart tremble. The first thing she noticed was the big Saint Bernard eyes, the face, smooth and clean. He looked *maduro.* Maybe thirty. He was dressed in crisp white pants and a shirt with bold vertical stripes of alternating teal and navy blue. His bare arms appeared to have been bronze-plated in Cancun.

"I'm afraid I don't know any appropriate *piropos* to toss at you."

My God! His voice was the color of cognac, low and mellow, dark and beautiful. "Oh, I pay no attention to them. I get that every day." She laughed self-consciously. "What can I get for you?"

"I need a six-pack of Corona and mineral water."

Candelaria didn't move. "You're not from here, are you?"

"No, how can you tell?"

"Tecate is a small pueblo. We know every face. And I thought I better tell you, the beer won't cross the border into the United States."

"It won't?"

"No."

"Then just give me the mineral water."

"Twelve pesos or two-fifty American."

The stranger paid in dollars. "It's a good thing you told me about the beer or they would have taken it away from me at the border."

"Is this the first time you are in Tecate?"

"Yes, and already I love the little town. Is there anything to see?"

"No."

"Is there anything to do?"

"No."

"Good, you will probably see me regularly."

Candelaria laughed. "Every day it's the same people, all saying the same thing. It is a tedious but wholesome pueblo, as a matter of fact. We've just grown used to it, and I suppose we don't appreciate it."

"What's your name?"

"Candelaria Perez Mesa."

"What a beautiful name."

"*Gracias.*"

The stranger extended his hand. "I'm Gabriel. Gabriel Carrasco. Of course, everyone calls me Gabi."

They stood there feasting on each other, with smiles just short of laughter. He appeared to be focusing for a snapshot. Her hair was as black as his own, feathery bangs drawing attention to luminous green eyes, the rest of her hair resting on her shoulders in big swirly waves. The mouth seemed poised for a kiss. The rest of her was not accessible for visual appraisal.

He released her hand. "Is there a place to stay in this town?"

"Decent?"

"Of course."

"No."

"In any case, I hope to see you on my next visit."

"Have a good trip." She stood watching the empty space where the apparition had materialized long minutes after he was out the door. A residual smile lingered on her face, and it lasted until it was five o'clock and time to head home.

Why couldn't she have met someone like him four years ago? That was the problem with Tecate. Small town, small minds. The *niños* you met in kindergarten became the same cowboys you grew old with. She had to fall in love with that *cabrón* Gerardo who disguised his lust as love. These machos were all the same. Strip a girl of her innocence with a kiss and a lie, then vanish when the baby comes. They are only out to destroy a girl's dreams.

At five o'clock the night girl arrived and Candelaria left. The bus deposited her on the corner of Sixth and Madero, choking in a cloud of noxious diesel fumes, then pulled away with a rude roar. She had two long blocks of dirt road to cover. Every time a car went by she ate a mouthful of dirt. She was thinking of a warm bath and a chance to get off her feet. Her legs felt heavy as she reached the last stone step and pushed open the front door.

"Mami! Mami!" Three-year-old Armida flew across the room and up into her arms where hugs and kisses came in bunches and for a moment she was the only one in the world. Candelaria held her daughter tight for a brief moment of sanity. Real life began the moment she put her down.

She looked into the living room. Six people were gathered for holy communion in reverent silence in front of the wide-screen shrine. Her brother Felipe was stretched out on the sofa with his head on his wife's lap. She was squeezing blackheads on his face. Beto, another brother, and his live-in girlfriend were tangled in an overstuffed chair. He had a lawful wife somewhere, but it didn't work out and he came home to Mother. Four children lay sprawled on the floor. One was missing. The Snot. Where was the Snot? A squabble was about to erupt when they wouldn't let Armida back to the place she left to kiss her mother, until Candelaria's mother yelled a warning. She was following the television drama from the kitchen stove where she was stirring something in a skillet that smelled awfully good. This morning's breakfast dishes were still scattered across the dining table where Candelaria's sister (the mother of the Snot) sat nursing her latest indiscretion while watching the *novela* on the screen. It was at full volume.

"Laura, get out of my house!"

"Your house? Your father's, you mean."

"I brought you here, and don't you forget it! I brought

you here because I loved you and believed with all my heart you loved me too. I know what you're playing at with my father—even the servants know it!"

"Listen to me, Nestor, your father is a lonely widower. I give him back his fantasies—and I'm going to stay here as long as he wants me in his bed!"

"Whore!"

Nestor stormed out. A door slammed. Laura stood alone in the bedroom curling a strand of her long red hair between her fingers. The music got ominous, then Laura looked straight into the camera with a sneer intended to imply triumph. A frosty can of Pepsi-Cola assumed her place on the screen.

Candelaria almost didn't see her grandmother, a living skeleton ravaged by years and woes unknown. She sat in a kitchen chair sorting beans into a bowl. Grandmother was deaf as a turnip, nearly blinded by cataracts. The poor thing, Candelaria thought, how can she stand it? Her grandmother acknowledged her arrival with a pink, gummy, loving grin. She lost every tooth she had by the time she turned forty. Candelaria put her arms around her and kissed her withered cheek. No one else seemed to notice Candelaria's arrival except her mother, who asked her if she remembered to bring home a liter of Fanta.

Candelaria headed straight for the bathroom and a soothing bath. The indignant voice screamed the moment she turned the doorknob.

"I'm in here, ox-head! Get out!"

The Snot. Probably playing with his *pito*. Candelaria walked back into the kitchen, looked at the sink stacked with dirty dishes. She stopped, grabbed an apron from the back of a chair and began the task. My mother provides free housing for all of them, a day-care center for their brats, she thought. She provides linen, maid, and meal service. You would think someone among this pack of drones would make an effort to at least rinse a glass.

By the time Candelaria had the dining table cleared and every dish washed and dried and put away, the credits were crawling past a freeze-frame of Laura and the horny old widower. The soccer game between Tijuana and Guadalajara was next. All the men assembled around the table to wait for food to be brought to them. The women served their children and their men. Candelaria served Armida and ate her dinner standing next to her. Grandmother was rinsing her mouth with a glass of buttermilk.

"Hey, where are my clothes!" It was not a question, it was an indignant demand. The Snot, the unfortunate result of a sixteen-year-old girl grooving in the bed of a Datsun pickup with a twenty-five watt × four-channel cassette player, stormed into the room naked but for a soggy towel thrown around his loins. He was fourteen, sullen, and on his way out to score. No one paid him immediate attention. "Where are my clothes!" he repeated.

Candelaria's mother answered. "I did four loads of laundry today. Whatever you want is probably in the basket. Go look on top of the washing machine."

The Snot shrugged his shoulders violently to demonstrate his displeasure. "But my shirt. My good one. It's not ironed."

The Snot's own mother made no move. It was Candelaria's mother who put down her fork and got to her feet. "I'll get you something to eat."

"I don't want to eat, woman, I want my shirt!"

"Then bring it here. I'll iron it for you now."

Candelaria fought back an impulse to hold her mother by the shoulders and tell her to stay where she was, then strangle the Snot with her bare hands.

The Snot came back dressed but for his "good shirt," which he handed to the stupid woman who was already struggling with the ironing board. Candelaria wondered if a good slap would erase the surly face.

The meal ended and, predictably, everyone filed into the the living area for evening devotions in front of the television. Candelaria could not contain herself another minute.

"I don't suppose it has occurred to anyone here that we've used every dish in the house."

"Ay Candi!" It was her brother's voice. "You're worse than a mother-in-law!"

Encouraged, her other brother threw another stone. "Don't be such a *bruja*, you'll never get a husband like that."

"If you are the models, I don't need a husband."

Her sister-in-law's voice entered the conversation. "Come on, Candi, sit down. We'll do them later."

Candelaria knew the dirty dishes would remain until this time tomorrow when she got home from work, but decided against the futility of doing them again herself. She joined the room full of free-loaders genuflecting in front of the TV set. She held out for about an hour, then picked up Armida and took her into her bedroom. She tucked her into a crib mattress on the floor next to her own bed, got undressed and slipped under the covers. She wanted to be asleep before her brother and his courtesan climbed into their bed on the other side of the room. She picked up her book and escaped in the pages of *Amor en el Tiempo del Cólera*. She loved Garcia Marquez. It took less than a chapter to feel heavy weights pulling at her eyelids. She turned out her lamp and let sleep take possession.

She woke once during the night. She could hear voices in the other room. The television. My God, she thought, they never turn the thing off. It's an addiction. Someone began to sing. It sounded a lot like Julio Iglesias. She listened for a moment then let herself drift off again. Was it minutes later? Or hours? Sleep could distort time. The man was no longer singing. He sounded in pain. No, it wasn't pain, it was ecstasy. And it wasn't Julio Iglesias. It was her brother and his sleep toy in the next bed. Dear God, find me a way out. I plead for a life of my own! Candelaria hadn't been to Mass in years. Not since the last wedding she attended. Yet she considered herself a good Catholic and often invoked His succor as proof of her faith. God, I need a place of my own. I'm dreaming! Even if I didn't give my mother half my earnings, I still couldn't afford my own apartment. I'm in prison!

Next day, Candelaria was grateful to have a job to go to. Work was boring but home was unbearable. She hummed while she swept the floor, sprayed Windex on the glass refrigerator doors to remove yesterday's fingerprints. She took out the trash and swept the sidewalk in front of the store. At ten, opening time for liquor stores imposed by law, she unlocked the front door. The same faces as the day before came in, bought the same things and tossed *piropos* to her.

Each boring day rolled past, today no different from yesterday, with a promise of an identical day tomorrow. Then at three o'clock one afternoon a liter of Coca-Cola slipped out of her hands and a dozen jumping beans nearly leaped out of her heart.

Gabi Carrasco stood in front of her. "*Buenas tardes,* Candelaria."

She heard her name every day. It didn't thrill her. She didn't even like her name. Today it sounded like it was set to music. "*Buenos dias*—I mean—*tardes. Buenas tardes*, Bagi—Gabi!" He's going to think I'm an idiot.

They laughed an embarrassed little laugh together. He put out both hands and she took them in hers. "I see you're still here working hard." It was a dumb thing to say, but Gabi didn't know where else to begin.

"Yes, here as always." Candelaria bit down on her lip. She nearly asked him what he wanted. That would be dumb. "How are you enjoying Tecate?"

"Oh, very much. I enjoy the tranquility."

"That's what most visitors say. You people on the Other Side must be under a lot of pressure."

Gabi was about to reply when a pair of *vaqueros* in tall hats sauntered in and *piropos* began to fly.

"Ay! What a bonbon and I'm on a diet!"

"*Hola*, Nacho." Her voice was friendly but unimpressed. She noticed Gabi wander off to the back wine shelves. "What will you have?"

"Give me a six-pack of Corona."

Nacho's companion spoke up. "And I'll have an orange Fanta, *por favor*."

Candelaria almost told him they were out of Fanta. She put the Corona on the counter and attempted to withdraw a bottle of Fanta with as little *nalga* squirming as possible. Where was Gabi? Still browsing the wine display, she hoped.

"If that's the plum, I'd like to see the tree!" She knew the speaker's eyes were glued to her bottom.

When she stood and regained her dignity, Candelaria looked up to see Gabi standing at the counter. He saw me! She rang up the sale and the cowboys ambled out, sniggering. She fought back a blush without a great deal of success but Gabi saved her with a question.

"Is there a good place to have dinner here?"

"La Fonda."

"Good place?"

"No, the only place."

"Would you join me? I really don't want to have dinner alone."

Candelaria almost reached for her breast to control the sudden renewed activity of the jumping beans in her heart but caught herself in time. "I don't get off till five when the night girl comes on."

Gabi consulted his watch. "It's three-thirty. I'll come back at five."

"I'll be ready." They exchanged nervous smiles. He wasn't out the door ten seconds when she was regretting the clothes she came to work in. Her hair was a mess and her face was ugly. Quickly she made two phone calls.

"Mamá, I won't be home from work till late. I just wanted to let you know."

"That's fine, dear, the dishes can wait till tomorrow." She laughed when she said it. "I have never seen such a gang of lazy people in my entire life."

"Blame yourself, Mamá. Why don't you ever say something?"

"No one pays any attention to me. They all grew up only to remain children and never move out. I've spoiled them already, I guess it's too late. Anyway, try not to be too late, and use a condom."

"Mamá!"

"I'm a practical woman."

"I am simply going out to dinner and I hardly think either of us is likely to strip our clothes off in the restaurant."

"When I was seventeen your father invited me out for a

taco, and nine months later your brother was born." Candelaria sighed. As long as memory served, her mother was always very *abierta*, open, frank, candid. "I considered it a blessing from El Señor when your father left me stranded with a clutch of four baby chicks the day after you were born. I couldn't afford to support him too."

She had heard it all before. "Mamá, I have to run, I have a customer," she lied.

"Just remember what I tell you, silly girl. One minute he asks you if you want to see his video, and before you know it he's plugged it in."

"Ay Mamá! I have to run." Sometimes her mother was too much. She rang off and made her second phone call to Casa Carol, the dress shop around the corner. "*Hola*, Tere? Candi. Listen. You know that pretty blouse in your window? The pink one with the little white design. Yes, that one. Bring it 'round right away in a size eight. 'Bye!"

Gabi was back in the store on the stroke of five and visibly disappointed to see another girl behind the counter. "You came for Candelaria?"

"*Sí*."

"She'll be right out."

Gabi looked up to see Candelaria coming in from the back room, where she had done her best to improve her presentation. Gabi was nearly blinded by the vision; eyes of green flame kindled in heaven, lips poised for his kiss. The pink blouse withheld no secrets. His head abandoned him and left him helplessly hanging on to his heart.

"Lead the way."

They walked side by side, and as new acquaintances often do, each tried to maintain a few discreet inches of neutral zone between them. It is possible that the bursting population of Tecate owes something to the *ingenieros* who planned Tecate's first sidewalks over thirty years ago. The little concrete strips are so narrow it is impossible for a boy and a girl to walk abreast and not achieve some degree of physical intimacy.

Candelaria was grateful La Fonda was nearly empty when they walked in. The news that Candelaria Perez Mesa had dinner with a stranger would spread like measles. The various vectors were already seated at their tables. Two of Candelaria's girlfriends from the bank were having a drink and said *hola* as she passed by more or less on Gabi's arm. She could feel their eyes following them, speculating. They would be in to the Deposito Corona tomorrow for details. She noticed Treenie Contreras at a table with two American men, but the table was too far to acknowledge. Treenie was Tecate's foremost matchmaker. He had offered to bring Candelaria the Blue Prince from the Other Side, but she didn't have three hundred dollars.

She swallowed a lump of guilt as she exchanged a tentative smile and a nod of recognition with Father Ruben, dressed in a blue denim shirt over a white T-shirt. He was having supper with two men she didn't know. He must be giving the six o'clock Mass this evening, she thought. Father Ruben was not a regular at La Fonda.

By tomorrow morning everyone in Tecate over the age of five would know what she wore, what he wore, and what they ate.

Gabi looked at Candelaria. "A margarita?" Gaining her approval he spoke to the waiter. "*Dos* margaritas."

Candi and Gabi chatted easily over their drinks. "Who was that man who greeted you just now?"

"Do you find him interesting?"

"In a way, yes, he looks different from the other men. No big mustache, his face is smooth, and he doesn't have that 'life is a struggle' look on his countenance."

"My, you are observant. That is Father Ruben, our local *sacerdote*."

"So you see him every Sunday."

"Not really."

Gabi motioned to the waiter. "I think we can handle another margarita." The waiter left to perform his duty, and Gabi turned to Candelaria. "You are a native of Tecate?"

"Almost. We're from Hermosillo. I was two when my family moved here."

"Then you still have your parents. You live with them, I suppose."

Candelaria did not think she needed to worry about a condom, but recalled another of her mother's candid rules. The truth is never a source of shame. No lies, no evasions, no euphemisms. Never allow a man to fall in love with what you're not. "Yes, and no. My father left us when I was a baby. My mother came out here with four children and her sewing machine. I live at home." The truth, Candelaria. All of it! "We all live at home and my mother looks after my three-year-old daughter." There!

The waiter removed salad plates and brought their entrées. "Is everything satisfactory, señores?"

"Everything is fine, *gracias*, Rafa," Candelaria answered for both of them. Then it was her turn to interview. "I'm assuming you were born on the Other Side."

"My parents both came from Guadalajara. They emigrated in the 1940s. But, yes, I was born and raised in Los Angeles. I live in San Diego now. How can you tell?"

"It isn't difficult."

"My language?"

"In part." She was not about to admit to having noticed his grammatical misdemeanors. "I don't speak a word of English, but I've noticed that people who speak both languages undergo a voice change when they switch from one language to another. They even *laugh* in English. But mostly your clothes, your mannerisms, I suppose."

"You mean, no big sombrero, no boots—and no *piropos*!"

She laughed with him. "What kind of work do you do?"

"Investments and money management. I work for my father. I am his financial adviser."

That was well over her head, and the first dance of courtship was over. They had coffee and flan then went into the plaza for the second *danzón*. They walked arm in arm now. The evening was deliciously balmy. They took a bench under the tall *alamos*. Garden lights illuminated the trees, turning the foliage above them into golden rain.

Nothing draws the attention of the vendors of Tecate like a young couple seated on a wrought-iron bench under the magic spell of the stars in the middle of the plaza. They circled the couple like moths.

"Hot *churros*, señores, hot *churros* to sweeten the conversation!"

"Corn on the cob . . . steamed tender for the elderly, freshly roasted for those with young hearts and good teeth!"

Candelaria waved them all away. But the corn man was quickly followed by a diminutive girl of maybe ten, in her big sister's old dress. She put them both under the magic spell of her smile, a smile that could melt hearts and mend souls. She held a single corsage of fresh miniature gardenias.

Candelaria recognized sweet blackmail when she saw it, and like every Mexican girl in this position, felt it was incumbent upon her to protect her escort from extortionists. But Gabi had a dollar bill in the flower girl's hand and took the corsage before Candelaria could wave her away.

"These little gardenias gladly gave their lives to lie near your heart."

Candelaria held still, allowing Gabi to pin the corsage. He slipped the sharp pin through her blouse with scrupulous care in the vicinity of the dangerous topography in an effort to avoid impropriety or shoving a pin through her flesh and drawing blood. For all his efforts, they were both aware of the back of his hand resting lightly against her breast during the brief ceremony. It was unavoidable.

"And I thought you didn't know *piropos. Gracias.*" Do I kiss him? she wondered. Her mother's voice never failed to make unsolicited comments. Don't give them everything the first night. That voice will still be coming to me when I'm an old lady, she thought, and expressed herself with a smile.

They sat inhaling the magic of the night with joined hands and learned about each other in whispers. Presently they became aware the plaza was deserted. Gabi did not want to look at his watch. He brought his lips to rest on her cheek. "I suppose I should be getting you home. It must be late."

"It isn't late for me, but you should know that the border closes at midnight."

Gabi brought his watch up to the light. "I have half an hour. I parked my car somewhere down on the main street."

She helped him find his car. He followed instructions through a labyrinth of rough dirt roads made treacherous by virtue of darkness, and pulled up in front of her house. The lights were on. Candelaria knew only too well the horror show that was playing on the other side of that door. Bring him in to meet my dysfunctional family, she thought, and he'll flee Tecate as though Mount Cuchumá were an active volcano and he was one stride ahead of the lava flow. Maybe, just maybe, he'll politely decline. The tenets of courtesy demand it!

"Won't you come in?" She held her breath like the accused waiting for the verdict to be announced.

"It's so late, another time."

Thank God for small mercies! The kiss was brief, tentative, almost not a kiss at all. Then, as though both mouths demanded more, a second kiss followed. Warm, long, wet.

"Next week?"

"Next week," she whispered. Her breast felt cool when he removed his hand.

And so began a courtship that could not contain the passion smoldering just beneath the surface. Two volatile hearts waited only for a spark from their lips to burst into flames. Every Monday, Gabi arrived at the Corona Deposito in the early evening just as Candelaria got off work. Every evening she came out looking gorgeous.

It seemed there was barely time for dinner at La Fonda, a walk in the plaza, and some surreptitious feelies in the kiosk before it was time to part. While they weren't looking, Eos, goddess of dawn that conspires against a man and a woman in love, repositioned the stars in heaven, and the clocks on Earth obeyed.

When they came up for air, there was just time for Gabi to get her home and to dash across the border before the clock struck midnight. Tuesday only prolonged the agony. It was Candelaria's day off, and this allowed them to spend the day sightseeing in Ensenada. They would have margaritas and a lobster dinner on the waterfront, then walk out to the end of the pier. But here too, Eos moved the constellations and pushed the moon to the other edge of heaven while they weren't looking, and the evening disappeared. Suddenly it was time to drive the two hours back to Tecate, deliver Candelaria, and race through the iron gate before American officers slammed it shut. And they weren't even through kissing!

The lights were on in the house when Gabi pulled up in front. Candelaria always adhered to Mexican protocol. "Won't you come in?" It was an impotent overture and they both knew it.

"*Gracias,* the hour is late beyond propriety. And the border will close in less than five minutes."

Their parting kisses increased in their intensity. The demands of the body for something more now became urgent.

A week later Candelaria had to pinch herself to confirm she wasn't dreaming. She was strolling in El Rubi, Tecate's largest furniture store, "I'll take this pink and white sofa and matching chair. The love seat too, of course. And these two lamps. And the leather-top end tables—and this glass coffee table." The sound of her own voice startled Candi.

"*Sí,* señora. You have exquisite taste. It is the best we have."

The man answered—she wasn't dreaming! "Now, I want to go upstairs and see the bedrooms."

"Of course, señora, right this way."

This was better than a dream because she was really buying all this furniture. The truck would really deliver it to her. Gabi really gave the man cash for the new apartment.

She saw him make payment with her own eyes. Gabi would really be here this afternoon to pay the store. He would insist that it be delivered immediately. And the salesman would slobber and bow and say, "*Sí*, señor, it will be done." No, she wasn't dreaming! She would deliver her body and soul to him in their new bed this very night.

Saturday morning Candelaria and Gabi made love, played house, arranged and rearranged furniture. They went to the open-air market, which was a novelty for Gabi. They bought things to bring back for lunch. Candelaria served him fish tacos, garnished with fresh cilantro, diced tomato, onion, shredded cabbage, and an incendiary *pico de pájaro* red sauce. She fixed him a mountain of guacamole and a side plate of beans cooked with corn, which was a new experience for Gabi. He ate everything on his plate then assaulted the serving bowls. Candelaria feared he would start on the silk flowers.

At three in the afternoon Gabi raced across the border. Candelaria decided to take a taxi home and pick up what few things she owned. She paused a moment to thank God for rescuing her from her nightmare and made Him a promise with the best of intentions. While at market they had bought with their eyes. She would take some of these things to her mother.

A blue taxi, number 26, pulled in front of her house. She instructed the driver to wait. Candelaria walked into her living room in time to hear a bloody scream and three ear-piercing gunshots in rapid fire. The family was watching the Saturday afternoon movie on Channel 12. They were deep in worship. Nobody stirred. Without realizing it, she identified five layers of food smells; beans, onions, coffee, scorched pork grease, and chile peppers.

Felipe lay on his back on the floor using his wife's lap for a recliner. She was stuffing something into her mouth. Beto, her other brother, took possession of the sofa. His live-in girlfriend lay between his outstretched legs, her head on his chest. Beto had his arms around her and was now massaging her breasts. She was a total stranger to Candelaria. He must have acquired a new sleep toy. The floor was covered with little children, Armida among them, but she was too intent on the drama to notice her mother's arrival. Loud and ravenous sucking sounds came from the upholstered armchair where her sister was nursing her baby. She took on a different color every time there was a scene change on the screen. Candelaria saw her mother sitting in a straight chair, totally mesmerized. Her pitiful grandmother sat on the other side of the table in her silent world, dipping bread into a bowl of milk. The Snot lay supine on the floor with his bare feet propped on the only vacant chair. He was in a Chargers T-shirt and red shorts or pants. They were too short to be one and too long to be the other. Once more she thanked God she and Armida would be out of this *infierno*.

Candelaria carried a large shopping bag in her arms. She walked over to the chair claimed by two bare feet and pulled it away.

"*Cabróna!*" hissed the fourteen-year-old Snot.

Candelaria ignored the obscenity, sat down and began to stack and arrange the Sierra Madre of unwashed dishes on the dining table in order to make room for the groceries. They probably think I'm about to wash their dishes, she thought. They're going to be disappointed when they learn why I'm here. She withdrew a kilo of tortillas and sweet rolls.

Next was a small wheel of soft cheese. She unwrapped it, and before the vultures could prey on it, put it in front of her grandmother in the wrapper, as there was no clean plate to put it on. She put her arms around the living relic and kissed her leather cheek. Her grandmother answered with faded eyes damp with love, then patted Candelaria's hand, which was resting on her shoulder.

There was a tight close-up of the screamer on the screen. Her swollen face dissolved into the toothy smile of Pancho Lopez Used Cars in National City, "*Hola* all my good amigos and *compas*. Need a good used car? Come in today and see your amigo Pancho. Cross the border and save!" The scavengers deserted their good amigo Pancho and swarmed around the shopping bag.

"Hey, your new *novio* must have plenty of *plata*!" Felipe said, rifling through the provisions.

Beto was too lazy to move. He sent his girlfriend up to investigate. Candelaria waited for some form of acknowledgment from her. There was none. "Bring me something good," Beto called out from the couch.

"You bring any beer?" the Snot snarled.

Candelaria ignored him. She was conscious of the waiting taxi and she wanted to be on her way. She spoke to her mother. "Mamá, I'm going to live in my own apartment." They knew she had a *novio*, but she had no intention of elaborating further.

Big round tears erupted on her mother's face. "You're going to leave us! Oh, how ungrateful one's own children can be!"

Candelaria made no move to console her. "I'll continue to give you the same weekly allowance I bring home now."

Her mother sniffed. "Oh, you're such a good daughter." The tears were gone. It was a brief emotional display.

"You're going to do the dishes before you leave, no?" Beto called out from the living room.

The Snot was on his feet. "Can I have your Walkman?"

"You have one," Candelaria answered icily.

"Somebody stole it. Let me have yours. Your rich *novio* can buy you another one. Isn't that the price of a night in bed?"

Candelaria swung out to slap his insolent face. Her mother was faster and connected.

"Cabróna!" the Snot screamed at his grandmother and stormed out of the room.

Grandmother sat quietly surrounded by profound silence, gumming little chunks of the cheese her granddaughter had put before her.

"My taxi is waiting, Mamá. I just want to collect a few things. My clothes, Armida's things."

"Armida's things! You certainly don't intend to take my baby."

"Of course, she's my daughter."

Candelaria's mother renewed her hysterics. She burst into tears and began wailing loud enough that someone in the living room felt it necessary to raise the volume on the television. "My baby, my baby, you're going to walk out of here with a piece of my heart! How can you do that to your own mother!" She pulled a tissue from her sleeve and emptied her reservoir of tears in hard, hacking sobs. "And who's going to take care of the poor baby when you're at work, tell me that! Some stranger no doubt."

"No stranger. I have arranged with Tere's mother. She's very reliable."

The woman became hysterical to the point Candelaria was sure she was going to pass out. Candelaria figured Armida was here all week anyway, it would be less disruptive for her if she stayed. "All right, Mamá, all right. She has to stay *someplace* during the week. You can keep her here."

Her mother gasped for breath then dried her eyes and tossed the soggy tissue into one of the bean-smeared plates on the table. The performance was over. A few sniffs and she was under control. "Maybe your *novio* could help out with some extra grocery money. And Armida could use some clothes."

Impossible woman, Candelaria thought. "I'll see to her clothes myself."

"Oh," came the answer, flat and dry with disappointment. "Well, I hope he's a good man and you've chosen wisely. I'm sure he won't mind offering a little financial help toward a new washing machine. You're not here to see how I slave all day with that old wringer machine."

Candelaria wanted to tell her that that would have been a wiser investment than the forty-inch shrine in the living room, but decided it was pointless. "I'll just gather up my things."

"Maybe you can bring your *novio* around so we can meet him."

Yes! The very day Cain achieves sainthood. Candelaria went to her grandmother and shouted into her ear. "I'm moving, so I'm giving you my bed, *abuelita*. You won't be sleeping on the sofa anymore."

The old wrinkled, toothless, stone-deaf woman patted her arm affectionately. "You're going to a movie? That's nice."

"No, no *abuelita*, I'm moving." Candelaria gave up. She

went into her room. She put her few things into a carton. Mostly clothes, books, and her CDs. The Walkman was gone and so was the Snot.

Candelaria called the man out of the taxi to carry her things down. She kissed her daughter, who was in a hurry to return to the movie. She kissed her grandmother.

"Enjoy your movie, dear."

No one looked up from the giant screen. Candelaria's mother walked her to the front door wearing her onion face. She looked down at her shoes and wrung her hands on her apron. Her voice was infused with a martyr's woes. "Could you leave me fifty pesos for some groceries?" She tossed her head in the direction of the devout assembled in their sanctuary.

Candelaria almost exploded. She knew exactly what her mother had done with the three hundred peso allowance she gave her only three days ago. She loaned it to one of the drones hooked up to the Saturday afternoon movie. Words formed on her lips, then she decided it would serve no purpose. Her mother would cry and wail and tell her that her brother needed some money for *gasolina* so he could go and look for work. Candelaria crumpled a fifty into the waiting hand and hurried down to the taxi, eyes stinging, big thick knots tangled around her heart.

"You're absolutely crazy, Candi. You know that?"

"Yes, I'm crazy. I'm crazy in love and it's wonderful. Magi, I have met Prince Charming!"

"El Príncipe Azúl appears only in fairy tales."

"Then I'm living in the pages of a fairy tale and I love it!"

Candelaria sat at the dinette in the house of her best friend, Magi. They were also cousins born a week apart, and over the years Candelaria and Magi became one. Even when Magi moved to San Diego and took the oath of citizenship, swearing allegiance to the United States of America, and McDonald's, and hot dogs and apple pie, the two girls remained joined at the soul.

Magi put grilled cheese sandwiches on the table. The potato chips were familiar to Candelaria, but the kosher dill aroused her provincial curiosity. It was strange, exotic. She felt her whole mouth pucker. Her eyes watered and she felt her sinuses clear suddenly. She decided it was an acquired taste.

"I'm so happy, Magi. For the first time I'm standing at the center of my life. He got me a small apartment. I went to the stores and furnished it with everything I like. I've never had my own life. You've seen my family."

"And mine. By the way, how's the Snot? I can remember he was repulsive even when he was a baby."

"I expect he'll be in jail before we finish lunch."

"I'm happy for you, *corazón*, but from what you tell me, you don't know a lot about your Principe Azúl."

"What's to know? Prince Charming loves me and I love him. Is there any more?"

"That's wonderful, but then he's putting the horns on Cinderella."

"Ay Magi!"

"Don't you think you should at least know what kind of a family he comes from, what he does for a living? How do you know he's not trafficking *drogas*?"

"Ay Magi! That's the first thing you always think of."

"And you know why."

"I told you. His father is extremely wealthy. He handles all his father's investments."

"Don't you think it's strange that he spends only a few days each week with you? And never on Sunday? Suppose he's married!"

"I've thought about that. And yes, I must admit, that bothers me. I wouldn't want to be a kept woman."

"We're all kept women. Our home life is so miserable we go off with the first man who comes along just to escape. We don't even ask ourselves if he's legitimate. We don't want to know! We have his baby then never see the *cabrón* again. Our mothers did it, you did it, I did it."

"I have to trust him, Magi. If he was using me for a plaything, he could do it for a lot less. He even thinks I should have a car."

"Dear God!"

Candelaria risked another uncertain nibble of her kosher dill. The jury was still out. "I'm telling you, he's the most generous man I've ever known. He puts the so-called machos of Tecate to shame."

"And what about *el sexo*? You used to think it was disgusting. How did you used to say it? Poked, mauled, and slobbered over!"

Her very words. Candelaria had to laugh. "Without love it's still a savage animal act. But when it's an expression of your deepest love, real love, it is nothing less than beautiful."

"I can't believe this is the same girl talking."

"I've learned things I never knew before, Magi. He gave me my first *orgasmo*. He showed me a whole catalog of lovemaking. He does everything to me and I've learned to do everything to him."

"Everything?"

"Everything."

Magi's voice dropped to a lower key. "I guess I just don't want to see you get hurt, Candi. I did the same thing, remember. A tragic mistake. That's why I came here to the United States to make a new life. I wanted to renounce the bitter legacy of misery we hand down from mother to daughter like a priceless heirloom."

"And did you break the cycle?"

"I'm sure I did. I'm engaged to a man I can respect as well as love."

"Mexican?"

"Irish. You'll meet Patrick tonight. He loves my little boy. By this time next year we'll be married. We'll plant flowers in the backyard together, we'll do the dinner dishes together. We'll talk to each other—all the things you've never seen a Mexican husband do."

"You sound so American."

"I *am* an American, in mind and heart. I never want to go back to the old ways. My eyes have been opened. I know too much."

"And how's *el sexo*?"

"Both beautiful and meaningful. And when do I meet your Principe Azúl?"

"Next week he's taking me to Cabo San Lucas for a few days. I'll call you when we get back. You can meet him then."

"I work, remember, I can only come down on a Sunday. After Mass, of course. Unlike some people I know, I never fail to attend Mass. And on Sunday your Blue Prince is in the counting house counting out his father's money."

"Ay Magi! You're always so suspicious. Then we'll drive up here during the week. You're going to love him!"

The Baja peninsula, a scaly, twisting serpent of volcanic mountains with irregular markings of brown deserts, jungle rivers, tropical lagoons, and secret coves hiding in its coils, dips its narrow tongue into the sea at Cabo San Lucas. It is here that the waters of the Sea of Cortes rush to meet the Pacific.

Candelaria and Gabi lay side by side on a beach blanket looking out at the Lovers, a geological epilogue carved by time. Two enormous sculptures of black stone rise up out of the sea to the height of a ten-story building. The two stone lovers stand about a quarter of a mile offshore, surrounded by crashing waves and turquoise foam. They appear to be treading water. "El" takes the form of a graceful archway reminiscent of the magnificent ruins of Hadrian's temple. It is large enough to allow a boat to sail through. "Ella" stands nearby just beyond the reach of his embrace at the moment legend tells us the lovers were turned to stone. Candelaria and Gabi were the only two people on the beach. They could have been the only two people in the world. They lay quietly, the sun smiling on their backs, dissolving the sediments of duty and responsibility that accumulate in the mind like algae in the tide pools.

This was the honeymoon she always dreamed of and never knew. She closed her eyes. Her thoughts were on her happiness, the beautiful man lying next to her who made all her dreams come true. She was also thinking of her conversation with Magi. The problem with both of us is the same problem shared by all Mexican girls, she thought. We've never known an honest man. She looked over at Gabi, who appeared to be dozing, his head cradled in his arms. She liked what she saw. Magi would approve. She kissed his sandy shoulder.

"I feel like a banana," she murmured.

"What does a banana feel like?"

"Warm, ripe. Carefree. I could stay here with you forever."

Gabi kept his head buried in his arms. "Yes, it's been like a dream. And I don't want this dream to end."

Candelaria wrote her name across his warm back with her fingertip. "There is someone special I'd like you to meet when we get back."

"Of course, *mi amor*."

"Do you think you could ever get away on a Sunday?"

"Impossible!" He said it emphatically, but with a friendly laugh and he rolled over on his back. He kissed the tip of her nose. "That is the one day my father demands that I be at his side. Sunday is his day. He won't let go."

She was about to suggest she would like to go up with him and meet his family, but she didn't want to push it. If she pursued it too vigorously, he could feel pressured and she could lose him. And she didn't want to lose him. Not ever!

Gabi didn't want the conversation to turn serious. He buried his face in her hair. "I think I liked you better as a banana."

As though by previous rehearsal, Candelaria rolled over on her back and received him in her arms. She liked the feel of his warm chest on her breasts. His lips tasted salty. His mouth played with her mouth for a while before he spoke. His voice was low, gentle, almost a caress. "You want some answers, don't you?"

She nodded. "Well, yes."

"Of course you do, and you're entitled to some answers. Am I married? Are you the other woman? Do I love you? Am I right?"

Candelaria answered with her eyes.

"Then let me be as honest with you as I can. You deserve that. I am not married. I have never been married."

Candelaria held her breath to keep from sighing. She just got the answer to her biggest question. His words removed the sharp thistle of doubt she'd been carrying in her heart.

Gabi continued in the same even voice. "Do I love you?"

"Do you?"

They held each other with their eyes. "I don't know. I know you are becoming an important part of my life. But is it a purely sexual thing or is it real love? I honestly don't know."

"You've been honest with me." Candelaria could feel her whole body relax. "I can't ask you for any more than that. I guess I'm just jealous of your life away from me on the Other Side."

Gabi buried his face in her breasts. His voice came close to breaking. "I can't, I just can't explain right now—"

"Sssh. Don't say any more, *mi amor*." She stopped his words with a kiss. "I love you and I trust you. I don't need to know any more than that."

In a sudden playful change of mood, Gabi slapped her *nalgas* and they raced each other up the beach to a *palápa*. They sat under the palm thatching and sipped a margarita while they watched the sun expire in flames over the Pacific.

Monday melted into Tuesday, and Tuesday was already a blur beyond memory. Wednesday was washed away by

Thursday, and on Friday paradise perished. On this their last night, Candelaria and Gabi left their clothing on their beach blanket and walked naked hand in hand across the ribbed sand that sloped down to the water, now covered with slivers of grated silver. They could see the silhouettes of the two stone lovers reaching out for one another, separated by the jealous sea.

They splashed and laughed and played in the warm water like two children taking their bath together. Time stopped. Then, as though by some unspoken arrangement, they headed back up the beach and stood facing each other in phosphorescent water foaming around their knees. Their arms went out at the same instant and they were clinging to each other in a desperate embrace against time. He held on to her so tightly she thought he would crush her. He made a low sound. For a moment Candelaria thought she heard him choke back a sob. Then his mouth found hers. Slowly, he slipped down and licked away the glistening droplets of sea-water beaded on her skin.

Together they dropped down on their blanket. Gabi covered her wet body with his own. Candelaria looked up at a million burning sapphires. She closed her eyes and listened to the voices of the sea. It was so beautiful she thought she was going to cry. She was so close. So close. She wanted to get there. To the other side of Time. It was getting dreamy. Then suddenly she found eternity in one shuddering impulse of her soul.

"*Hola,* Magi, can you stand some company?" Candelaria was so ecstatic she was shouting into the phone.

Magi pulled the instrument away from her ear. "Hey Candi! When did you get back from your honeymoon?"

"Ay Magi! We got back yesterday."

"I would love to see you. I'm dying for another episode of the Blue Prince. It's better than television."

"Magi, you're terrible. He's taking me to Acapulco next month and he told me to buy some clothes. I thought we could go to Fashion Valley Mall together."

"*Magnífico!* When do you want to go?"

"Saturday would work for me. I can even stay over if I won't be in the way of your Irish *novio*."

"As a matter of fact, I'm all alone this weekend. Patrick is at a Catholic retreat and little David is spending the weekend with friends. I'll pick you up at the bus station."

"*Magnífico! Hasta pronto.*"

By ten-thirty Saturday night the two best friends were already in their nightshirts. They were exhausted. Magi's bed was covered with new clothes. Candelaria bought a black one-piece swimsuit cut high in the leg with a zipper front, and a vibrant red two-piece that would require major tonsorial attention before she could wear it on a public beach. She found three sundresses, two sets of shorts with matching tops, and three pairs of raffia espadrilles. The two girls were admiring everything all over again.

"It's a funny thing about new clothes. They always look better when you get them home."

"It seems to me you bought everything in the stores."

"I'm afraid I spent nearly everything he gave me—five hundred dollars!"

"Ay *por Dios!* And how did the Blue Prince manage to get a whole week off?"

"We leave on Monday and return on Saturday."

"And have you met his family?"

"Well, not yet. You're still suspicious, aren't you?"

"Of course I'm suspicious. You've been living together for six months. Why is he keeping you a secret?"

"You can put away your doubts. I think he's going to ask me to marry him."

"Ay Candi, that's wonderful! Has he actually asked you?"

"He hasn't put it into words yet, but I can tell he has something on his mind. He was asking me if I had a passport."

Magi put her arms around her best friend. "Oh, Candi, forgive me. I've become a distrustful, cynical woman who suspects everything and everybody. I'm so happy for you." She squeezed her tighter.

The two girls admired the new things all over again, then, high on exhilarating exhaustion, dropped into bed and turned out the lights.

"You're happy, aren't you, Candi?"

"I have never been so happy in my life. He fills the hollow places in my soul."

"I'm so glad for you. You deserve it."

"Do you know what it means to be fulfilled?"

"I think so."

"I even love the sound of my name on his lips. Are you going to tell me I'm being silly?"

No answer.

Magi was sound asleep, and in the next breath Candi joined her in dreams.

The church of Saint Bonifacio on Ivy Street in San Diego was crammed to overflowing. "You would think it was Easter! Is it always like this?" Candelaria asked as they ran up the stairs.

"There must be something special going on. We may have some difficulty finding a place together. Follow me."

"I can always wait outside."

"Follow me!"

They didn't really find a place. They *made* a place at the end of the penultimate row. The air was heavy with the smell of two hundred people, flowers, incense, candle wax, and piety. Candelaria could feel her nose plug up. She couldn't see anything that was going on. The Mass was said in English and she immediately turned off all her senses, the rote so ingrained she could go through the motions of any Mass without thought. Her mind drifted off to Cabo San Lucas, the warm sun, the kisses, making love on the beach that night when the sand was coated with silver. It wasn't until during the Elevation of the Host that she came back to her pew at Saint Bonifacio.

"Magi, I don't feel so good. I'm going outside."

"Ssh!"

"Magi, I'm going to be sick!"

Candelaria ran from the church followed by a hundred eyes. She made it to the front doors, ran into the fresh air, and gasped for breath. She still had her arms around a eucalyptus tree when Magi found her.

"Candi! What is it?" Magi put her arms around her. My God, she thought, she's pregnant.

Candelaria could hardly talk. She spoke to Magi in gasps. "I'm—I'm sorry I made a such a scene. Is Mass over?"

"Yes, I just took communion and came right back to look for you. Candi, what is the matter with you?"

Candelaria burst into tears. "The man who gave you the flesh of our Lord is El Principe Azúl."

A Man of Common Sense

There are no strangers in Tecate. Everybody knows everybody. You could ask anyone on the street about Albino Reyes de P. Mendoza and they would tell you, "There goes a practical man." Albino himself would agree. He saw himself as a practical man. A man of common sense. He drove a practical car, wore practical shoes. He was neither tall nor short. He was fair of face. No mustache. Just wouldn't be practical. His hair was thick black curly wool. He kept it cropped short. Practical, you know. His ears, a little larger than necessary for their intended purpose, the wide nostrils and the smooth muzzle, gave him a remarkable resemblance to a sheared Suffolk lamb.

Albino Reyes de P. Mendoza had a good wife, attentive, obedient, docile, subservient, and manageable. All the qualities a good Mexican wife should possess. She also made very good tortillas. He had three good kids, and, more or less, a pretty good job. But Albino was also an unfortunate man. The source of all his misery was his common sense; he knew the difference between how things were done and how things *should* be done. Predictably, this unfortunate insight brought him into daily conflict in his human relationships in Tecate. Albino had one other tiny flaw in his character that contributed to his malaise. He was vocal about it and this may have been the main cause for his substance abuse. Albino had a serious dependency on cherry-flavored Mylanta New Stronger Formula antacid for fast relief of heartburn, acid indigestion, and sour stomach. He suffered from a chronic gastroesophageal reflux disorder that robbed him of the basic human impulse to sing in the shower, smile at children, smell the flowers, and other simple pleasures.

He sat at a small table in the kitchen grousing into a cup of coffee. His ideal Mexican wife, still in her blue robe, with her hair pulled back and tied with a red hair bow, put a plate of sweet breads in front of him along with a full bottle of cherry-flavored Mylanta.

"I'll fix you some oatmeal." Maria began the procedure, it seemed to Albino, by banging every pot and pan in the kitchen and slamming the refrigerator door unnecessarily. The stomping of her carpet slippers was excruciating.

"Don't bother with the oatmeal. Who can eat? I didn't sleep the whole night. On the Other Side they have zoning regulations, you know. We wouldn't have a body shop next door. Not here in Mexico, oh no, here I have to listen to an idiot pounding out a fender at four in the morning." He shook the first pink tablet of the day out of the bottle, crunched, and washed it down with a swallow of coffee.

Maria made no comment. After nearly twenty years of marriage she knew to let him run his course.

"Then the idiot behind us turns on his grinders to start

making the day's tortillas. On the Other Side these shops would be confined to commercial areas. We wouldn't have to suffer heavy industry right next door. Believe me, I know what I'm talking about. I've lived there."

Maria heard this complaint every morning for the nine years they lived in this house. She was careful to utter no sound, display no movement, offer no gesture however subtle, that could be misunderstood to imply encouragement to continue his litany. No point in lighting the way for the Devil.

Albino broke the sweet roll, took a bite, and nearly gagged. "Where did you get this bread, señora? Don't tell me. Only El Panadero Gomez could make bread this bad. I've told you not to buy his bread."

Maria, like any wife, easily anticipated every mood of her husband. She already had two warm tortillas and a pat of butter in front of him. "And yet yesterday's bread was good. You said so yourself."

"That's the problem. El Panadero Gomez is a moody man and his bread invariably takes on the flavor of his disposition. One bite of his bread and I can tell you his humor at the hour that he made it."

Maria answered with no answer. Why throw more kindling on the flames?

Albino finished his breakfast and rose from the table. "I'll see you tonight," he grumbled, stashing the bottle of Mylanta in his pocket.

Maria did not kiss him. She put her hand on his forehead and drew the sign of the cross in the air in front of him. *"Dios te bendiga."*

Albino ignored his next-door neighbor who was still

hammering out the crumpled fender of a Toyota that looked like it had been in a couple of street fights. He got in his own Chevrolet, born in 1976, the same year as his oldest son, Albino Chico. He left a trail of pungent blue smoke behind him as he pulled out.

He wasn't looking forward to going to work. Working for the city of Tecate was a secure job, paid all right by Mexican standards. It had other benefits too. If he stuck it out for twenty-five years, he would receive a miserable pension that might cover the cost of a kilo of meat if there were no more currency devaluations. And that was about as remote as the Mexican army retaking California and hoisting the flag in the Presidio at San Francisco. But by observing people who were worse off, he considered himself in good shape.

But the job! The very thought was enough to incite his sensitive stomach to rise up in rebellion like the insurgents at Chapultepec and attack his vital organs with fire and flare. Here he was, nearly forty years old, come within a fingertip of becoming an engineer, and he was the assistant—yes, the *assistant*—to Cosme Carranza, Director of Public Works, who didn't know his *nalgas* from his *codos*. If it hadn't been for the devaluation of the peso, he thought, I would have graduated with my credential as *ingeniero* and I would be the *directór*. He pulled into a parking place in the municipal yard and raised his face toward heaven. "God, I swear to you, my son will finish his engineering studies if I have to go beg in the plaza!"

A short walk brought him to the door of his office. It was a huge steel door on casters. He slid it open, walked into the dark warehouse, and went immediately to his desk, a four-by-eight sheet of plywood supported by two stacks of El Gallo cement. The only thing on his desk was a layer of fine white dust and a stack of work orders in a plastic in-box held together with a wooden clothespin. There was no out-box.

He riffled through the papers and headed toward his boss's private office. To Albino it looked like the throne room in Maximiliano's palace. Cosme Carranza, Diréctor de Obras Públicas, sat behind a walnut conference desk the size of a soccer field. The leather tufted swivel chair with an eight-foot back seemed to reduce the size of the occupant, who, if he stood on a box, could scarcely reach a doorknob owing to some genetic practical joke. The director's feet dangled idly a few inches above the floor, his big nose, in constant danger of chafing, barely clearing the top of the leather-edged desk blotter. There was an in-box and an out-box in a walnut finish. And something else Albino didn't have. A telephone.

"*Buenos dias.*"

"*Buenos dias,*" Cosme answered. He slurped at his coffee and drew out a pack of cigarettes. "Change of plan this morning."

"What is it?"

"I want you to take a crew out and find every *pinchi* pothole between here and the border and pack them with dirt. I'm getting too many complaints."

"Let's do it right for a change. Let me take a load of asphalt out there and stop the complaints."

"No, no, dirt is good enough."

Good enough! Jesus! he thought. Is that the limit of the municipal mentality? "Believe me, Cosme, it's the same amount of time and manpower and effort. And the job gets done right."

"And just where do we get the asphalt?

"There's a mountain of it obstructing part of the playground at Tierrasanta school. The sisters have been begging us to get it out of there."

"We can't use that. That's earmarked for the new bridge to Colonia Juarez."

"That bridge is a local fable. Those poor people have to wade through water up to their *nalgas* to get to their homes. It's been like that since I can remember."

"You're starting to sound like one of those *pinchi* complaining residents. For your information, the state government has announced plans to start on the bridge, and we will have the responsibility to pave it."

"But we both know they'll never get around to it. In the meantime we can have decent streets."

The phone rang at that moment. The *directór* picked it up and waved him away like a housefly. The rude dismissal started a small fire somewhere in the vicinity of Albino's belt buckle. He knew when he had lost a battle. He munched the second Mylanta of the morning and headed out to the yard. He walked to the end of the chain-link fence. He recognized his men swarming over a fish taco pushcart that rolled in every morning.

"Chito! Nestor, Pablo, get over here. We have to go to work."

The three men responded to the summons and came over to him with their tacos. *"Buenos dias, jefe,"* they all greeted.

"I'm not so sure. The three of you grab shovels and get in the pickup. We're filling potholes on Revolución today."

Albino went over to a green Mitsubishi pickup truck with the great municipal seal painted on the door, got in, and started the engine. In a few minutes his men were back. Two carried shovels, and Chito held a push broom, the bristles worn down to the wood.

"*Cabrón!* How much dirt do you think you can shovel with a broom?"

"We could only find two shovels," Pablo explained for all of them.

"All right, all right! The two of you get in the back. Chito, get rid of the broom and get us some water so we can be on our way. It's going to be like the Sahara out there today."

Nestor and Pablo made one last run to the taco cart and jumped in the bed of the pickup. Chito showed up with a Styrofoam cooler, placed it behind the passenger seat, got in, and closed the door in three bangs.

"*Vamonos!*" Chito sang.

"To the devil," Albino answered, and they drove out of the yard.

They drove out to one of the many *colonias* with dirt streets that terminate in vacant land where tall weeds flourish and effectively hide the beer bottles strewn across the fields like land mines. Nestor and Pablo began at once to shovel dirt into the pickup. Albino read his newspaper. Chito sat in the passenger seat, looking out like a supervisor. When Albino felt his impatience start over the edge, he commanded Chito to go take alternate turns at the shovel with the other two. By the time Albino got to the sports page, the truck was full. The men took their customary places and they headed for Avenida Revolución, the northernmost street in Tecate that parallels the U.S. Mexican border.

Albino brought them to the east end of the avenue, found the first pothole, and stopped. The men jumped out and began to pack the holes with dirt. This end of the street had so many it was useless to get back in the truck to go to the next one. Albino crawled and stopped at each one. The men followed behind on foot and filled them in. Some chuckholes were not much bigger than a dinner plate, but most of them were deep enough to snap an axle, and there were a few that were navigable in winter.

They worked their way west. It was hot as a kiln in the truck. Albino got out. It was cooler out here and he could watch his crew.

"Nestor! Pack it in tight, *cabrón*. What you're doing won't last the day." Why did he have to supervise such stupid people! "Pablo, look what you're doing! Take the rocks out of the hole first before you fill it. And you, Chito, when you get tired of watching, why don't you take a turn?" God help me!

They were coming up to Calle Cardenas, the only street that leads to the U.S. border crossing, and traffic began to back up like a laundry sink as the cars got caught behind the slow-moving crew. Occasionally an intrepid driver would swing around them in order to pass. Some made comment.

"That's right, fill them in with dirt so you can do it again tomorrow, *buey*!"

Now, as we've seen, Albino was a sensitive man, and being called an ox by a member of the same species did not sweeten his disposition. A Yaqui dart dipped in curare embedded in his flesh could not have been more painful.

"Stop putting our taxes in your pocket and go out and buy some asphalt!" some wise *cabrón* yelled as he turned toward the border.

A taxi passed in the opposite direction, giving the passenger a clean shot. "Viva Mexico!"

The drive-by insults became too much for Albino and he decided to get back in the pickup. He would bake like a clay pot, but it was better than providing a live target for the benefit of stupid idiots. *He* knew how it was supposed to be done!

Albino saw a car full of Americans come slowly by, heading west. They were all gaping, unquestionably fascinated by the procedure they saw in progress. Albino knew the Americans would never say anything, but he knew exactly what they were thinking. He turned his head in the other direction to hide his embarrassment.

By the time they gained the intersection, the sweet strains of "Ave Maria" floated across the town to announce meridian, and the noonday pile-up began to stack up on all the cross streets.

A police car arrived on the scene with blue and red lights strobing. The cop parked in the middle of the street and walked over to Albino. "The gringos must be mad at us again. They're slowing down the line just to create a traffic jam. I'll hold the traffic back for you while you get across the intersection."

"*Gracias*," Albino answered in a tone that was as much thanks as it was fury.

The men piled into the pickup and Albino started the engine. At least that was his intention. He turned the key and listened to the starter turn over, but the engine refused to come to life. "*Madre!*"

"What's wrong?" the fat cop asked.

"The animal is out of *gasolina!*"

"That's the problem with these machines. They're useful but they are addicted to *gasolina*."

Albino didn't like the look of the cop's big, dumb, fat face. The cop probably didn't finish the third grade and here he was being smart-mouth with him, an educated man. Nearly an *ingeniero*! "For your information, señor, none of the gauges work on most municipal vehicles." Put that in your tamale trap and chew it!

The cop blew his whistle, waved his arms, and the cars parted like the Red Sea.

The entire crew climbed out of the truck and began to push the metal carcass with the official city seal on the door while Albino steered. Once across the busy intersection, the crew resumed their task. It was Mylanta time.

The cop came up to Albino carrying a plastic milk jug and a thin hose. "You might as well take a gallon of mine. It all comes out of the same cow."

Albino was grateful for the offer but he did not say *gracias*. He was not in the mood to say *gracias* to anyone. None of this was his fault. He was the victim of *stupidity*! Instead, he laughed louder than required at the cop's joke and this satisfied both parties.

"Chito, get over to the squad car and suck out a gallon."

Albino decided it was time to call a lunch break. The men must be hot and hungry and thirsty.

The pushcart peddlers of Tecate possess the same hunting instincts as a school of barracudas. They can smell a traffic jam from miles away at any given hour of the day. No one can ever go hungry or thirsty in Tecate. In a matter of minutes, carts offering calf-head tacos, cheek, tongue, or brains (sorry, we're out of eyes), bean burritos, fresh fruit, and flavored ices, were swirling in the vicinity. The tamale man rolled in on an oversize tricycle to join the feeding frenzy. A day this bad could only get better, Albino speculated as they dug into the tamales.

But he was wrong.

After the lunch break and a round of cold Fanta paid for by Albino, they prepared to resume their work. Albino fired up the engine and they were off hippity-hoppity like a three-legged bull intending to exit the bullring before the fun turned rowdy.

"*Madre!*"

"What is it?" the crew asked all at once.

"A *pinchi* flat tire is what it is!" Dear God, when will it end? He received no immediate answer.

"Are you going to let me out?"

Albino looked up to see a woman who was about to back her car out of her driveway. Did she hear the profanity? Albino was a gentleman. Quickly, he bit down on his lip in an effort to capture the second obscenity that was about to escape from his mouth. "Ay *perdon*, señora, of course. I will get out of the way immediately. So sorry."

Once again the trio got behind the pickup and pushed while Albino steered the lurching vehicle out of the way. He waved amicably to the señora as she pulled out. She did not wave back.

"Chito, get the jack and the spare."

"*Sí, mi jefe.*"

"Nestor, Pablo, you two will have to walk ahead to the next pothole while we make repairs."

"We have a *problema*," Chito said.

He could feel a painful gush of gastric lava working its

way toward his heart. "I cannot imagine otherwise. What is the problem?"

"We have a jack, but there is no spare."

"Are you sure? I don't believe this."

Albino searched for a spare and concluded that Chito, while not very smart, was at least telling the truth. Maybe it's all a bad dream, he thought. No, his skin was on fire from the relentless sun, he could feel his bones beginning to melt inside his body. He would die here on Avenida Revolución, the victim of stupid idiots! But he saw Chito standing there in front of him with a vacant look in his eyes and a jack in his hands. Indisputable evidence that this was no dream.

"Jack up the vehicle, remove the tire and take it to the nearest *llantéra*, and bring it back." Albino said this in the calmest voice he could affect. He could have been saying "It's nice to be out on a day like this."

Chito recognized the danger hiding within the calm voice. A calmness that precedes the hurricane. He had the tire off but was shy about asking for funds.

Albino dug into his pocket. "I also finance the city. And you might as well come back with a gallon of *gasolina* or we'll never make it back."

"Are you going to let me in my driveway?"

Albino looked up in the direction of the voice. It came from a woman who was intending to turn left into her driveway. *Ay Dios mío*, no more. PLEASE! "I am so sorry, señora, so sorry. *Perdón, perdón! Sí*, of course I will get out of your way immediately. *Perdón!* The boy just took the tire to the *llantéra*. He should only be a tiny minute." He wanted to disappear into one of the potholes and never come out.

"You municipal people are all the same. You throw parties with our money, you don't do your job, and then you come here and discommode the citizens."

Albino searched for a courteous answer and couldn't come up with anything appropriate for a señora. God was not on his side today.

"I'll park on the street. Maybe you will have the kindness to help me with my *mandado*."

"Of course, *inmediatamente!*"

Nestor and Pablo came over immediately and helped Albino unload the woman's groceries from the car and deliver them to her front door.

"*Gracias,*" the señora said, bringing a light frost to a scorching afternoon.

An hour later Chito was back rolling the tire with one hand, holding a jug of *gasolina* in the other. He had the tire back on in minutes. Nestor pulled out the rag that served as a gas cap and emptied the gallon of essential nutrient into the tank.

Albino got behind the wheel. "*Ah que la chingada!*"

"Now what is it?" Chito inquired.

"What is it, Chito?" It was that dangerously calm voice again. "I'll tell you what it is, Chito, let me explain it to you. When there is *gasolina* in the tank, and you hear the starter grind like that, it means *the* madre *won't start!*"

Chito tried to make himself invisible.

"All right, *muchachos*, get out and push this *madre!*"

All three men got behind the pickup and provided enough of a run that Albino was able to pop the clutch and get the *madre* started.

"What's next, *jefe?*" Chito asked as Nestor and Pablo caught up and climbed into the back of the truck.

Albino did not answer. He could feel his intestines twist and squirm like a hungry boa constrictor gripping a wild boar in its coils. He pulled out the pink plastic bottle, put it to his lips, and emptied the entire contents of cherry-flavored tablets directly into his mouth, then ground them to powder.

Without a word of explanation Albino turned left at the next street. He knew exactly what he was going to do. He was going to return to the yard, dump this Mitsubishi *madre* with the city seal, and send the crew home. Next, he was going to walk into Cosme's office and demand reimbursement. Let him try to get it back from the city. Good luck. It was best to let this day end. Let it take its place among all the other horrors of life stored in the farthest corner of the brain where they might never be recalled.

Albino Reyes de P. Mendoza did not resemble a sunbeam when he pulled into his driveway at home. He saw his eleven-year-old son shooting baskets in front of the house. Oh, how he loved that little boy. The sight nearly removed all the bitter taste of the day. He got out of his car and walked toward the house. The man next door wasn't pounding out a fender, but the penetrating smell of lacquer threatened to give Albino a headache. At least the tortilla factory was silent at this hour.

"*Hola*, how's my *campeón?*" he called out to Raulito, who had just put another one through the hoop.

"*Hola, Pápi!*" Little Raulito dribbled over to his father to hug him without missing a bounce. "I'm setting a record. I've made ten in a row, *Pápi*. Now you're about to see number eleven." Raulito spun around and sent one dead center into the hoop. "Now for number twelve!"

"*Muchacho!* You're holding the ball all wrong. Look, one hand here, the other here. More control, see? Now try it."

Raulito followed instructions. The ball traveled smoothly, hit the edge of the hoop and bounced off. Raulito didn't even bother to chase after it. He kicked at the dirt. His eyes filled with youthful tears of frustration he could not vent in the presence of authority.

Albino walked in the house and immediately took refuge in his chair. He had a jackhammer in his head, and a colony of fire ants appeared to be attending a political rally in his digestive tract. Immediate medication was required. Preferably something he could take orally. Maria came into the room with a blouse over one arm. "I'm almost finished here and I'll get your supper on the table."

"You know, if you learned to organize your work, manage your time better, you wouldn't be ironing at six o'clock in the afternoon."

Maria made no answer. She left the room and returned in seconds with a cold Bohemia in an amber bottle. His hand was already in position to receive it. He pressed it to his lips. After twenty years of marriage they could have lost the power of speech totally and it wouldn't have made a lot of difference. They communicated remarkably well through a complex network of airborne vectors known only to the married.

The cold beer subdued the fire ants and laid unction to his troubled soul. "Where's Socorro?"

"She's at a friend's house." Maria called out from the kitchen. "They're doing their homework together."

"Why can't she do her *tarea* here at home?"

"Now, you know how fourteen-year-old girls are. They have fun doing their homework together."

"Fun! Since when does schoolwork have to be fun?"

"As long as they get their work done, what does it matter?"

"These kids today! They think life is going to be one big

Disneylandia. They'll find out. And Raulito is out shooting baskets. Can I assume he's done his *tarea*?"

"He's finished with his work. I told him he could play outdoors until you got home. Then it's bath time."

"And I suppose Albino Chico has a class tonight?"

"Yes, he does." True, Albino Chico did have a class in Tijuana tonight. He also had a *novia* that would keep him out after midnight. But there was no point in going into that. "I had to give him money for *gasolina*." She did not ask for reimbursement. Her instincts told her that in his present mood, this was not within an acceptable range of practical politics.

"And I had to do the same thing for the city today." He took another long pull on the bottle. "At least Albino Chico takes his studies seriously. He's going to make a fine *ingeniero*." Albino finished his beer, got up, and went into the bathroom.

Raulito was standing at the door in his underwear with his towel, ready to go in when Albino came out. He gave his father a forgiving smile. Albino rumpled his hair affectionately, and now it was his eyes that filled. Raulito would get over it by tomorrow, *he* would never get over it.

"I'm going out for a while, Maria."

Maria knew where he was going and when he would be back. Long after everyone in the house was sound asleep. They read their lines to each other from their silent scripts.

Don't drink too much and don't get back too late.

I'm going to have one small glass of wine. I shouldn't be too late.

Albino headed out the door.

On the north side of the plaza, in the opposite direction of La Fonda and the Diana, stands the most remarkable can-

tina in Tecate. Maybe in all Mexico. Maybe even in the
Third World. It is right next door to the Cine Tecate, our
pueblo's only movie house, with eight hundred seats, no pro-
jectors, and no movies. It was toward this cantina that Albino
Reyes de P. Mendoza now migrated. The sign above the door
reads:

CANTINA EL HIGADO CONTENTO
Cayetano Mesa, Prop.

The Contented Liver Cantina has no windows. You enter
through a splintered wooden door that appears to have been
removed from an old house by a wrecking crew. Once inside,
even the casual observer would notice the dissimilarity to
other wine shops. The first thing that becomes apparent is the
absence of a bar. You might reasonably conclude that you
mistakenly walked into someone's living room. Two pseudo-
Victorian sofas, presently in molting, face each other across a
knotty pine coffee table. One is covered with a brocade the
color of cooked spinach, the other in a red plush once popular
in bordellos of the Mexican revolutionary period. At one end
is a massive morris chair, ugly and lumpy, that guarantees its
occupant low-back pain. It is said that it was donated by the
local chiropractor. An even uglier platform rocker encloses
the other end of the "conversation group." Similar groupings
of mismatched Goodwill furniture are arranged along the
length of the cantina. Lighting is provided by a number of
atrocious Tiffany lamps dripping red and amber and green
beads. A lighted vitrine in the French style displays an
apothecary jar wherein floats a human liver that Cayetano
Mesa, prop., claims to be his own.

The walls are decorated with stylized human liver cartoon characters. They have arms and legs and happy faces or grouchy faces, depending on the caption.

A boy liver says to a very pretty girl liver in a yellow frock: "Did I ever tell you, you look great in yellow?"

On the another wall is a big liver saying to a little liver: "Of course I'm bigger. Priests require a bigger supply of bile!"

The cartoon behind the sofa shows a liver with a huge goblet in his hand. He points upward. "That's nothing, mine has four-on-the-floor and a 2.5 liter gullet!"

There must be dozens of these cartoons. You could spend a good part of the evening just browsing. The cantina is quite low-key. It never gets rowdy. And yet no woman has even been seen within the homey atmosphere of the Contented Liver. It may be the fact that there is no ladies' room. There is but one rest room, and word of this may have gotten around Tecate. There's another cartoon on the door. A little blob with a fierce grimace, intended to represent a bursting bladder, appears to be in tears. Next to this is a cartoon figure of a liver who is saying: "Why are you complaining? At least you'll get some relief."

Albino groped his way through the gloom and found his friends gathered over a bottle of the special house *vino tinto*, a robust ruby red vinegar posing as Burgundy. He assumed the hostile morris chair.

"*Hola!* We were just starting to wonder about you."

"Let me pour you a glass."

"You look like you've had a hard day."

Albino took a sip and immediately felt the gradual discharge of his overloaded magnetic field. These were his friends. They understood. It was a congenial collection of old comfortable friends who came to the Contented Liver and stayed late in an effort to escape the blanket lecture that usually began as soon as they were under the covers of the matrimonial bed. Present at this evening's symposium were the lawyer, the doctor, and the dentist, who shared a sofa. Seated opposite were the temperamental baker, the auto mechanic, and the foreman from the electric power company.

"What a day," Albino sighed. "A total dismother."

"Forget your day. That's why we're here, no?" *el licenciado* remarked, but then lawyers have a tendency toward the interrogative phrase. "I was just complaining to the group here that wherever I go, somebody wants free legal advice. Even if I'm at a party, someone will always get me in a corner and tell me his case to see what I suggest."

"That's true of all professions," *el doctor* answered, draining his glass.

"How do you handle it?" *el licenciado* asked.

"Very simple. I tell them to take their clothes off."

"That's *magnífico*! I think I'll try that next time."

"How can you do that? You're a dentist."

"Still, it could work," *el dentista*, now well basted, answered hopefully. His marriage knot was coming unraveled and he was known to have several extramarital friendships. He didn't have a very large practice, and this could be, at least in part, because no one in Tecate had ever seen him sober.

Albino turned to *el panadero*. "What did you do to your bread today? It tasted like you made it with burro dung."

"Is *that* what it was! My wife gave it to the dog," *el mecánico* chimed in. "I took the dog to the *veterinario* this morning."

"I had a fight with my mother-in-law," *el panadero* confessed. "I haven't spoken to her in six weeks."

"Six weeks!" several ejaculated simultaneously.

"She gets furious if I interrupt her."

"I'll remind my wife not to buy your bread tomorrow."

"Tomorrow's bread will be nothing less than delectable." *El panadero* kissed his fingertips with a loud smack to give emphasis to his meaning. "The old viper left for Guadalajara this morning and my *vieja* went with her."

A phone rang. Cayetano Mesa, prop., put down the glass he was polishing. "It's for you, Doctor."

El doctor left his friends to answer the call. Chispas Gutierrez suddenly came to life. He was a maintenance foreman for the electric power company in town, and it was only natural that his friends all knew him as Sparky. "Bring us another bottle of poison," Chispas called out to the proprietor, and turned to Albino. "Didn't I see you with your crew today filling potholes with dirt?"

"*Por favor!* I'm here to forget today—to erase the events from memory forever. And are you the smart *cabrón* who yelled out "*Viva Mexico*'?"

"I swear to God, I did not. But what's the matter with you people?"

"*Por favor!* Don't say 'you people.' I am not in charge. If I were the *directór*, the streets would be repaired with asphalt, the bridge would be finished, the traffic lights would work—everything would be done right."

El doctor returned to his friends.

"Anything important?" *el dentista* asked.

"The Holy See. She always knows where to find me." *El doctor* poured himself a refill and continued along the theme in progress. "I don't understand the mentality at city hall. There is an open trench running halfway across Avenida Hidalgo, and it's been eating up cars for weeks. What's the problem?"

"The problem is that the great *director* is a dumb *cabrón*. It was opened for the water department to make repairs. If I were the *director* it wouldn't be ripped open until the water crew was standing there. And it would be closed as soon as they finished. It's just a matter of common sense!"

"But every problem has a solution," *el licenciado* insisted.

"Of course!" Albino agreed. "But you need brains to see it. Listen, Albino Chico, my twenty-year-old son in his first year of engineering school, already knows more than Cosme Carranza, the great *director*."

"Why don't they put you in charge?"

"Politics! The man actually shimmers with stupidity, but he's somebody's *compadre* so he gets the job."

"Of course, the standard tragedy down here! That's why nothing can ever be done right," *el licenciado* lamented.

"All it takes is a little common sense, I repeat. But he won't let me do anything my way. Jealous. He's afraid I'll make him look bad."

"You should do something about the trash pickup. They haven't picked up at my house for two weeks."

"It's been three weeks in my *colonia*."

"What is this, National Dump Caca on Albino Day?"

"No, no, we're your friends. Here, let me refill your glass." *El mecánico* poured. "Let's talk about something else—beautiful women!"

Chispas could not adjust to the sudden change of theme. "I wish your *director* would do something about our power pole over on Calle Nayarit. The curve is too sharp, and every Saturday night somebody who's had a couple of *copas* too many plows into the pole. The whole town goes dark and they get me out of bed to restore service. I'll bet you we replace a utility pole every week."

"Why did you install the pole in the tightest part of the curve?" Albino asked.

"There was no other place to put it. But certainly there has to be a solution."

"Of course! There is a solution for everything. All it takes is a little of this," Albino pointed to his head, "and a little of this." He pointed to his heart.

"What would you do?"

"The simplest solution would be to build a low wall all along the curve. This would protect the pedestrians and the shopkeepers as well as your utility pole. Nothing extraordinary, just plain common sense!"

"That's very good! The drivers would quickly learn they can't take that curve at full speed, and no more power failures."

"I told you I'm a problem solver. But I'm not the *director*."

"Just one moment! We are all forgetting just one thing." *El licenciado* began his opening argument.

"What's that?"

"We are in the land of the *compadres*. We are not fixable. Whatever solution you come up with, Albino, the incestuous system will betray you. That's why nothing works and never will. I don't care how you fix it. As long as we straddle a braying ass and see a white charger, disaster is guaranteed."

"What a pessimist you are!" they all declared at once.

"Objection! I'm a realist. Look around you. When we repair a water line in one place, a leak pops up in another. You can't win!"

"You're such a pessimist that if you heard Mexico's monetary crisis was over, you'd be afraid it might be true," *el dentista* accused.

"No, no. Let me give you an example. The city recently erected a steel pedestrian bridge across the highway, right? They installed traffic signals. That was intended to keep cars and people from tangling up with one another, right?"

"A sensible solution!"

"Except nobody uses the bridge. They solved the wrong problem! Our pedestrians cross the streets like cows who have just seen green grass. They have never been taught to cross a street or trained to use the bridge. My little second-grade nephews on the Other Side understand traffic lights better than any adult in Tecate. On top of that, there is no such thing as driver education down here. If you have fifty pesos, you've got a driver's license. No written test, no driving test. So the money is spent in the wrong place and the problem continues." This impassioned speech left the speaker thirsting for a draft of liver tonic. He drained his glass and summed up his case for the prosecution. "Nothing is going to change. I don't care what you do, it won't work! Gentlemen, I rest my case!"

The next morning was no different from yesterday morning for Albino. No sleep, burning indigestion, and sweet rolls a mentally challenged pig would refuse for fear of hog scours. Maria gave Albino His blessing, a fresh bottle of Mylanta, and he left for work.

Albino went directly to his desk as usual, and found it listing dangerously. I can't believe this! he thought. Some stupid *cabrón* needed a bag of cement, and he took one off the stack that supports my desk. Not a good omen. Albino prepared for another bad day. He took a sheaf of work orders and walked to the director's big office. He popped three

Mylantas en route and prepared for the worst. But once again he was wrong. Fate, it appears, took an unexpected turn to the right.

"*Buenos dias*, Albino."

"*Buenos dias*," Albino replied as he sat down. The tone denied meaning to the words.

"I have to go to Mexico City. "I'll be gone a week. You will have to manage without me, look after things in my absence."

Albino was momentarily struck dumb by this piece of news.

"You don't really have to do anything. I have all the work orders and a schedule all made out for you."

Still nothing came out of Albino's mouth, but a lot of dialogue was running through his head. Of course, I'm just another dumb peon. I won't even be required to think. Just go out there and do the same stupid things we've been doing.

"Don't look so tense. You can manage for a few days. I leave on Monday and return the following Monday. I don't think you can get into too much trouble in seven days."

Albino was momentarily dazzled by a sudden flash of celestial light. This was as a message from God! He nearly shot out of his chair like a skyrocket. It took all the strength at his disposal to force back a smile that threatened to stretch his face to the point of pain if he didn't do something to control it. His whole body was celebrating. He had to hold on to his chair to restrain himself from turning cartwheels and leaping, backward double flips. He wanted to burst into song, and scream and shout, and yell, and dance on the ceiling! He wanted to set off a Roman candle! He took a firmer grip on his chair in an effort to control his ecstasy. "We'll try to get by as best we can in your absence," he said in a gray voice that barely tethered his joy.

Monday morning Albino woke early and bright-eyed. The body shop next door and the grinding tortilla mill in back did not invade his sleep. Maria had his coffee waiting for him when he walked in the kitchen and a new bottle of cherry-flavored Mylanta tablets in front of him.

Albino pushed the jar away. "I will not be requiring those today." He bit down hungrily on a fresh roll. "Hmmm! The sweet rolls are wonderful this morning, *mi amor*," he crooned, as though giving her full credit.

"Yes, *el panadero* must have been in a happy mood yesterday. Why so early?"

"This is the week of the creation."

"What are you talking about?"

"I have seven days to re-create Tecate!" Albino stood by the kitchen door to receive his wife's blessing and went out with a light heart. If the fender pounder next door had been listening he would have heard Albino humming a stirring battle hymn.

I am saddled. I am mounted.
The reins of leadership have been thrust upon me.
Sword in hand I lead the crusade against mediocrity!

"*Buenos dias,*" the work crews called out in unison as he drove into the municipal yard.

"Where is Nestor?"

"At the fish taco cart."

"Send him in to me right away."

By the time Albino sat at the director's desk and began

to peruse the work orders, Nestor was standing in front of him dripping red sauce from a fish taco. "You need me, *jefe?*"

"Yes, I want you to put two crews together and fill potholes today."

"We just did that a couple days ago. The dirt should last at least a week."

"But today you're going to fill them with asphalt."

"Where are we going to get *asfalto?*"

"There is a mountain of it in the playground at the Tierrasanta school. The sisters will be glad to see it removed."

"I thought that was for the new bridge."

"First we answer the sisters' prayer, then we can all pray for the new bridge."

Nestor looked at the work orders. "This is every street in Tecate. You want all this by the end of the week?"

"We only have eight paved streets, Nestor."

Nestor took his orders and his dripping taco out to the yard and began immediately to assemble two work crews. If he had been paying attention, he would have heard a diabolical laugh similar to that uttered by Pancho Villa when he declared war on Mexico.

Now the fun begins! Albino picked up the phone and rang Sanitation. "*Buenos dias*, let me speak with Chuy, please."

"Who is calling?" a woman's voice, officious, challenging.

Chuy must think he is the *Presidente de la República.* "Albino Reyes de P. Mendoza."

"Oh, *buenos dias*, Albino. Chuy is out. Can I do anything for you?"

Albino! Where does this woman acquire her insolence? he wondered. And why is she addressing me in the chummy 'tu'? Albino had no doubt as to Chuy's whereabouts. At this hour he would be holding court over coffee and rolls at the coffee shop across the street, and he would be there until noon.

"What did you have on your mind, Albino?"

She must think she's talking to some peon. "Have him call me as soon as you see him. I'm on the director's phone."

"And should I tell him what this is regarding?" Her voice climbed the scale like a flute.

Albino dipped his voice in amaretto. "Oh yes, please, if you would be so kind. Tell him there's no rush. It's regarding his paycheck. And by the way, we have been ordered to make some cutbacks. He may have to give up his secretary." He covered his mouth to prevent another spasm of diabolical laughter from escaping.

"*Oh, sí, Señor Albino*! I'll have him return your call the moment I locate him. *Sí, señor, gracias, sí, Señor Albino.*"

Albino put down the phone with a gap-toothed grin reminiscent of the perverted Garfield when he's contemplating a nasty prank. Now it was *Señor* Albino. And it was *usted*. He barely had time to mambo over to the coffeepot and back when the phone rang.

"Albino! Albino, old friend, how are you? I don't get the opportunity to talk to you very often. *Que onda?*" Chuy's words came through a wad of cake and a swirl of coffee. He may have been running. He was puffing.

"I'll tell you *que onda*. The *director* has gone to Mexico City and I'm taking over for him." Albino was careful not to reveal the duration of his improvisatorial command. These dumb *cabrones* could twiddle their mustaches for a week. "We're going to have to install additional phone lines to handle all the complaints. The trash trucks don't get around on their appointed days. Some *colonias* claim you haven't had a truck out there in several weeks. What's the *problema?*"

"Oh, is that all? No problem, Albino. We'll get it caught up. Don't worry yourself. I'll take it up with Cosme later over a *copa*. How long will he be away?"

A gush of exasperated breath escaped Albino's pursed lips. That's exactly why this town looks the way it does, he thought. You have to talk to these *cabrones* in a language they can understand.

"You don't understand. Cosme is in Mexico City for an undetermined period. I'm taking over in his absence."

"Oh."

"I want every trash truck in the fleet out in the *colonias* picking up. I want all five *colonias* done by the end of the week. You can do one a day."

"I just don't know if we can get all that done."

He still doesn't seem to grasp my full meaning, Albino thought. "Chuy, remember a few months back when the pay-checks were a couple of days late?"

"Yes, I remember. What a nightmare."

"Well, if one single citizen calls in and says his trash barrels have not been emptied, the paychecks are going to disappear for a couple of weeks." Suck on *that* one!

"We're starting immediately, Señor Albino!"

Oh, what a beautiful morning! Oh what a beautiful day! Albino could have put the thought to music.

In a dark corner at the other end of the Public Works building, a stout little man who had nothing to do and all day to do it, sat reading the morning paper. He had a cup of coffee in his left hand, a cigarette smoldering between yellow knuckles. His phone rang. He put down *El Mexicano* and picked up. "*No! Sí? No!* I can't believe it. *No! Sí? No!* Thanks for the warning." My God! the director was in Mexico City and there was a monster loose in the municipality!

Only nine-thirty in the morning and word was starting to get around.

The stout little man almost snapped a salute, sending his coffee all over the floor when the monster walked into view. "*Buenos dias*, Albino, can I get you a coffee?"

"*Gracias.*"

"Can I get you a newspaper, a sweet roll, a chair, a *chamaca?*"

"*Gracias.* Pablo, we are getting more than the usual complaints from the citizens of Tecate. Streetlights go out and the bulbs are never replaced. They claim their streets are dark as a cave. I know mine is."

"We do the best we can with what we've got, Albino. I can't replace bulbs if I don't have them. Look around. See any lightbulbs? When I ask for them, they tell me there's no money left in the budget. What can I do?"

"Follow me."

Pablo waddled behind Albino to the director's soccer field desk. Albino pulled out a form, filled it in, signed it, and handed it to Pablo. "This is an authorization for the purchase of one hundred lightbulbs." The Great Municipal Seal was imprinted on every word. "Get them in here, and get them installed before the end of the week."

"Did you say the end of the week?"

"You spend too much time in Rocco's Disco. The noise is beginning to damage your auditory nerve. *End of the week!*"

"I'm on my way."

"Oh, by the way, Pablo."

"Yes?"

"That traffic light on the corner of Revolución and Cardenas. It's cockeyed. Both streets get a green light at the same time. Take care of it."

It was a wonderful feeling. Albino was just beginning to see how much you could get done with a little initiative and a few lies. It was going to be easier than he thought. Just tell these *cabrones* what you want done and hold a threat over their heads, and they respond like trained pigs.

Every morning Albino danced into the director's office, took the seat of power, and continued his march against ineptitude. Every afternoon he would drive through the town to check and see that things got done. Next morning he would begin his crusade again. He was so tired and so amply rewarded by the end of the day he hardly had time to put in an appearance at the Contented Liver. Also, he was having too much fun!

Albino picked up the phone and dialed a number.

"*Buenos dias*, this is the Water Department."

"Let me speak with Enrique, *por favor*."

"I'm sorry, he's not here."

"I expected he wouldn't be. Please have him call Albino at the municipality."

"Should I tell him what this is regarding?"

"By all means. His job." Albino was just in the act of putting down the phone.

"He just walked in the door!"

"*Buenos dias*, Albino. And what can I do for *you?*" It was a rhythmic voice spoken in salsa tempo with the accent on the last syllable. Albino expected to hear the rasp of a *güiro* gourd and a cha-cha-cha. "And what can I do for *you!*" Cha-cha-cha!

"We excavated a trench for you to make a repair in a water line. It goes halfway across Avenida Hidalgo. It hasn't been repaired yet. May I ask why?"

"We've been waiting for a *part*." Cha-cha-cha! "We've been waiting for a *part!*"

"For two months? What exactly do you *need*?" Albino realized he was picking up on the other man's salsa rhythm.

The music stopped and the tone became more serious. "As I recall, we need a four-inch elbow with a female thread at one end and a male adapter at the other."

"How very *interesante*. I want you to go to the adult sex shop and buy one this morning."

"We don't have an adult sex shop in Tecate."

"The plumbing section of the Tecate *hardware store*!"

"Of course, Albino, *absolutamente*. Immediately! I assure you we'll have that all done by the end of the week."

"You may be too late."

"I don't think I understand."

"Then let me put it more within your reach. At four o'clock this afternoon my crew is going to fill in the trench and pave it. If your work isn't done by then, the *presidente* told me this morning he will have your balls, and the citizens who have been without water will have your *nalgas* on the barbecue."

"We'll have it done by *noon*!" Cha-cha-cha!

I've never had so much fun! Albino thought. He could not contain himself, a cheerful tune escaped. We'll have it done by *noon*. Cha-cha-cha! We'll have it done by *noon*! It's amazing what you can accomplish when you know a little about behavioral science. Now, who's next? Ah yes! That utility pole that Chispas has to replace every week. That would be Ricardo, foreman of all our heavy equipment. Albino picked up the phone.

"*Bueno*." A man's voice, rough and indifferent.

"Let me speak to Ricardo."

"He's not here."

"Never mind, I know where to find the *cabrón*."

Albino got into his car and drove into the center of

town. He felt like he was sailing on air. Of course! The potholes were gone. He took a left and came down the main
street. There was the crew from the Water Department knee
deep in a trench making repairs. When he got to the traffic
light he saw a man in the basket of a cherry picker working
on the cockeyed signal. Albino was coming close to burst
ing into tears of joy. He took a right on Cardenas, double
parked, and walked into the Diana. It was dark. He smiled
cordially at the naked Diana on the back bar. The place was
nearly empty. Nearly empty. When his eyes made adjust-
ment to the sudden light change, he found his quarry in the
back corner.

"*Hola*, Ricardo."

Ricardo was holding what appeared to be a tall, frosty
Cuba Libra in his right hand. His left rested on the soft thigh
of a *chamacona* with the most extravagant body Albino could
ever remember seeing. He knew he had never seen her
before. Imported from Tijuana, no doubt.

"*Hola*, Albino." Ricardo's voice was cautious. Had
Albino caught him out, or had he caught Albino slipping
into the Diana during working hours? It was too early in the
conversation to tell. Richardo not only shared the actor's
name, he also saw himself as a young and gallant Ricardo
Montalban. He tilted his head toward the voluminous girl
and gave Albino that characteristic smile that devastated
two generations of women. The gesture implied that he was
winning the señorita and Albino should get lost.

"I've been looking for you, Ricardo. But don't let me
interrupt you."

Ricardo saw the official work orders in Albino's hand.
"Where is Cosme, *el director*?"

"He's gone, I've taken over and I have some work orders." Albino did not elaborate further.

Ricardo took the work orders from Albino. "It's a little late in the day for these. I'll put someone on it first thing *mañana*."

Albino studied the face for a moment and saw nothing that indicated Ricardo got the full meaning of his message. He would try a more direct approach. "No problem with me. I'm on my way to a meeting with the *presidente*. I'll explain the situation to him. I know he'll understand."

Ricardo Montalban turned his charming smile and his eyes of molten topaz toward the young thing whose thigh was providing a convenient armrest. "Please excuse us, my pretty flower, *con permiso*. I'll only be a moment, but your absence will leave a wound in my heart that may never heal." He even *sounded* like Ricardo Montalban. He came to his feet and followed Albino toward the front door.

"Have you seen these work orders, Albino?"

"Of course."

"You want me to grade all these dirt roads listed here?"

"You catch on quickly. They're supposed to be graded once a week. But it's been months. The roads become riverbeds during a rain and they're all but impassable with a car now. The residents are tired of losing a wheel, breaking an axle, and puncturing an oil pan."

"But these are half the residential streets in Tecate!"

"You better get started."

Ricardo dropped his voice to a whispering hiss. "But what do I do with her? She was just coming around when you walked in here! I am about to see her noble parts. You're a macho, you understand."

"I understand perfectly."

"I knew you would, *compa*."

"But I don't think your wife would understand. And I know your mother-in-law would have an opinion."

"I'll get on it at once!" Ricardo Montalban went pale. He looked more like Boris Karloff in *The Return of the Zombie*.

"Good. One more thing."

"*Sí?*"

"Send a crew over to Calle Nayarit and have them start digging a footing the entire length of the curve. Then I want you to raise a low wall, maybe a meter and a half. We need it done by Friday."

"I'll get Sylvino over there right now." He nodded his head toward the *chamaca*. "You have not seen me here today, no?"

"No."

Saturday night Albino marched across the plaza with his head high. He stood as tall as the enormous bronze Benito Juarez that towers above the plaza. He could hear his national anthem, complete with blaring trumpets, drumrolls, and cannons.

> *Boom! Boom!*
> *Mexicanos al grito de guerra . . .*
> *Boom! Boom!*

He provided his own timpani. He nearly shouted *Viva Mexico!* Albino Reyes de P. Mendoza was not exempt from pride. He crossed the street and entered the Contented Liver in triumph.

"There he is!"

"The man of the hour!"

"A magnum of my special estate bottled champagne for our *héroe!*" Cayetano Mesa, *proprietario* of El Higado Contento announced as he popped a cork and filled everyone's glass.

"*Salud*, Albino!"

"*Arriba*, Albino!"

"*Bravo*, Albino!"

They were drinking a tart green juice pressed from Thompson seedless grapes. A shot of Cliquot Club quinine water was added to warrant the word *sec* on the label. Cayetano Mesa, prop., swore the bottle had been aging peacefully in his dark cellars for over half a day.

"You've done it, Albino, you've done the impossible!" *El doctor* gave him a firm *abrazo*.

"I take it all back!" *el licenciado* burst out as he threw his arms around his friend. "You proved me wrong. You've proved what a man with some common sense can do!"

A flurry of *abrazos* followed and the men took to the sofas and chairs. Albino claimed the ugly morris chair.

"Look, you even made it in the papers!" The coffee table in front of them was covered with newspapers.

"Listen to this," Chispas said, and picked up *La Semana*. " 'Something of a miracle has struck Tecate. It is unrecognizable. We no longer have to weave in and out in traffic to avoid the potholes that have become a Tecate trademark. They have all disappeared as if someone waved a magic wand over the pueblo. The huge trench that has victimized a score of motorists who travel Avenida Hidalgo is miraculously paved and the avenue is no longer a threat to our safety—' "

"Listen to this!" *el doctor* interrupted. "You even made it in *El Mexicano*. '"Citizens of the outlying *colonias* of Tecate walked out this morning and could not believe the sight that greeted them. Their trash barrels were empty! . . .'

"There's more on the next page. 'The riverbeds that pose as roads have miraculously become smooth and negotiable streets.' "

"Here's another one . . . 'Cosme Carranza, Director de Obras Públicas, could not be reached for comment. He is believed to be out of the city. Fulanito Perengano, *presidente municipal* of Tecate, said, "I don't see the mystery. We promised all these improvements to the people before the election and we have fulfilled our contract with Tecate." ' "

The reports stopped long enough for another round of boisterous laughter and a drink, then resumed. They read from all the newspapers. They reported on the restoration of lighting, and traffic signals that actually worked.

A phone rang in the back. Cayetano answered. "Hey, Chispas. It's your dispatcher. Someone just plowed into the new protective wall on Calle Nayarit."

Albino, bathing in his moment of glory held up his glass and turned to Chispas. "But you notice the lights didn't go out."

"You're right!" Chispas replied. He drained his glass and put it down. "But I suppose I better get over there anyway and see if I'm needed."

"I'll join you." Albino emptied his glass and the two men left the Contented Liver with their arms around each other's shoulders.

"Bring us another bottle of your vintage Clorox 'ninety-six!" *el licenciado* called out. "We have a lot to celebrate."

Cayetano obliged, glasses were filled, and there followed a brief rest period from the jubilation. They began to settle down, and the subject turned to other things.

"How is the new baby at your house?" *el doctor* inquired of *el mecánico*.

"Fusses all day, cries all night."

"I suppose you help your señora out, *si*?"

"Of course. I call her when the baby is crying," *el mecánico* answered, and turned the tables on *el doctor*. "Do you help at home?"

El doctor's reply did not get the opportunity to see light.

"What a depressing subject!" *el licenciado* grumbled. "I see how my relatives live on the Other Side. Over there hombres wash dishes, they do laundry, they even take out the trash."

"No!"

"He's right. I've seen it!" *El mecánico* shuddered in agreement. "They've exchanged their *pantalones* for an apron. It's another world over there. A man has no control over his house on the Other Side."

"I was going to leave my wife, but I think I'm better off right here in Mexico," *el dentista* admitted.

"And why didn't you leave?" *el licenciado* asked.

"I couldn't find my clothes. And anyway, I would miss my girlfriend."

"I'm not going to give you a lecture on safe sex," *el doctor* interrupted. "But I'm going to assume you have enough sense to take precautions."

"Of course! She's way over on the other end of town."

The front door opened at that moment and Pistolas Martínez, an old retired cop they all knew well, came rushing in. "Where's Albino?" he gasped.

"Hey, Pistolas!" they all cried out at once. "Sit down and join the celebration. Albino will be right back."

El dentista poured a glass for the new arrival. "He went

with Chispas to see about a crash. They won't be long. Sit down and have a drink."

"Oh dear God, dear God!"

"What is it?"

Pistolas tried to control his voice but the choking sobs escaped. "The accident. It was Albino Chico. Died instantly."

ABOUT THE AUTHOR

DANIEL REVELES was born in Los Angeles of Mexican-born parents. He has been involved in some aspect of the entertainment industry since his youth as a songwriter, late-night disc jockey, and producer of commercials. He has written and directed a wide variety of foreign documentaries for American television, including countries such as Africa, India, Turkey, Mexico, and Guatemala. He lives at Villa Mirasol, his rancho, on the outskirts of Tecate, Baja California, where he devotes his time to writing and playing chamber music.